HEART I:

THE SILENT

GODS

FREDERICK GORDON KENNEDY

ISBN

Hardback: 978-1-965134-31-3
Paperback: 978-1-965134-32-0

About the Author

In 1969, Mr. Kennedy graduated from Berklee with a diploma in Arranging and Composition. More interested in a career as a trombonist, he joined a newly formed Swallow, billed as a blues-rock band, culminating in a recording contract with Warner Brothers Records. Mr. Kennedy concluded his instrumental career in 1973.

Joining the workforce, Mr. Kennedy has worked part-time at a drugstore soda fountain and full-time for an automobile parking company, rising to management. Following that, he worked as a 'flask rigger' at a grey iron casting foundry in Connecticut. Returning to the Boston area, he found work in an electronics factory as an assembler, encapsuler, test operator, shipper, and, finally, at that company's help desk.

In the years that followed and throughout his time in Connecticut, Mr. Kennedy answered an inner call to write, finishing several short stories, teleplays, a screenplay and several book length science fictions, one of those self-published.

Dedication

I want to thank all those who helped me move forward in the arts and this literary effort.

Do you know the true meaning of *Pittean*

Slan?

A long, long time past had seen a star blink and dim in a far part of another, an unknown galaxy. grown nearly cold and barren.

Circling it, a cylinder world. Built In those final years Modallas was to serve a few, last beings.

The mammoth structure was more than a satellite and more than the planet that spawned it. Modallas went out to find The Heart.

Possession of The Heart meant possession of the galaxy.

Table of Contents

1

Tyrus Orbit

Borter peered across his panel sleepily, maneuvering Soarer around the corner and onto the light side of the planet, crossing the terminator. Daylight began to gleam brightly on the distant horizon, reflecting off Soarer's exterior. The viewport umbra responded, shading the cockpit. He turned, shouting back into the tube. A dim light winked on in response to his voice. "Planetfall in thirty minutes," he announced. A dark shape moved, searching for clothing.

Borter calculated his entry angle into the thick atmosphere of Tyrus. The Tyrean horizon shifted noticeably as the nose tilted down toward the planet. All the panel lights read positive, green for go, and the onboard computer computed the angle. His thoughts briefly turned to power dots; they were three short. Reggia had burned them out—actually, Borter had, while escaping that planet. The mission there had cost them more than they had made.

Helio stumbled into the cockpit, showing the effects of insufficient sleep. The mission-gone – bad to Reggia had cost him, too, as Borter's full partner. "You look green," commented the pilot. The statement would have made more sense if the Dillisome's natural color hadn't been a very pale blue. Borter's skin was a robust bronze, common to all Magnean's. "An unnecessary reference," the Dillisome noted easily. "Just tired," Helio replied, familiarizing himself with the ship's status. All the settings were good. "You'll feel better soon," his partner chirped. Borter had not slept himself, preferring to watch as Soarer gained on Tyrus. "We need power dots, and we need 'em bad," he muttered to himself, half to Helio. "I hope there's cargo for us here."

The Dillisome tilted his thin, intelligent face, now fully awake, toward Borter. "Tyrus has been good to us before." Borter had no reason to disagree except for bad nerves. He improved the angle of his glide another degree. Tyrus Control came on, giving approach instructions. There was something reassuring in the sound of it after so long away.

Leaving the planet, there would be a full tube going somewhere else. Another of the sub-system planets, he supposed. Perhaps another system altogether. They were, as all sub-systems were, the backwater of the galaxy, some areas within them completely unknown. Universal buzzed in his ears reassuringly.

Helio placed his hands on the controls and relayed data to Borter. Tyrus rushed up to greet them as Borter turned Soarer around, the aft end of the little freighter toward the planet, and fired the good engines, slowing their descent. A return to Reggia would have to wait for another day. Their cargo was gone; they had done well to escape.

Had Soarer not been in such good repair, they would have lost everything. Lost cargo, well, that was a hazard common everywhere, not only in the sub-systems. Pirating was epidemic. It happened to all sooner or later, some had more luck than others.

Borter pushed the throttle forward and escaped the controlled freefall. Soarer then described a slow circle, gliding easily on its wide, outstretched wings. Moments later, they broke through the cloud cover and sighted Bouley itself just ahead. They were on track, in the slot, with nothing more than routine matters left. This was Borter's favorite part of the ride – a favorite spaceport.

It was a shipping terminal, the last civilized post before the outworlds. Some said due to that favoritism, it was no longer quite civilized. Freighters of every description lined the runways on either side, Bouley being part of the galaxy.

"We're clear," Borter said needlessly to Helio. At times, he readily apprised him of situations he was already familiar with and information he already had or had received simultaneously. True to his nature, the Dillisome made the proper acknowledgments to each update and thought nothing more about it.

A paved strip suddenly came into view, and just as quickly, Borter set Soarer down on it. Other ships, already berthed – some taking on cargo, Borter thought – whizzed by on both sides. Helio switched on the shields and angled them back to deflect engine thrust.

Berth 435 was assigned to them by the Port Controller. Helio picked out the marker, and Borter swung Soarer's nose toward it. Borter left the ship in Helio's hands. Bouley had long been familiar to the Magnean. Before his partnership with Helio, long before, it had been his base.

2

Targans

Morning came early to Nine, a Ranger base on the edge of the Targan Forest. Two of their number stirred earlier than usual from their relaxed breakfast. Arranging their weapons securely around their already armored bodies, they moved with customary swiftness toward a small, much-used trail into the forest. Patrol had fallen to them that day. In the forest, it was still night. The two felt the clammy dampness beneath even the smooth wrappings of their armor.

Armor covered them completely, head to toe, but weighed next to nothing. Both men waited for the warming sun to reach through the enclosing branches overhead. To them, even such limited warmth could feel good. Very soon, they would leave the comparative ease of the trail.

Neither man spoke for long periods, concentrating only on making progress through the underbrush. Trouble was afoot, much trouble. Targans again roamed near the forest's edge in ever-increasing numbers, ready once again to follow the path of The Forest Spirit. Both kept a sharp watch. If Targans got onto them, it would not go easily despite their superior weapons and fine armor. Targans attacked only in strength.

A few kilometers ahead lay the results of the last work done by Targans. Slowly, they were making themselves known, reasserting themselves, choosing not to confront the Marcelleans directly for the time being.

The Rangers would pay a visit to old Torbo that day. There had been several night raids on other settlers in this outlying area, and Torbo was the farthest out. By midday, they were less than two and a half kilometers from his place.

Torbo was old – old, and getting older. He was very special to the Rangers at Nine. A hermit most of his life, he took naturally to the frontier. They visited him often, as a matter of course, on their long patrols. They loved to drink his homemade wines and hear his wild stories of Marcellus' distant past as much as he loved to tell them.

They never quite knew whether he composed them as he went along or actually had earned them from his own experiences because there were so many. In quarters, the Rangers passed the time during lonely nights repeating those stories, wondering even longer at the truth of them. As boys, they weaned on such a diet of fantasy and mysticism. The tales intrigued them and were rich in history and excitement, but often, the truth of them eluded their young minds.

Marcellus possessed an antiquity even greater than they suspected from which the present was drawn, reaching back many, many eons into indecipherable fragments.

A few hours before dawn, they came. The forest fell silent, more so than if Targans were merely skirting the small farm on their way by or just having a curious look. It quieted the way it did when they came silently in large numbers. It was always a sure sign, and Torbo heard it; rather, he heard nothing, only silence.

They approached with greater confidence than usual, meeting the darkness evenly, on its own terms, with their dusky skins. Torbo quickly readied himself in the single room of his shelter. The single door was bolted and barricaded. The old man stood in the clear center of the room, waiting, weapon in hand.

At last, with a shrill cry, the door jamb shattered and crashed inward, Targans spilling in behind it. For a moment, all that could be seen in the room was the blue of old Torbo's ion blade. The blade sent first one, then another to death, and The Forest Spirit. That night would see more of them there before Torbo went over to The Heart.

Suddenly, the room burst into flames as the Targans rushed him again through the matted gore of their fallen comrades. They used blasters hurling photon energy before their last headlong dash.

It was nearly the second hour of the afternoon before the two Marcelleans crested the ridge overlooking Torbo's small farm. At a glance, they knew something was terribly wrong. One of the young warriors reached a stud on his left shoulder and pressed it.

At once, a small voice came to life in his ears, "Sensors show no life," it said sharply. The Ranger ordered the Shoulder Falcon, as the device was called, to keep him informed. A torrent of information followed in a babble. The second Ranger followed the example of the first.

They moved down the ridge cautiously toward the shelter, forgetting the weariness of the day. Following the brush line as far as they could for cover, they reached the shattered doorway.

Everything they saw told the story of Torbo's death. They found him there, stretched out across the smashed door jamb, the ion blade beside him shattered and useless. The shelter itself was scorched but not badly burned. Torbo's few possessions were there intact. They had not come for loot.

Torbo was buried deep in his own soil, with the hope that The Heart would accept his spirit. There was little else to be done except return and report to base. With him gone, there were no others left to warn.

3

The Snow Beggar

It was a place far different from where Soarer had landed, on Tyrus, a place that did not have the wide, smooth, and well-kept streets of distant Marcellus, the city, nor any of its high-throne architecture to speak of. In the blowing mountain snow, there was a single dwelling of the humblest design and a well-worn path to its door. The Snow Beggar alone walked the upper regions of Marcellus, the planet.

The door had not stirred in several days, and snow piled high against it. The wind howled darkly, bringing more snow against the door, and rasping against the windows with the voice of its frozen crystals. It was the only sound to be heard in the place. This was the house of the Snow Beggar.

It was no more than a rude dwelling, given the tastes of most Marcelleans – really a hovel. But it served well for one who chose it as his home, savoring above all the sanctity of solitude, cut off from the contacts of Marcellean life. After too many years, one day, he decided to leave the world of Marcelleans and keep himself to other things.

Inside, the hearth crackled now and again, barely alive, waiting for more fuel to burn. Except for the dying fire, there was no other light or heat provided in the single room. Yet, there seemed to be a purposeful warmth, perhaps the warmth of satisfaction and peaceful repose. He would have to open the door again soon to gather more fuel.

For the little time it took, the door would be flung wide, and the cold and ice would invade the tiny room as a body – an unwelcome guest without regard for peace and sanctity. For these few minutes, the world turned inside out as nature ran amok, reclaiming that which was its own domain alone. This puny man would seem to be driven out, and all memory of his encroachment would be erased.

Simple shelves lined the walls, placed over the inner boards of the shelter, themselves covering no more than the bare beams. Against them, the wind constantly threatened, and the old man knew it. It was his manner of joking to leave the door open as he went out, as if to invite the eternal enemy within his own small fortress to do its worst. To do damage inside it could not do with all its windy threats from outside.

Then, he would come back, his arms greatly burdened. He would stand for a moment, then bluster, "No, you haven't got me yet. I am still too strong for you. See how strong I am," he referred to the load of wood held in his arms. "I'm still standing, not tired, not breathing hard. I'm just as I always was when I cut down your brother, The Forest Spirit, and his horde of savages."

He laid down the heavy load and turned slowly back to the door, closing it firmly. "Still too strong." The room quickly warmed with the addition of new fuel to the fire, which, reborn, made a happy crackle. In the new light, small articles could be seen all around the room. A ragged book or two lay haphazardly against each other, on end, side by side. A lamp rested on a small table beside a large chair. It remained unlit in favor of the hearth, except when he chose to read the books.

He'd read everything there, not just a few times, but many, and had many pages in his memory, having nothing else to do. A stove for cooking worked when called upon. Finishing the list of sparse furnishings was a bed.

Nothing prevented light from reaching through the windows when there was sunlight. They were bare and puzzlingly bleak spaces in the walls. From one, he looked down, far onto the lowlands, still desolate in the perpetual snows.

Beyond the lowlands lay greener lands, lands of warmth he had not crossed for those years, keeping to himself in the upper ranges of the mountain. The other window showed only the upper peak, the only thing built higher than the house itself. But it had always been there, longer even than him.

Clouds laden with moisture crystallized into snow and disappeared over and around its pinnacles. They were still higher than the old peak. He wanted nothing else to conquer. Instead, he chose not to conquer because they were there. There were things higher and things lower and the things that were in between. It was fine that way; he'd long before decided.

The room held little else except for the ancient suit of battle armor and the somewhat undefined, special, quality that came from the few other possessions of the man kept together.

All in all, there was still the peace the old man wanted there. The snow and the wind howled by and clung to the outside, not the inside. There, it was warm and out of the wind.

Something brushed against the door that was not the wind. The old man rose and forced it open against the elements. It seemed that another arm as strong as his own pushed with him, and the door opened. "Ah, there you are," he said, smiling with deep affection in his voice. A hollow rumbling came from something large trying to enter.

"Ah, 5D, I wonder where you've been. It's been weeks – " A huge something like a tongue, checkered black and white like the rest of him, stopped the old man midsentence, licking his face. The old man sputtered, stepping back, trying to draw a breath. He laughed.

A huge form pressed at the door frame, looking for entry. 5D, a swirling checkerboard of black and white squares, whirled one after another, bent as if pulled at one corner, each into an angry vortex that was his mouth.

The bulk of his form rubbed against the door frame, stretching the black and white squares, making a hissing sound as he pushed his way through. He still licked at the old man's face. The rumble from within it went on.

"Come on, then." The Snow Beggar reached up to pat the massive shape. The tongue, all black and white squares, licked out at him. "Now, now, you. That's enough," the old man laughed.

5D's shape of happily undulating squares stretched, disappearing, then reappearing one after another. Indeed, the old man was pleased to have him back, his only companion. The weight of the big animal pushed him back.

"I wonder where you've been, you old devil?" he playfully pushed back. The big chair tumbled over on its back while the table moved halfway across the room, nearly losing its lamp. The game ended suddenly when cooking utensils crashed to the floor.

The beast stood still. As 5D stopped, his squares slowed. His visual sense followed The Snow Beggar as he went to the small cabinet where food was stored.

"Where have we been this time?" demanded the old man. "Out scaring the pants off half the galaxy? How many worlds did you get into mischief on this time?" He held something out in his hand. 5D gobbled it down quickly with a loud, wet smack. "Get tired of chasing around, did you? Decided to come back home? I thought it was about time," the Snow Beggar chuckled.

The old man reached up and gave 5D, a creature of the fifth dimension, another pat on what he reasoned to be a head.

The squares were soft and mobile to his touch. 5D rumbled contentment from deep inside. The squares continued to move inward, then out from another side or from the same place. Then, all over again, from another direction. The Snow Beggar struggled again to close the door.

There was little room left with the added bulk of his friend from the fifth dimension in the humble shelter, but he would make do. Finishing with the door, he turned back to his friend.

"I thought you had gotten lost," he scolded, wiggling an admonishing forefinger, making 5D rumble apologetically. "All right, I'll stop, but you stay a little closer from now on." 5D came forward in a definite loving manner.

"You're the last of your kind. You'd make me feel better if you didn't go traipsing around the galaxy like that, looking for adventures. If you want adventure and want to be of help, why don't you go to Modallas and grab that Helmsman by the seat of his pants?"

The Snow Beggar picked up his chair and settled himself gently into it. "Not as young as I once was," he murmured. "But I can still push you around a bit."

5D lay on the floor in front of the chair, a great lump on the floor. It was a pleasant scene, the remnants of the fire glowing, casting half-light that filled the room. The Snow Beggar sat for a long time, a heavy blanket around him with only his gray head sticking out above it. The feeling was warm inside the blanket and secure in a world that had never really known peace.

It was a peace the old man had found for himself in the most remote spot on the Marcellean world. It was his wish never to leave this place. He could only guess at the worlds 5D had seen, even as recently as the past week or two. While he was rooted to the top of that snow-covered mountain and its enveloping bit of solitude, 5D was not. Though he suspected that 5D searched for a mate and was not merely sightseeing as he preferred to think, he would not admit it fully into his thoughts.

"Oh, I wish I could phase like you, we'd have adventures together, we would. We'd leave this troubled mudball of a planet. First, I'd make that Helmsman some trouble. He'd not forget us soon. He's as bad as Markham, if not worse." He leaned toward 5D, "He doesn't like you at all, you know," he whispered as if they were not alone.

The old gray head nodded reassuringly to 5D. "You're the only being in the galaxy he has a real terror of. You are the last of your kind and the best. And you don't like Modallas, do you?" He laughed gently, like a grandfather speaking to his child's child. "Lord Soal will have to look after you soon, won't he?"

The Snow Beggar shook his finger at him, admonishing him to remember, "If something happens to me, you go to Lord Soal. He'll be your new master. You've got brain enough to follow that command. You give him the big flash of light when you materialize and scare the pants off him the way you did when he was a boy. That will be one on him."

The fire glowed in its last embers, growing dimmer and dimmer. "I'll have to get more fuel before it gets darker and the night wind blows too hard." With that, the old man threw off his blanket and made his way in the fading light to the door. It would snow again that night, he could tell easily. The wind blew far too gently at the wrong time and it smelled different as it would when more snow threatened.

Above him, the stars of the galaxy did not show in the sky. A fresh layer of snow readied itself to drop on the little house. Before the snow came to his door again, the Snow Beggar had laid in days of fuel and closed the house tightly against the winds that would drive the snow. 5D lay at his feet, listening to one story after another that night of the old days of Marcellus.

He had been a gift years before, 5D. The Snow Beggar, then known by another name, a name of great honor, had been delighted to accept him. Then, the breed was rare and was to become rarer. The animal grew quickly, becoming large even for its kind, larger than the tallest Marcellean and broad. He flashed from place to place, instantly, playing games with the old man's youngest, Lord Soal.

Finally reaching maturity, his little jaunts in time and space covered vast distances, often far from the planet itself. Though he always returned. Standing in their midst suddenly, often at the wrong moments, sometimes at the right ones, interrupting parental discipline of the young Lords Soal and Markham. The Snow Beggar often suspected that it was done on purpose, but he could not prove the beast was intelligent enough to make even so simple a plan. He simply functioned as his biology dictated, as a large, bumbling, rumbling pet that had delighted his children.

Once more, the days pressed upon him without this, his last companion. In recent years, he had been given to talking to the creature. He had no idea if 5D had any speck of understanding in his constant speeches. The senses of this creature of five dimensions perceived the lonely feelings of this old man.

Indeed, this formidable creature of the galaxy always returned to him. At no equal interval, he would appear and disappear only to return at another time, always the same as he had left, unscathed by his travel. It was not difficult to reason why. The Helmsman feared him above all creatures and things Marcellean. After their first encounter, The Helmsman had gone to great lengths to avoid a second.

4

The Helmsman

A day later, the old man carried his armload of fuel toward the little house. Snow covered all of it except for the door, which he continually had to force open. During a letup in the Winter storm, he went to a woodpile and brought in his own fuel with no small effort. His feet crunched in the snow as he walked.

5D had not been seen that day. Gone, he supposed. It would not be long before he found his way back. The animal was never away more than a few days, usually. The Snow Beggar found himself lonely at times in the peaks but stayed anyway, no longer taking part in the affairs of the Marcelleans below. Other than 5D, none came to see him. A few knew where he was, or that he still lived.

He longed for those he knew as The Warriors of The Black Cragg, The Companion Blades, or his old friend, also long gone, The Red Spirit. In those days, there had been many of them, friends. And, Targans to kill, more, though there were fewer Marcelleans. Those days of adventure would never return. He reached his door with his firewood. Numbness from the intense cold began to overtake him.

He hurried his steps along, muttering as he went about an old man's bones. His breath froze in the air, and new snow covered his broad shoulders as he reached the door. It swung easily as he pushed it open.

A fire still burned in the hearth. It had not quite weakened to cinders and ash before he'd decided to go out. It was as if he'd left it only moments before. His simple bowls, pans, and other utensils were all in their places. The bed, with its heavy covering, was undisturbed. The spare chair and little table were all unmoved. Nothing, it seemed, had bothered his snowy sanctuary during this brief absence. The place was beginning to get to him, he thought. 5D would be welcome back when he came.

The door creaked behind him. The old one turned to face not 5D, but a Targan in full Modallian battle armor. As the Targan raised his blaster, he met the tip of the old man's ion blade. The body collapsed in a heap at his feet.

"So, I am found, even here. Well, let them come. I'll take them all on my way to The Heart. Come along then, I know you're out there."

Feet shuffled outside in unsteady snow. "In a hurry, I suppose." The Snow Beggar stood, his blade ready, facing the door, waiting for the next Targan to show himself. Suddenly, a voice crackled behind him.

The residual light from a teleportation tube reached all corners of the house. The sound of it was both present and far away. It seemed, at the same time, as if it were caught in an echo between the rock pillars of the notches above. He turned.

"Do you really prefer this to the comfort and honors accorded you on once great Marcellus?" The voice was that of The Helmsman.

"Once great?" The old man spat the words. "Don't tell me you've pulled us down so quickly. And yes, I preferred it until you soiled it with your presence."

"Ah, forgive me, Lord Snow Beggar, that is how you prefer to be called now, isn't it?"

The Helmsman laughed in no good humor. "My ploy was a simple one, was it not, but effective? Perhaps, simply wanted to assess the sharpness of your mind."

"My welfare is no business of yours, Helmsman." It was a child's trick. "You forget I have raised two sons of my own."

The Helmsman withdrew his laughter and his false manner of cordiality, becoming stern.

"You forget, I have one of them," he snarled.

"It is not to your credit he is the only Marcellean you have managed to subvert to your evil in all these years you have forced yourself on us."

"And in turn, your eternal shame that he is your son, old one." Once again, there came the sinister laughter ringing in the little shelter.

As The Helmsman heaped shame on the old man's suffering, he eyed the ion blade held ready by him. He paused, unmoving, watching the blade. "An ion blade," he said, "the mainstay of Marcellean weaponry and honor, I believe." He looked at the body lying behind the Snow Beggar on the floor. The old one said nothing.

"And now, old man," he faced the Snow Beggar impatiently, "the Marcellean Heart. I know you have it." No words came from the old one. "I warn you; it has been a long, hard search already to reach you here. Quick, the Heart." The Helmsman made his demand. He circled the old man warily, outside the reach of the menacing ion blade. The Snow Beggar followed with his eyes.

"You are nowhere near the Heart of Marcellus; you are a fool; I don't have it."

"You do not have it?" The Helmsman laughed to himself. "As I expected," he sneered. He looked at the ion blade.

"If you do not have it, you will tell me where it is," He pointed a finger at the old man.

"I can kill you where you stand," he roared. "I can kill you as easily as I materialized in this little house." A beam of light leaped from the end of his extended finger, catching the old one in the shoulder.

The Snow Beggar winced painfully. Smoke curled up in a gray wisp from the deep wound in his shoulder. Involuntarily, the shoulder lowered a bit. He said nothing.

"Where is The Heart?" The Helmsman again demanded.

There was no answer. The pain stung and grew worse. The old man could do nothing; attack was impossible, the ion blade hanging loosely in his other hand useless, glowing bluely. A moment passed in silence; The Helmsman seemed in no hurry. He stood easily, no longer afraid of the blade.

"Marcelleans love a bit of irony in their lives, don't they?" He ignored the old man's struggles to remain on his feet against the pain.

"Old one, would it not be irony of a kind if one of The Heart's greatest was killed with his own blade?" The Helmsman looked at him as if expecting an answer. It came in a voice unafraid but trying to find its strength, at the same time realizing the hopelessness of such an attempt.

"My death is not irony, but vengeance is always ironic."

"I will have The Heart now, old man, give it to me," The Helmsman repeated the demand.

The Snow Beggar crumpled to the floor. "Not I," he gasped!

"What?" The Helmsman charged across the space between them. "What?"

"The Heart prophesies its key will be your death. Your efforts are for nothing."

"I will have The Heart, old man, or I will have my irony."

"You will have an irony, but not one of your choosing," The Snow Beggar could only whisper.

Taking the ion blade from the Snow Beggar's helpless grasp, he positioned himself to use it above the old man.

"Now, old man, tell me." The Snow Beggar said nothing. There was a quick thrust, and it was done. "I have irony enough," he said. "Let us see if you have yours when I have, in my hands, your blade and the Marcellean Heart." He turned from the body.

"Captain."

A second Targan appeared at the door, coming stiffly to attention. "Captain, tear this place apart. Bring me The Heart of Marcellus!"

"Yes, Helmsman." The Targan saluted grimly and turned in the door, signaling others outside. He stood to one side as the entire shelter was razed to the ground and each piece of the wreckage examined. It took only minutes. The Targans gathered with empty hands behind their captain, facing The Helmsman. It was then that 5D returned.

Fortunately for The Helmsman, 5D materialized with the Targans between them. The Helmsman disappeared that same instant 5D was on them, pulling them screaming, helpless, into his checkered, twisting mouth.

They would be an expensive loss. Disciplined Targans were rare, but he had more aboard Modallas and at other places in the galaxy.

There were only two, The Helmsman and 5D, who could teleport their own matter at will. In 5D, it was natural; for The Helmsman, it was a development of ancient Modallian technology that only he held. He could match 5D with it in most ways, except in distance, and he required bulky machinery aboard the cylinder world; 5D did not.

One day, he would leap to Modallas, this plodding, shifting thing of the fifth dimension; there, he would find his enemies.

In him, there was no conscious wish for revenge; instead, there was something else telling him what a pleasure it would be to rip the life from The Helmsman's body.

The hair's breadth saving The Helmsman from 5D's dimensional maw was the beast's inability to sense Modallas. That refinement was coming; very soon it would be easy to sense the artificial as it already was to sense a planet. That and the animal hatred of the thing he was were what The Helmsman feared most. One day there would be no place to hide.

That day, he left 5D amid the cries of dying Targans and the body of The Snow Beggar, his beloved master. The notches of the mountain echoed with his great cry, a mournful sound to be known on Modallas itself, soon.

5

The Oasis

In the hours that followed the landing at Bouley, Helio successfully did what Borter could not. He booked the cargo. Borter returned from the shipper's agency discouraged and exhausted. The Dillisome went out, letting him sleep.

Helio was a man of many interests. Many things caught his eye as he wandered from the berth. 435 was a dismal heap serving the passage of time more than the passing of space freighters. The buildings around him looked dirty and rotten.

He wondered who had been there and who was there now. Helio wondered at all things. He walked into The Oasis. It had been a long time since his last drink. Until strangers had come to Dillisome, the drink was unknown. Helio grew to like it and continued the habit.

This was a place where a flyer could get a drink. Curiosity, he thought, was the reason he stayed with Borter. The Magnean was the strangest man he'd ever known.

At first sight of him, he wondered, "Why has he come?" Helio left his planet knowing that the few Dillisome who left never returned. Since then, the pair had been to more than fifty worlds, but never back to Dillisome.

Dillisome was a barren rock of a planet. Nothing more than ice and snow year-round. It was barely habitable. Borter came hunting Waugreb. Helio guided him across the ice until he'd killed one, almost killing himself in the process. The man completely mystified him.

At that time of day, The Oasis was almost empty. The few men inside looked as if they also crewed aboard freighters.

The only Tyrean was the barman. Helio moved to a table in the corner and pulled up a chair. For a long time, he sat there quietly.

Time passed slowly as Helio sat, immersed in his thoughts. The first of the evening crowd, a crew of Tyrean shippers, barged in, boisterous and loud. They began playing Tyrean music from a coin-operated machine, the same song on repeat. The noise drove everyone else away except for a dark-cloaked figure in a far corner, the bartender, the Tyreans, and Helio himself. No one else lingered.

Helio surveyed the room once more, contemplating leaving. More patrons streamed in, none familiar to him except for the recognizable planetary types among them. They hailed from near and far, but none hailed from Dillisome. At the bar, two burly men conversed in hushed tones with the bartender, covering their mouths against the din to prevent lip-reading. Occasionally, they glanced back over their shoulders at the cloaked figure seated at a corner table behind a nearly empty glass. The figure slouched forward slightly, with two blinking dots of light on one shoulder, the only discernible features being a closely cropped humanoid head.

The bartender, a nondescript Tyrean, whispered, "I tell you; I gave him enough to knock out an army. He should be on the floor." One of the two men snarled something at him, leaning across the bar. The bartender recoiled, keeping his distance from the Tyreans.

The dark figure rose slowly but steadily from his table and approached Helio. "Are you a freighter crewman?" he asked.

"Half owner," Helio replied.

"Is your ship available?"

Helio nodded, and the man sat down at the table across from him, his back to the men at the bar.

"I require transportation to Marcellus and can pay," the man said.

Initially disinterested, Helio inquired, "Are you in trouble with the local authorities?"

"No," the red dots on his shoulder blinked once, "but there is a strong element of danger and a need for discretion."

"How will you – pay?" Helio asked.

"I pay in high – quality power dots," the dots blinked again.

"I am interested. You can depend on us," Helio said calmly.

The two nodded, and a second meeting was arranged. Up close, the stranger's striking features could be discerned, something others might call noble.

"Berth 430, one hour," Helio instructed.

"I will be there," the man confirmed, glancing toward the bar, now devoid of other patrons. The bartender had turned away, busying himself with wiping glasses.

"Are you armed?" the man asked, noticing Helio's belt.

"No," Helio replied.

"Follow me out, but keep a few paces back," the man cautioned. They rose from the table, the cloaked man struggling slightly. Helio followed behind as they made for the door.

Outside, the man scanned the area carefully. Helio hesitated at the door while the man positioned himself in the center of the street. It wasn't apparent in the bar, but his passenger wore body armor unlike anything Helio had ever seen before.

Stopping at the entrance to an alley beside The Oasis, Helio took a moment to assess the situation. Then, he turned, surveying the narrow street. He noticed another alley on the opposite side of the bar, identical to the one they stood by. As he walked between them, a man from the first alley rushed out, brandishing a blaster. In a flash of blue light, the blaster fell to the ground, and the man collapsed, lifeless.

Meanwhile, the cloaked passenger was already in the other alley. There was a brief recoil from a blaster, then silence.

Emerging from the alley, his client sheathed his ion blade and walked away, his cloak billowing, without a backward glance at Helio. The Dillisome hurried back to Soarer and Borter with his news. Borter remained asleep in his rack in the cargo tube, taking a moment to fully awaken to Helio's excited revelations.

6

Lord Soal "Berth 430?"

"And you saw him kill two men?"

"Not exactly. He went outside, and they attacked him. It was over when I got out there."

"You're hopeless, like a child with a new toy, whenever you see something new. Where is Marcellus, anyway?"

"The Varian sub-system," Helio answered quickly. "It's supposed to be quite amazing, a place of former glory."

Berth 430 was only five berths down from their own. Upon arrival, no one was in sight. "Where is he?" Borter snapped. "The police probably have him. We've been stood up." As he spoke, twin points of light blinked in the dark alley next to 430. "There," Helio pointed. Straining his eyes, Borter tried to make out the figure in the darkness. Helio led him forward. "This is Borter," he introduced proudly to the Marcellean. Borter seemed surprised to find the Marcellean a humanoid, with regular features, after seeing only the blinking lights from his Shoulder Falcon. The Marcellean nodded. "We are observed," said a synthesized voice.

"This way," Helio began to lead. The Marcellean slumped against the wall, causing Helio to start. "What's wrong with him?" Borter demanded, crouching beside the Marcellean to check for signs of life. A blink of light from the Shoulder Falcon with a synthetic voice replied, "Strong drug, I request assistance." The two flyers helped the man to his feet.

"To your ship," the Shoulder Falcon ordered urgently. "Quickly. Enemies are closing in." Struggling, they made their way toward berth 435, the Marcellean assisting when possible. Borter wondered who the enemy was and where they were; he hadn't seen anyone. Soarer wasn't far. Passing the gate to their berth, heavy footsteps thudded behind them. An order in Tyrean to halt was given, perfectly translated by the Universal translator, but neither Borter nor Helio understood. The two flyers maneuvered their passenger into Soarer. Helio settled the Marcellean into a seat while Borter went forward to start the engines.

"Helio," he shouted back, "if he's paying in power dots, get them now and throw them in. We're going to need all the help we can get." Helio located the container in Marcellean's cloak and placed it in the left power pod.

"Shields up," the Magnean called. "We have power." Helio ran forward, and they taxied onto the runway. Borter angled the shields at the back, amazed at their newfound power. Energy burst against the aft shields ineffectively. Tyrus Control came on; Borter requested clearance for takeoff but was denied. "Control, I request emergency clearance," he tried again, with no success. Hesitating for a moment, Borter realized they had no choice. The throttle levers moved forward on their own, surprising both men. Soarer rocketed down the runway, rising vertically at almost ninety degrees. Borter had never taken off at such a radical angle.

Once above the cloud cover, they calmed down, and control returned to the cockpit. Borter eased Soarer's launch angle to something more normal. "We'll have to watch for interceptors now," he said. Helio nodded, acknowledging, "The Tyreans will want us bad." They remained silent for a moment, the roar of Soarer's engines filling the space. Interceptors appeared almost at the edge of the atmosphere. "I think we can outrun them," Helio said, monitoring the ship's systems. "Maybe not!" he added as blaster energy slapped against the atmosphere around them. The throttles were pushed to maximum. "They're fading," he announced after a tense moment. Leaning back, both pilots sighed in relief as the fighters disappeared from their screens. There would be no further pursuit from Tyrus.

Borter nodded toward the tube, "Our friend must be something special to rate that kind of attention. Something very special, indeed." Then, he recalled the power dots Helio had shoved into the left three-pod. "Those power dots – pretty good. Take over, will you?" He said, getting out of his seat. The Dillisome nodded, taking the controls.

Borter went aft. The sound of footsteps woke the ailing Marcellean, who looked up, his head bobbing a bit. "I'll fly my own ship, if you don't mind," Borter snapped, speaking from what he thought might be a safe distance, trying to appear authoritative and angry. "You got us in plenty of trouble back on Tyrus. I suspect there won't be much cargo from that direction anytime soon."

The Marcellean replied slowly, "My powers grow dim." The Shoulder Falcon answered for its wearer, "Modallain agents, Targans only dressed to fool you. If they'd gotten close enough, they'd have your ears by now. Thank the Inevitable they did not."

The Marcellean passed out, his head sinking down toward his chest, lapsing into a long unconsciousness. His breath came easily. Borter loosened the seat restraints, allowing this strange passenger to rest more comfortably.

Of the Marcellean himself, nothing more could be known until he awakened. Even the mysterious box, the Shoulder Falcon attached to his body armor, was silent. He rested, asleep, giving no sign of movement, no indication of when he'd regain consciousness.

Borter smiled a curious, even wry smile, pausing momentarily, looking with deep admiration at the new power dots running his ship, then returning to the cockpit.

For several days, Borter and Helio moved around the sleeping form, going about their business, looking at him curiously from time to time, examining him from a distance. They were familiar with body armor but had seen nothing like this before. Marcellus was days away from Tyrus. They would never be able to go back to that planet again, Modallians or not. The inability to do that took from them the prospect of much lucrative shipping available nowhere else. They could forget that part of the galaxy.

From the Galactic Atlas, Borter learned Marcellus was one of the galaxy's former giants. Also, they would be able to walk without artificial aid. Former glory, Helio had called it. Helio was too enamored with dingy, worn-out places, Borter thought.

He longed for something besides another broken-down subsystem planet. Soarer had never taken them to the Varian Subsystem before. Judging from the diversity they had encountered in other systems, he didn't know what to expect and tried not to bother himself with more speculation based on as little information as this sleeping Marcellean and the Atlas could readily provide.

Borter paced the length of the tube while Helio sat in the cockpit. Space passed by outside, quiet, mysterious to them, even after all the light years they'd logged. Borter sensed, despite his best efforts, a certain haplessness in this mission. They were walking into something. He knew it.

7

The Sky God and Marcellus

Borter never denied Helio's intelligence but wondered at his friend's weakness for newfound curiosity. He guessed it was the same bug that had bitten them all since they left Dillisome, and it explained why they didn't want to return. All things considered, could Helio recognize danger before walking into it? It wouldn't have been the first time his curious and trusting partner had landed them in trouble.

The new power dots were the finest Borter had ever seen. He couldn't deny that. With only the original three left to Soarer after the Reggian debacle, it would have been no contest with the Tyrean interceptors. Even with a full six of the old dots, it would have been a much closer contest. Bouley had been a good base.

At times, Borter hovered closely around the Marcellean, examining his face, body armor, and the Shoulder Falcon itself. Borter referred to it as "the box." The man appeared to be in his mid-fifties, tall and heavy. Borter had never seen either the ion blade sheathed at his side or the Marcellean himself before.

Borter busied himself wandering by the Marcellean, occasionally sitting in the cockpit with Helio. He frequently glanced back into the tube; once, he was sure he saw the Shoulder Falcon blink. Five hours from Marcellean space, there was movement in the tube.

Startled, Borter looked up at the Marcellean's sudden presence at his side. Recovering, he said calmly, not knowing what else to say,

"Five hours." The Marcellean said nothing but bent forward to look out the cockpit window. The planet, Marcellus, was nothing more than a speck in the distance.

"The men outside the bar, they weren't police?" Helio asked.

"Modallian agents," the Marcellean responded softly.

"Modallians?" Borter interjected. "What is Modallas?"

"Modallas," the Marcellean began thoughtfully, "exists in orbit around Marcellus. The Targans call it Sky God, but they are a very superstitious race." Borter looked over at Helio, confused, wondering what they had gotten into.

"The Modallians work against us through the Targan. Targans follow Lord Markham, who is, in turn, the slave of The Helmsman," the Marcellean continued. "I am needed on my planet."

"Just who are you?" Borter finally asked.

The Marcellean drew himself up as much as the bulkhead would allow. "I am called Lord Soal." There was a deep silence as Borter and Helio absorbed the new information, trying to bring it all into perspective. Lord Soal glanced forward at the oncoming planet.

Helio thumbed through the Galactic Atlas. "This is unusual; I don't recall the planet having a natural satellite."

"Modallas is not a natural satellite. It is artificial and alien, made by intelligent beings, possibly from another galaxy. His evil brings destruction to the planet. You will see soon enough," Lord Soal explained.

"There is more danger," Borter interrupted. Helio's face fell. Etiquette soured in the space between them. "Can you give me a good reason why I should not turn this ship around and take you to a neutral planet?" The Marcellean did not hesitate.

"Three reasons," Lord Soal answered. "First, you are being paid. Second, there will be no neutral planets if The Helmsman is not stopped here. Finally, I am about to make you an offer, one I'm sure you'll not refuse." Borter swallowed hard.

He continued, "We are about to meet a Marcellean flyer." Borter consulted Soarer's instruments, "Nothing on the scanner."

"I have sent for it with my own equipment."

"Impossible," Borter snapped. "We would have intercepted any signal."

"Unfortunately, your equipment is not as subtle as my own. Your sensors should activate your deflector array in five seconds," the Marcellean said calmly.

There was a full five seconds of silence. Helio shrugged at the sound of a beep from the sensor panel. "Deflectors coming on," he announced. Both men, astonished, looked at Lord Soal.

The panel beeped a second time. "A small flyer," Helio spoke softly, "speed 4.4, gaining."

Slowly, the Marcellean flyer came into sight and pulled alongside. "You mentioned a deal," Borter said flatly, raising an eyebrow as he did.

"Yes. I will pay in advance, Marcellean currency," the Marcellean looked from one to the other, first to Borter, then to Helio.

Borter listened carefully, wanting more. "Sounds good, so far," he said. "What's the mission?"

"Do you know the planet Menad?" Helio nodded. Borter followed suit dumbly. "You will journey there after I transfer. Your cargo from Menad is something you have carried before; the destination is Marcellus."

"What cargo?" Borter spoke up.

"A journalist—named Parnak. He speaks of you often; I'm sure you remember him," the Marcellean smiled wryly.

The pilots looked at each other, measuring their response; neither smiled. "Your third reason, gentlemen."

The Marcellean went on smiling, "You know that Parnak reports only on warfare. I must tell you that a constant state of war exists on Marcellus, a conflict that will escalate before your return. You will have to run a Modallian blockade to reach the planet, a difficult undertaking. Parnak says you are the ones to do it!"

The airlock clanged heavily on Soarer's hull. Seconds later, it was secured and operating. Lord Soal had nothing else to say before leaving Soarer except to request that his chief engineer be allowed to inspect Soarer's space-worthiness as a courtesy. The pilots agreed.

Before transferring to his ship, payment was transferred to Soarer and stowed aft. He did not wish them luck as he departed, neither did he look back as he crossed over.

A moment later, in place of the Marcellean lord stood an officious-looking little man of supposed authority and no small gravity of manner. Helio made a proper greeting to the Techno-Dwarf while Borter merely nodded. "I am Old Face," the little man's self-introduction came. "Do you speak?" He demanded, eyebrows raised, looking from Helio to Borter.

"I am Borter."

"I am Helio, and if there is nothing you require of me, I'll go to the cockpit. There are things that demand my attention."

The little man said nothing but nodded, as did Borter. Helio went forward to the cockpit.

Having boarded without any visible equipment, the little man stalked from place to place in the tube with long steps for one his size, Borter's gaze on him all the while. He whistled annoyingly the whole time through a gap in between his teeth.

Once, he looked briefly at Borter as if he'd lost something. Borter pointed casually, "The pipes are over there," indicating the heavily shielded tubular units.

"I can see 'em," scolded the dwarf. "The day I can't, you can bury me." Whistling softly, Old Face released the opaque shield covers and peered in. The glare, shielded by yet another translucent cover, lit his face eerily, giving him the aspect of mystery as well as great age. The cover slammed shut.

"Pipes," he growled, "ya got yer pipes." He tapped them with affection. "Little beauties, our power dots."

His whistling became more absent-minded as he retraced steps toward the airlock. Finally, turning as he stepped across the bulkhead. "She's a strange one," he pronounced Soarer worthy, if not her crew, "but she should get you to Menad and back." The airlock hissed open, and he went back to the Marcellean flyer without another word.

8

The Search For Parnak

His long legs stretched out toward the summit. The slope didn't look too steep for him. He'd crossed worse in his time, he supposed. Then again, there was no point in having come if he did not go on. It wasn't long until he was able to look back into the rough scrub valley and ravine he had just crossed to the slope itself.

Beyond the scrub valley was a small plain enclosed by sharp mountains. He had been let off to walk by the convoy carrying supplies and reinforcements. It had been his own idea to walk, saying it would do him good. His short walk had already covered several kilometers.

In the distance was the adventure of solitude. Among other small benefits, it allowed him to express his own thoughts. He used the time traveling in the wilderness to collect and sort ideas. Sometimes, they seemed to tumble down uncontrolled, with no end of them in sight. Even to an old workhorse like him, the torrent seemed at times unbearable.

Vast loneliness was the only cure. He enjoyed the diversion as strange as it was for one of his necessary social backgrounds. Nothing else was going on then, on Menad. Had he the flying transportation, he might have chosen an easier sort of escape from the ghosts that followed him, if only at a slightly greater distance.

That day, it was raining, no new military developments to report in the rain. The entire apparatus of the war shut down when the skies on Menad opened. He shouldered the supply column before the first drop touched the ground. Enough time had been spent in different parts of that world to know what was happening in the sky. It was down to a science.

He brought very little equipment with him on this little foray. Most of his equipment was stored in a transport in the convoy. A miniature recorder and his constant companion, the Universal Translator, were all he carried on him. Not far, but well out of sight and earshot, the column wound through the dust of the road. The vibration of the heavy vehicles was apparent through the ground.

His walk had not much farther to go. Not far ahead, the road made a great bend to avoid a mountain standing in its path. With his quick pace, it would be no problem to intercept them and rejoin that drab procession, letting it carry him comfortably into the night through the rain that would surely come, making traveling, in its way, sticky.

No reason would be served by staying out in the downpour. Without the drenching rain to slow them, it would have taken only two days more to reach the back area of the war. The big tires of the transport would keep them away from the mud and moving toward their destination. That was something he liked about them, the inanimate wheels carrying on, conquering everything in their path. For long periods, sometimes, he would stare down at them, crunching along on the road.

As he crested, his view improved. Just beyond lay the bend in the road where the convoy would catch up to him. They should have walked, he thought, although they would not have been able to match his pace. He looked down onto another plain. It was cut by a river. Perhaps it was only a large stream.

He did not know exactly which it would be called by the standards of Menad. The planet was not overly watery, except for the rains. Great stretches of it were barren, rocky deserts most seasons. Not all of it, however, for Menad, too, was a place of teeming life.

Many days' travel from the hilltop on which he stood, Menad boasted great cities, great enough to be known throughout the central part of the galaxy. That, however, was not the primary attraction of the planet. The high mountains gave way to low hills reaching in from both sides of the plain. Their dull hues held more wonders for him than did the densely populated areas farther away.

For the better part of the afternoon, clouds of white vapor hung low on the plain of the little river; he couldn't tell whether or not they reached the hill or actually hovered over them. In his mind, he tried to work out the meteorology and found that he did not have the necessary information to formulate a prediction.

Looking out, he spotted the bend in the road where the column would pass. He would have to wear shoes again before he rejoined them, though they were a discomfort. The soldiers tended to stare at his mechanically jointed appearance, particularly his feet. To avoid unwanted attention, he would accept the inconvenience.

Parnak started down the ridge. The steepness of it did not bother him at all; he drove straight down. His curious feet, the single, obvious insectoid feature of his body, held him in good stead, moving him quickly across the ground. The trek had been enjoyable, a recreation compared to an uneventful ride with the convoy.

For three days with the convoy, he had been bored and had grown increasingly restless. The bouncing ride over the primitive roads made it impossible for him to do even the slightest work. Thinking had been almost as difficult. The hard bed of the truck rose up to smack his backside at every bump. The common soldiers, he found, were a good lot. They were the kind almost always found in wars like this. They had their rough spots, their hopes and desires like all the others, and to be sure, there were the brutes and cowards among them. This he found in other places too, if not all.

The occupation of a journalist in a war zone, his continual assignment, was rough. Parnak, however, minded it little and probably would not take it well if relieved of his duties. Other times, it was just plain hard work, but he was bred to that if nothing else. And the warring? That was hereditary, too. His people could not get enough of the stuff. He transmitted to them continually from many strange places, places where his smooth exterior was mistaken for body armor. Common soldiers remembered that he was never without it and never questioned further. Parnak allowed them to believe as they wished. He did not believe they would knowingly or easily speak with an alien. It had been workable, or he would have abandoned it long before.

He wondered if they would speak at all to an insectoid, a thing that trod underfoot for millions of years. They would not wait, nor would they even slow down for him. The rumbling pace of the trucks combined with the lack of good roads made them easy prey to his quick run.

Reluctantly wandering from the river basin back to the plain, feeling the pull of the not-far-distant convoy, he gathered to the pace and began to jog toward it leisurely. Reconnecting the translator before he embarrassed himself, he gathered to the pace and began to jog toward it leisurely. The pace came easily; the prescribed mechanics of the outer skeleton made his manner appear quick, gliding extremely tireless and efficient. Parnak rarely found himself fatigued at the end of a run, no matter what the distance. It was all work to him, and he loved it all. The shoes swung easily over one shoulder, rocking with the jogging motion.

The dust cloud rose tinted the sky behind it. A kilometer or two, he thought. It was an easy run; in a few minutes, the river and the surrounding territory had slipped behind him. The rest of the journey by transport would not be so brutally monotonous now that he had managed to give himself a few hours to clear his mind.

The time spent was just finding its place in his memory when something shattered the idyllic scene, something like a pane of ordinary glass hit by a rock. A thing startlingly fast whistled closely overhead. Instinctively, almost before it could be heard, he went flat against the ground, making his way to the sparse cover that offered itself near the roadside.

A rebel aircraft shot by overhead, then another, a part of the coming storm of destruction they were. Explosions shook the ground. A third aircraft zoomed past after them. Before they began strafing the column, Parnak was back on his feet, trying to get to a better place to take action. Seconds later, black smoke boiled up into the sky. Something had been hit. Flames leaped from burning trucks by the time he got to his vantage point. The road was newly littered with hot debris scattered by intense blasts. Parnak stayed well back. Except for the small recorder with which he stood surveying the scene, he was completely unarmed, save his natural strength.

Rebels poured onto the road, driving the convoy defenders before them. Their flyers still buzzed above, keeping loyalist heads down as the convoy advanced. Smaller explosions ripped through the convoy, destroying other vehicles and scattering more defenders. The smell of burning fuel mingled in the air with that of explosives.

Parnak moved cautiously, farther away. It appeared that he would be treated to a long walk whether he liked it or not. His recorder faithfully took in the whole attack. Flanking the column to cover the road from a better angle, this time more dangerously, in the direction the Loyalists came, forced out by the burning wreckage as they pulled back farther away from the fighting. Smaller explosives continued to fall on them as they fought back hard for their lives. The camera recorded as their numbers diminished in the open, where they were caught. Debris began to rain down all around him. A customary stubbornness held him in place until he had enough footage.

Parnak then ran hard to escape it himself. He backtracked, circling the battle as widely as possible. The bombardment became more intense at the lower level. Rebel flyers continued to strafe farther down. A few vehicles in the convoy broke the ring of desperation and bounced down the road at full speed on their big tires. The small explosions followed them until they drew out of range. The rebel flyers swooped quickly after them, pounding the trucks until they were left a mass of rubble, destroyed.

The lot of war, Parnak offered his wisdom. He had not come to save lives or do any serious moralizing. His words were descriptions and, as such, objective. Parnak bore no regrets over death. He regretted only the loss of the greater part of his equipment.

The fight was over suddenly; only a distant crackle of small arms fire could be heard. The last fuel tanks of the convoy's vehicles had exploded minutes before. He'd observed it had all been very precise and quick, very efficient. Turning away, he strolled down the slope away from the fighting. It was over.

The distance to the next post was not known. It would not be a difficult journey on foot for him. The walk he'd enjoyed that day had likely saved his life. They would have to do without supplies and reinforcements for a while at the outpost. It was supposed that they were being worn down, deprived of supplies and fresh troops they would weaken, ripe for attack. He set his way for the outpost, two days away by foot, at least, he thought. He would record the outpost's siege, too. So, very little was missed by his recorder. The words that became his narrative, recorded in his own language, gave a vivid picture of all that happened. In his own world, they would regard his work and make criticisms. Of course, he would hear none of it; he rarely saw the finished product and did not care to.

Rebels scurried among the wrecks. Several bedraggled prisoners were marched away. None of them appeared to have any fight left; the light artillery disappeared back across the little river and the abbreviated plain into the hiding from which it had come. The rebels themselves began to fade into the landscape and their flyers back into the sky. All except five soldiers.

The five plodded down the slope. About thirty meters below the dusty roadbed, they entered a deep gully. They followed it solemnly for a time. Occasionally, the leader would turn and look at the others to be sure they still followed. The gully was long and winding, and they did not move on top of the other but were spread far apart. Five men were not much along its length.

The gully was empty and dry that time of year. Other seasons swelled it with rain, rushing along in torrents. The men moved silently, treading with the great skill born of necessity. Dust moved like light powder; more than once, the wind gushed up the ravine, raining dry particles with a soft rasping sound, forcing some to stifle a cough or a sneeze. The gully turned itself out some kilometers distant. The five Rebels fanned out. The road was just beyond their reach ahead, where it split into two trails, one high, one low. They dropped to the ground and waited.

They were men, more somber than dark, coarsely dressed, intent. Their eyes did not wander from the fork in the road.

Though looking ragged, they were professional soldiers, revolutionaries, as they thought of themselves. However, the direct calling was unimportant to the one they sought. Time wore on slowly, but they did not have to wait long. The stranger had taken the wrong fork to the high road.

The Rebels looked around at each other. The anticipated mistake by their quarry had been made. It would be a short day for these men who usually drew the difficult assignments. Containing themselves was beyond question as the dark one they sought followed the wrong trail to the bluff nowhere.

When Parnak had gotten out of sight, they advanced behind him cautiously. Mistaking the outer skeleton for body armor, rarely seen on this planet and worn by no other than great warriors, they planned to capture this bold survivor of their most destructive attack. Pacing slowly, they covered the space to the roadway and pursued their quarry. This one might be taken alive since he'd already helped them by taking the wrong road. When he reached the edge of the bluff, they would be right there, behind him. The ground was old and soft, hiding their footsteps. Had the ground been hard and rocky, their stealth would have produced the same result.

Parnak climbed what simply was another hill that would lead him easily down the other side along a winding road back to the plain. There were many of them on this part of Menad. Unfortunately, he had forgotten his map; it burned with the remainder of his equipment in the bombed-out convoy.

He stepped out onto the unexpectedly level bluff. It was covered with a light green grass, the kind found in many places on Menad. It was not long before Parnak came to the edge and looked down over a sheer drop to the plain below. The correct road wriggled out on the ground far below, seeming to mock his normal efficiency. A false step from behind made him turn. The trampled-looking men stood quietly behind, giving each other quick glances, smiling and nodding to one another.

Parnak faced them calmly. His features could not change, nor therefore smile, allowing any gesture of friendship toward the men. Their weapons remained pointed at him. After what seemed to be an appropriate time, Parnak spoke through the Universal Translator. Long ago, he had learned all there was to know about the facial expressions of humanoids. To him, they were like reading a book.

They wanted him alive; there was no danger. He would allow himself to be led off and make his explanation then.

All this was not to be immediate, however. Blank stares and more smiles greeted his translated words. None of the men had the slightest idea what language Parnak spoke to them. They gamely tried several of the most dominant on Menad. Parnak then had another realization, that the translator did not have in it any of the languages the rebels knew and did not have any of the applications necessary to code them from scratch. Surrendering became less difficult.

Still, he could use that to his own advantage. They must be made to see that he was something quite special. He hesitated at taking the recorder from the case on his belt, careful that the hillmen did not think it a weapon and open fire. Parnak gestured happily in what, for him, approximated a cheerful greeting. He buzzed happily at them until they got the message.

The leader motioned him forward with the barrel of his blaster. He walked forward. The buzzing that was Parnak's native language stopped. All talking stopped. The man looked Parnak over, from his feet to the antennae at the top of his head.

The man scratched his head. It was beginning to dawn on him that this creature was unfamiliar, even unknown, something that he had never seen before.

Parnak gazed down at the man who was about a head shorter. Parnak's feet told him this was no mere armored shell. He stepped back and looked again. Raising his blaster, he stopped smiling his stupid grin and motioned his prisoner forward with the weapon once more.

Before long, Parnak found himself in a crude stockade with several other prisoners. Looking at the recorder that he'd been left strangely, Parnak decided to make the best of it. When his body was not found among the convoy dead, inquiries would be made. It could take months, years even. He did not have recording supplies for that long a stay; rescue, therefore, would have to come sooner. He sat down, preparing for a long stay.

9

Tienan

Breaking from Menad orbit, Borter and Helio prepared to meet the atmosphere of the planet. Soarer nosed over, the pilot's eyes skimming the dry surface of the world below. It was his favorite way of looking over a planet upside down. Helio sweated over the onboard computer and had little time to admire the view. They were on a planetary glide path, taking them to the Loyalist sector of Menad.

"I have Menad Control," Helio swept across the console, flicking switches. Borter took no special note. It wasn't time for landing instructions. "They appear to be under fire," Helio glanced around at the unconcerned Borter, who merely grunted. "They appear to be under fire," Helio repeated. The pilot was unmoved.

"War going badly, is it?" Borter replied finally. He leaned back in his chair. For some reason, he'd been unable to sleep the night before and now felt drowsy. Menad was not his worry. Parnak would probably be there when they landed to greet them. A few moments after that, Soarer would be loaded, and they would be on their way. Time spent there would be minimal, and they would return to Marcellus in a matter of slightly more than three days - mission accomplished.

The Dillisome worked feverishly over the console as he listened to the space chatter coming over the headphones. Things quieted, and Menad Control came back with landing instructions, which

Helio passed along to Borter, who'd already heard them for himself. He made no comment on the repetition. Soarer veered down. Borter slotted the craft toward Menad Control at Tienan.

An hour later, with Soarer safely on the ground, they walked from their berth toward the main terminal. "What do you think?" Borter asked.

"Terrorists," the blue man answered in an easy tone, "they come, and they go. The voice of the powerless," he said, noticing several smoking craters.

Borter looked around at him impatiently. "No. I mean Jibba's ship. Did you see it?"

"No. Where?" The Dillisome looked around. "Don't," Helio looked, "turned, " – look now. Some of his men are standing over there."

Borter nodded casually. Several roguish men loitered not far away. "It's Piquar. I'd like to even things with that one," Borter glared, almost letting the old hatred out. "Let's go."

The area surrounding the main concourse was cordoned off following the rocket attack. It smoldered in several places, as Helio had noted. They passed quickly through and left the spaceport for the city. In the search for Parnak, any vengeance on Jibba would have to wait, for a while, at least.

Their first destination, port-of-call, was a local hotel frequented by journalists covering the warfare on Menad and others there on separate business. Both kinds of customers favored the place for its uncomplicated style and especially its cool bar where long afternoons, when there was a lull in the fighting but not the heat, they could sit and drink, telling their adventures to one another. Then, when it became late enough or when they were drunk enough, dinner could be ordered.

Generally, Parnak and his friends might be found weaving through the wide Tienan streets at all hours. He was not there and hadn't been for days, said the room clerk. Borter expected as much. Through his malfunctioning translator, the room clerk said one day, the week before Parnak had packed his kit and said something about an outpost under siege in the hinterlands. His room had been paid for until the end of the month and he'd given orders to hold all messages.

Borter became annoyed. The room clerk's translator sputtered unintelligible, half words in Universal. "What?" Borter asked over and over. He turned to walk away, but the clerk called him back.

"eee . . . aid so. . . thing about a . . . convoy."

The man removed the ailing translator from its holster on his belt and tapped it hard on the desk. "I said, he said something about a convoy. You'll have to get in touch with the army supply headquarters for more information on that one."

"Thanks," Borter called back over his shoulder, already heading for the door. He called to Helio, who was making his second circuit of the lobby, admiring the expensive curios and decorative appointments. They walked down the street at a new pace. "We'll have to go to the army for anything more."

"What did you want to do about Jibba?"

Borter walked another few paces before answering. Jibba and his man Piquar had cost them the Reggian cargo and three very expensive power dots. "I'm working on it," he replied irritably. "Any ideas?" Helio smiled and shook his head no.

This was Borter's area of expertise. "I'd like to give him what he gave us," Borter confided.

"What if Jibba's an honest man here?"

Borter shook his head, giving Helio a look of great despair. He spoke in a quiet voice, "The idea is that Jibba is an honest man nowhere. That's what will make it easy. Come on," he said. "We've got to find out where the army assembles its convoys around here. It's the only lead we've got."

Much later, the two found the proper depot. A young officer remembered Parnak, "A dark, tallish fellow, all in battle armor, antennae sprouting from the forehead." It was a good thing Parnak put in such an appearance. The young man sighed and looked up at them sadly. "I'm afraid that convoy was attacked and destroyed en route. However, this fellow, Parnak, was not one of the dead or the few others who escaped. He's likely a prisoner of the rebel hillmen."

They were led to a small, spindly man who wore a field command insignia. Borter doubted that the man had ever seen combat.

He rose from behind a large desk and weakly shook hands with them. Borter thought it going a little far to display field rank; everyone knew the real fighting was done by mercenaries. This man could be no more than an efficient clerk, a bureaucrat, a skilled paper coordinator.

"Ah," the man moaned, "took us by surprise, I think."

Helio paid attention dutifully. Borter made questions from the new information he'd been given.

He asked, "Why don't you clear the rebels out of those hills?"

"Can't—wouldn't have happened years ago. The caliber of mercenaries has gone very low, don't you know? They've stopped spending the money to attract the really good ones. I think it's an indication of the way things are going for us, don't you?" The officer turned to his papers.

"There are too many of them and too few of us," He said. "At least out there. You must understand this has been a long, hard action. To make it worse, they are well entrenched. Without an impossibly massive commitment of men and materials, we stand no chance at all."

He paused once more, shuffled through more paper and this time checked his computer. "There is something going out that way next week if you'd care to wait. Nothing else 'til then."

The man smiled at them with a little side-to-side shake of his head.

"Of course, it will be better protected than the one your Mister Parnak was on." The man's brow wrinkled. "Are you planning something on your own?"

"Unless you can suggest something better," Borter replied. "And, unless these rebels execute their prisoners immediately."

"No," the officer shook his head, 'rarely, very rarely, indeed. The Gas Mor hillmen are vulgar but not savages." He looked briefly at Helio, who remained the attentive listener, then back at Borter.

"Where can we get a small vehicle?"

The supply officer thought for a moment.

"Suitable for the terrain around Fourth Peak in the Gas Mor Hills?" He asked.

Borter nodded. The man eyed him strangely and gave directions.

10

Revenge

Back in the streets of Tienan, Borter stepped up to a paid communicator. He picked up the receiver and dropped in the appropriate coin. Looking away, vacantly down the street, he spoke several words to a person on the other end. Rejoining Helio, they walked away.

The center of Tienan was like the center of many cities with spaceports: dusty, with long straight streets intersected at regular intervals to form square block after square block. Life seemed to be a variety of confused light vehicles buzzing by, seemingly without a set destination or pattern.

As they walked, Borter and Helio noticed the same glut of alien life they saw at all such places. There was nothing they had not seen before somewhere else. Beside them strode proud Borreans, overdressed for the hot climate of Menad, moving slowly in the thoroughfare. Their long, bristling manes waved in the wind, back and forth with each step like grass breaks on some arid Savannah. Borter knew by the look of them they were mercenaries hired by the Loyalists. Despite their penchant for grooming and excellent manners, Borreans were good fighters, rough and ready. In many ways, they were like Marcelleans. His mind ran back to Lord Soal, the only Marcellean he'd ever seen. Like Marcelleans, he thought if Lord Soal was par. Helio followed after Borter, who was making his way through clots of them crowding the streets.

They made a stop to buy translation dots for the language spoken by the Gas Mor Hills tribes. White medical uniforms came next. Borter smiled but gave no answer when Helio asked what they were for. Instead, he handed them to the Dillisome, and they moved on to the vehicle rental. They picked up a small four-wheeler that would fit Soarer's tube perfectly. The color was metallic blue, Borter said to the pretty rental agent with a wink and a smile to match Helio.

The rest of the way back to the spaceport was easier with a vehicle. Near the main gate, Borter stopped abruptly and stepped out. "Looking for Jibba?" Helio asked.

"I'll settle for Piquar if Jibba isn't around," said Borter. "He smells pretty rotten, too."

Helio agreed, "I'd feel perfectly justified if Jibba was not available."

Borter leaned over to Helio mockingly as if disclosing some worldly truth a sheltered child might have missed growing up, "He never liked you, you know?"

"Which one, Jibba or Piquar?" Helio played along, asking stupidly.

"Both," Borter revealed with even less credulity.

"No," Helio feigned amazement.

"Yes."

Helio recovered slightly, "You never told me."

"Well, I know how much their goodwill means to you," Borter consoled.

"When did you find out?"

"Oh," Borter spoke in mock confidence, "the last time they tried to kill us - I think."

Borter got back into the car. There was a flurry of activity ahead of them at the spaceport.

"What's going on?" The Dillisome asked.

Borter smiled wryly, "I think maybe they've raided Jibba's ship." The little vehicle moved forward slowly.

Passing the gate, he showed his papers and asked the guard in plain Universal what was happening. The guard did not answer, moving them along with a jab of his thumb.

"How did you know it was Jibba's ship?" Helio asked as they drove along.

Borter smiled, "Dumb luck, just dumb luck and the fortunes of Plan B."

Helio laughed. Borter rarely had a Plan A, never mind a Plan B. They boarded Soarer and launched uneventfully.

Parnak languished in the small stockade. The Gas Mor Hills had proved less than hospitable to him, especially in the hot night. From several low buildings, a variety of prisoners emerged, many not natives of Menad, crossing the clearing. No one approached Parnak, fearing his strange appearance; they thought he wasn't a prisoner at all but an informer or worse. His distant manner did not help. At one time or another, he caught all the others staring at him.

Parnak refused to enter any of the long barracks made of crude materials for the prisoners. The outside seemed more hospitable to him. The yard was bounded by a high wire fence. He spent much time sitting on the ground, looking out with his big, shiny eyes into the thick trees and vegetation surrounding the camp.

The guards and their blasters were the things he feared in the camp. At night, he could easily cut through the linked wire of the fence, but it would not be soundless. Then, perhaps, with his speed, he could make it into the deep brush before drawing fire. If he encountered resistance, his strength was great enough to kill or disable one or two guards before others could answer a call for help.

It was then he was reminded of his old friends, Helio and Borter. Parnak wondered why he thought of them just at that moment. He managed the equivalent of a smile. He thought of Helio as one who finessed with courtesy. Borter, on the other hand, was someone who could sneak vulgarly. To be sure, he could make use of both their talents at that time.

Parnak felt a special closeness to Helio and had always. They were both men of ideals and loyalty. The blue man was as faithful to his friendship with Borter as he was to his own people. A simple explanation of the difference in their loyalties would be to say Helio had acquired what Parnak had been born with. In the end, both loyalties were as profound as the vast numbers populating their home planets.

Borter had entered with something else. If only they were there. Still, for a while, there had been that odd vibration in the air. It was inexplicable, something he hadn't experienced in some time. A brief sensation brought on by the unaccustomed captivity, too good to be true. He put it from his mind.

All through the night, Parnak sat in the same place. The guards did not move the prisoners into their barracks, but all went, except Parnak. There were no lights in the compound. Guards were minimally stationed. He wondered how the prisoners were kept in. A little later, he got an answer. They did not care at all that he sat outside.

A few meters beyond the wire fence, something snarled in the brush. The snarl was deep in pitch and came from a large throat. It crashed through something suggesting vegetation, making no attempt at stealth. Two guards walked with it, groaning under their breath as they strained at heavy leashes. It could not be made out clearly, a brutish glistening something about one meter tall.

He never saw it clearly in the meager light carried by the guards as they jerked along. Once, he caught an evil – looking glint from the creature's eyes as it pushed by. That brief, distant encounter was close enough for the journalist.

The struggling trio vanished into the darkness. Parnak did not see them again. The dense night lingered with him. He had lost track of the days since he had come to Menad. It had even been several days since he had last filed a report with the home office. The last one dulled even the old loyalty; it flagged, and he almost did not send it in.

He did not often think in these terms. His life was to report what he saw. That was his reason for living, for being. Life seemed full enough without bothering with other unnecessary considerations. Situations could be handled.

These other questions were of the kind that were never properly answered and only led to others like them. Parnak looked up into the night sky. Lights flashed through it. He had seen enough ships in the night sky to know it was a ship and not a meteor. It was not a Rebel craft; theirs were black-hulled and did not reflect light.

It had to be a Loyalist ship or that of an off-worlder. The odd vibrations returned, chilling him again. He wondered, standing before he realized he'd done it.

Far down the plateau, Rebel flyers leaped into the sky, showing off their powerful afterburn as they went to challenge an intruder. He watched the lights of the little fighters taper off into the sky. They were the ones who had attacked the convoy the day before. He hardly wished them luck, the memory of the smashed convoy fresh in his mind and in view of his present circumstances.

Most often, he was unaffected by the destruction and death all around him. There had been that convenient insulation of his professional dedication; at times, it slipped. At other times, he became trapped in it and wanted to stop. He had not. Actually, what it amounted to was more articles, several in his personal doubts. They were not well–received at home by a people innately dedicated to spare, plain lives born of the necessity of eons. They were an old race and changed slowly.

Shortly, several bright streaks appeared in the sky and landed on the plateau. He assumed their mission went satisfactorily. Whatever action there had been happened out of sight. Parnak had seen or heard nothing with his remarkable senses. There were four lights returning.

The sun rose over Menad slowly, giving the horizon an angry orange hue. Clouds of ice crystals gave the sky a streaked appearance. Parnak rose from the dampened ground and walked the worn paths inside the stockade. They did not lead far. Soon, he turned and then turned again. He circled the small enclosure again and again, seeking an exit he could not find, hoping for a plan he did not have.

Other prisoners dribbled at length from the barracks. There seemed no set regimen; they roamed at will. Parnak saw no one from the convoy. Those in the stockade were one and the same with their pitiful appearances. How long had they been there? He did not know, but whatever length of time had taken its toll on each, no matter how long or how short.

They drooped, thirsty, to the ground one after the other, daubing at the disappearing moisture on the blades of short grass. Parnak would have no part of it, refusing even to look. In a befuddled order, they straggled one after another toward the stockade gate to see if breakfast was coming. Then, they dawdled along the same path Parnak had walked. For a long, long time, they trudged the hard ground. Rebel mercenaries were in plain sight all around.

Several mulled the space in front of the main building of the compound. Others stood guard. They were not the same hillmen who brought him in the day before. These men stood like regular soldiers. Far away were the hillmen, he thought, though he could not make them out clearly in the distance.

An hour and a half more dragged on before food was brought. A big pot was moved out from somewhere behind the main building. Parnak caught a bit of its smell and wondered if he would be able to eat it. His early survey of the planet before coming showed several substances dangerous to him, but none were known to be included in any food.

The stuff was awful. It dripped between his hard lips, down his chin, and onto his chest. It was almost completely liquid with a few lumps of mysterious, unknowable paste floating in it. Parnak wiped away what he could, putting the hard shell of his forearm into service in the effort. In all his years, this was perhaps his first really disgusting experience.

The rest of the morning continued much the same as it had begun. Parnak did little. Once in a while, he got to his feet and walked, his exposed feet becoming a big attraction among his fellow prisoners. A little after the noon hour, four mercenaries in smart-looking uniforms escorted him to the main building.

He was led to a marked door. It slid sideways before him. He was put into a bare room without windows. There was nothing to be heard on either side; his guards did not speak among themselves. His feet clattered and scraped on the hard floor, making him wish for his shoes, though he liked them no better than before. There he remained, waiting for a long time.

He concluded escape was impossible.

His inner clock, a sort of biological intuition bred in all his people, did not help retain the delicate balance between day and night, between activity and rest.

Interrogation was expected. It would not be gentle, he knew. Waiting served only to disorient him. The harsh light from overhead was not like the sun in any world where he had ever been. The silence of the place brought by the lack of industry was his next thought; he could not work. It nearly overwhelmed him.

11

Parnak

Later, Borter lay back in his chair. He looked across at Helio. "She runs nicely."

Helio looked back. "What did you expect?"

"Why don't you go back and get some rest?" said Helio.

"I'd like to, but I still have some things to think over," the pilot replied.

There was a silence, unusually long for the pilot. "I'm amazed we got out of there," he said, staring straight ahead out of the cockpit into endless space ahead.

"Yes, Tyrus is quite the place, even at the worst times."

"We got out," Borter smiled.

"Yes," the reply came dryly back from the Dillisome. "All the way out."

Borter was beginning to drift. They called him The Bug, but not to his face. It was difficult to anger Parnak; you had to threaten his life or that of someone close to him, only then things opened up. The strength in those spindly insectoid limbs was as great as he was slow to anger.

They had been in the main city of Jinzyka, Pi. Crummy place, he remembered. It was in a bar, of course. The war there was just beginning to attract interplanetary attention. The city was full of flyers. Parnak had hired them; he forgot just where they had run into each other to move him from place to place in the fighting.

Helio noticed his friend's somber expression. "What are you thinking?"

"Parnak," was the answer. "I was just remembering that time, back in the bar, on Jinzikan. That was a battle worthy of a correspondent of Parnak's abilities."

Helio smiled briefly, "I think that was the last time anyone tried to throw The Bug out of a night spot. It will be good to see him again. If there are more like him – they are too few in the Inner Galaxy. His species are fewer than Dillisome."

"Besides yourself," said Borter, "there is only that – Pak, the sub-commander with the Kithronese fleet that I know of – that is rare. I wonder if he's changed much?" Borter smiled. "Not unless he's grown out another set of arms. Parnak worried after us like someone's grandmother. The first thing out of his mouth will be why haven't we settled down?" Borter laughed. Parnak understood next to nothing of the physiology of life forms, his own included. Predictably, he supposed that the two were mated and expected to hear the patter of little feet in Soarer's cargo tube. Arguments to that effect were common from him. "You two are biologically compatible for the creation of new life, aren't you"? He'd asked once. "Quite a gentleman, that," Borter murmured, bordering on admiration. Helio nodded in agreement. "Remember the time we shuttled him in for that battle on Trasurus?"

"Yes, those kid troopers heading for the front on the polar cap will never forget The Bug. They thought they'd left him behind, hundreds of kilometers back, in the staging area. But there he was, standing on the ice, waiting for them. We got around faster than they did. That had made them think he was really important. Only their generals traveled that fast. That got them to talk to him."

By then, Borter had flown Soarer, alternating with Helio, for three days with no more than an hour's sleep at any time.

"Those troopers," Helio spoke, "they'd never understand a thing like that." Borter agreed. Moving much faster than the soldiers on either side, they were practically immune to interception. Parnak's credentials as a journalist, a second safety, shielded them on whichever side they landed.

Further, his word was good, as well as his basic ethic not to endanger a source through any report, was accepted as a fundamental precept of his profession by all. The fact that Parnak often had knowledge useful to one side or the other did not place him in danger; a journalist meant non – partisan, which meant he was ineligible, totally exempt from what one side dealt to the other.

"And, that thing, on Claudius Major," Borter stopped for a minute, remembering what he'd seen there. "Planets pushed into the near sun? Cosmic war, I won't say it's a good thing, but there's certainly nothing else like it." Helio nodded in agreement.

"I'll bet Parnak and that Old Face character would be a perfect match, pals. Remember Marrus V? I've never heard such complaining. He didn't even stop when I threatened to make him walk. I'd love to be there when those two square off."

Helio laughed. "It would be interesting."

"I wonder what kind of war will be raging when we get back to Marcellus?" Borter shrugged.

Helio did not attempt to answer. They continued on their way without trouble.

The pilots knew each other well after years of shuttling cargo from planet to planet in the Inner Galaxy. Usually, they felt no need to converse beyond the normal exchanges in the performance of routine duties. When they felt no need, the ship fell silent.

The Marcellean Mission, as they would call it, was forcing something else, something new, into the unique relationship between them. They chattered on as if reviewing their entire partnership, paying little heed to the passage of long hours traveling or any other pastime kept aboard for the occasion of long voyages.

Parnak was an interesting part of their past, a part they enjoyed wholly when he was not there. The two valued adventuring somewhat for its inherent dangers. Parnak's penchant for warfare brought them that opportunity. He was not a sentimentalist. At least, he was not the type of sentimentalist the two pilots seemed to be.

Though it had been several years since they had seen him, any greeting from him would more than likely be minimal. A quick word or two, then on to business. They would probably find him knee-deep in his current work, a recorder with him, surrounded by whatever else were the current tools of his trade.

Borter got up, remembering to check the Universal Translators. They would certainly need those for anything other than communication in sign language with Parnak. The buzzing of the insectoid serving as a language was understood by few others in the Inner Galaxy. From the time already spent with him, Borter and Helio could pick up a few meanings, but their humanoid physiology made it impossible to do little other than pale imitations of sounds they thought they heard.

Borter liked to try out his meager skills each time they met after a long separation. Helio, not wanting to share the embarrassment Borter claimed for himself in each attempt, kept quiet. Usually good-humored at the effort, no matter how bad, Parnak tried to teach him the basic sounds. At one time, he actually sat Borter down and explained that he simply did not have the biological equipment to create the necessary buzzes, rattles, and most certainly the electronically produced wave signals transmitted and received by the antennae grown from his smoothly rounded forehead.

Without certain factory – made electronic equipment, these signals were undetectable. Borter never gave up. Parnak liked that quality in anyone and showed exceptional patience with any, even the inescapable, like Borter, who showed the virtuous *stick – to – it – ness* he so admired in his own kind.

Parnak, himself, always carried such instruments. In his work, it was hard to say just who he would come across or where and what story he would miss by not having the device with him.

Most planets had them, either making their own or buying them from some off-world supplier. Borter and Helio had flown several shipments of them, all to different worlds. Helio remembered out – loud Borter's continuous complaints about the constant glut of Parnak's stuff, things in the way, nonessentials in Soarer's tube.

At one time, it had nearly filled the tube, spilling now and again into Borter's space, a no – man's – land reserved there. He considered it sacred ground and argued that nothing was to be placed in it, threatening to throw anything out that was left there. Parnak argued he was renting the entire tube, and Borter had nothing to say about it.

Helio had no trouble obeying the new rule since his physical possessions were few, and those he had were small. Borter, at times, was meticulous, keeping things in faultless order. However, when Parnak was busy, things fell everywhere. Parnak usually avoided such situations.

Borter's rants eventually stopped and became a thing of the past. Helio was happy. Parnak was happy and had only his work to think of, not an angry pilot. With a clear gangway, Borter also had little for complaint and had nothing to worry about.

Once, however, Parnak had run out to cover a nearby firefight, leaving the path impassable. Borter entered with the same enthusiasm as Parnak had when he left. About midway in the tube, Borter tripped, sprawling headfirst in the dark, flailing away in an unstoppable spill toward the cockpit, trying to catch hold of something, anything that would stop his fall – nothing came to hand or to mind. He landed flat with a loud thump near the bulkhead. Helio, in the cockpit, turned around in the dim light as the pilot came to that ungraceful rest on the deck.

On his feet quickly, complaining, he nursed small aches and pains gingerly. He refused any help Helio offered – injury far worse to his self-esteem.

Borter's full uttering was not repeatable. Helio would have left the ship if only to avoid the noise but was unable to make a path to the loading ramp.

Finishing his verbal tantrum, Borter returned to the tube and began throwing the offending clutter, not just from his sacred gangway to other parts of the ship but outside as well.

It was at this time Helio chose to leave. He wanted no part of the uproar between the two when Parnak returned. Other places provided more peace in greater quantities, if only by comparison.

The alternate shoutings and buzzings subsided at length. For several days longer, the two did not speak to each other or spoke only through Helio, who finally grew tired of that arrangement himself and threatened to leave the ship again, this time never to return. Neither wanted that. Borter wanted to end their contract with Parnak, who, in turn, wanted to end his arrangement with Borter, but not Helio. Instead, he offered to back Helio in the purchase of a new flyer. Helio refused to hear that, as well, insisting that the two settle their differences in an adult manner. At even greater length, that was done.

Parnak appointed Helio keeper of his train. Though reluctant to keep the brittle peace, Helio accepted the task. In the days that followed, Parnak rid himself of much of the extra equipment that had formed the once-curious, winding path toward the cockpit, the pilots' haunt and Helio was relieved of his duties. With some discomfort, Parnak became used to the new tube, thanks to Borter. Conversations slowly grew between the two and then got to normalcy. Borter apologized, and Parnak followed suit. It did not take long for them to mend relations. The war after that was covered with engaging professionalism.

From above, Borter engineered daring photography of engagements large and small while Helio, at the controls, dodged missiles and killer satellites, to whom their client was unknown, or if he was known to those who controlled them and did not care at all. Parnak's search somewhere below during that time for other news, particularly those of common soldiers, went forward. They were his heroes. Creeping among the shell craters, he would locate them and extract their stories whether the next minute they met their death or went on to victory on whatever dust ball of a world, forever lost in the backwater of galactic space, they were on.

At times, between battles, when other sources proved reliable, and Parnak had moments to himself, even he wondered in awe at life. On planet after planet, there was life. Then, after it, death occurs in an unending array. After that, more perishable and more fragile life. It was the puzzle that awed him. It was the same no matter what the danger. In his own world, there were always the soldiers, those who lived and those who died. For those whose life poured out on the ground or burned out in particle fire, Parnak was always there to record it.

Usually, he never fit himself into any part of the struggle. His life never mattered that way. When his life stopped, that would be that, and he did not worry about how or when. All life would not stop; there would be another, as there was for all things. He was just an observer of the cycle. Another would follow him. Others thought of it every minute. At times, he saw fear, sometimes bravery. Parnak supposed both to be based on necessity since giving or taking ground meant only superior numbers on one side or the other. Courage was expected from all. What was it that pressed him on?

"Halfway to Menad," Helio called back. Helio looked around at the sound, not really paying attention to the words that were spoken. One day and a half to Menad, he thought to himself finally. They had already been through all the old stories about Parnak they could remember. They had even repeated a couple. Now, both lolled in the empty tube. There was nothing in front or behind them except open space. The automatic pilot flew the course for them. The mission had become quiet. Borter had time, even, to check the containers holding their payment for the mission. It was there as promised. They did not know the exchange rate for Marcellean currency against any other currency. They would have to leave the answer to that for whatever planet was at the end of their journey after they brought Parnak to Marcellus. He glanced at the cockpit instruments and spoke to his partner, "Halfway to Menad!"

It was a possibility, something Borter had mentioned to Helio, that Parnak might hire them for the duration of the time he was on Marcellus. Helio shrugged when the suggestion was made to him. "What is it you want to do when we're back on Marcellus?" Helio looked back at him across the vacant space of the tube. Borter's face wore no expression as he'd looked up. He made a polite smile of it and flung up one hand in a sort of shrug. There were two answers in his mind, and he gave the most obvious. "Quit working for the Marcellean. Maybe work for Parnak, like we said." Yes, things were coming together now that he'd had time to sort through them.

12

Rescue

Late in the afternoon, it must have been late, he thought. His guards returned, the same four who had brought him from the stockade. Each took up a position in the room. The door did not slide back into place as before; rather, it remained open to admit the people whose hard-soled shoes he could hear pacing the corridor as they approached. Three sets of feet, each plainly audible.

The first men into the room wore white uniform smocks. They looked at him, then at each other, and once more at him. Next, they faced the officer who entered behind them, a young captain in the Rebel army.

There was silence, then, "Ah, yes," the man smiled, "it's him."

Borter shrugged to Helio, who shrugged back. He turned to the captain, and Helio assisted the game with a stern look. "I suppose he's told you that wild story about being some sort of... what is it... a war correspondent?"

"Actually, not," the captain replied. "He's new. We haven't a corresponding translator for the one he wears."

"Well, nevertheless, he'll tell you that. Tragic case, this one. Been on Muse for five years, Captain," Helio nodded in wise ascent.

"Try mine," Borter offered his translator. "It's keyed to the words and signals we've worked out with him. Mind you, it hasn't been easy. Comes from a lost world, you know?"

Borter smiled cordially, "There aren't many of his kind in the inner galaxy." Helio showed only the slightest trace of a smile.

Parnak was stunned by the pair's entrance. "Helio?" Of course, it was Helio. Who else would be traveling with this madman? What other Dillisome did he know?

"Borter?" The words buzzed from the translator in a language the captain could understand.

"Ah, he remembers us. That's hopeful." Borter beamed at him. "Though chances of recovery are remote, we have not given up, have we, my friend?"

"B-Borter?" Parnak stammered in amazement.

The pilot stretched his ability as an actor to the limit. Putting a hand on Parnak's shoulder, he spoke soothingly, "There, my friend. We've come to take you home. All your friends are waiting back on Muse."

Parnak stared down at the hand on his shoulder. He made no attempt to brush it away. "Won't that be nice?"

"Where are you from?" demanded the captain.

Parnak sputtered. "Uh-uh, Muse." Casting his large eyes at Borter.

"The isolation planet?" the Magnean helped him. "How did you get here?" The captain took a turn, this time a little less demanding.

"At last, the Universal language. I'm a war correspondent, a journalist," Parnak brightened. "I am simply doing my job. I'm Parnak, the Jillian."

"Never heard of you." The captain looked at Borter, who shrugged, then at Helio, who had an equally apologetic expression on his face.

"He really doesn't understand." Borter gave a sad roll of his eyes toward the ceiling and, with a forefinger, made a circling motion by the side of his head, to which Parnak took instant offense. He attempted to step forward and protest. The guards advanced, changing his mind. He stopped.

"Gentlemen, gentlemen, he's harmless, like a child." Borter interceded, "It's good you're ridding yourselves of him. He's difficult to care for, *has the strength of ten, you know?* Imagine the manpower to guard him, just to prevent his hurting himself."

Parnak relented. Borter continued to talk about him to the captain as if he were a small child and not there. Helio watched the conversation calmly, somberly, as was his usual disposition.

He looked at his guards, who stared back, indeed, vacantly at him. It was not they who should suspect his sanity, but he theirs — he thought. For some minutes, the discussion went on. Finally, Borter smiled, nodding to Helio. "Doctor?" He said with dignity. The two moved forward, each gently taking an arm.

"Come, Parnak. We're taking you back home." Borter smiled at him broadly, which seemed designed to reassure and satisfy the captain. Down the corridor, they led him without incident. Soon, they would leave the Rebel stronghold and be on the way to Marcellus.

The captain motioned the guards forward. Outside, the rented vehicle waited with a Rebel carrier behind it. The four guards climbed into that. After Helio and Parnak sat in the car, Borter moved the car out smoothly. It was not like flying Soarer, but he was in no position to complain. Soarer itself was not far away at the landing strip on the lower plateau.

Parnak sat cramped, his long legs jackknifed almost to his chest, in the back seat. Helio turned toward him, "Don't say anything until we've gone," he instructed. "So far, everything has gone well." As long as the guards were behind them, Helio refused to deviate from that plan in the slightest. The landing strip was coming into view. Soarer was still in place near a wing of sleek Rebel fighters.

Borter quickly boarded and lowered the cargo ramp. Borter and Parnak drove up the ramp into the tube. The car secured; they could take off. Helio called Rebel control. All was in order. Once again, they rolled down the runway. Borter inspected his instruments quickly. Helio took the controls, guiding the ship. Soarer nosed into the air.

Parnak hovered nervously at the bulkhead behind the cockpit. Until they reached orbit, he remained quiet. As Soarer leveled off, he talked to both of them, though neither turned from their duties. If they listened at all, neither showed it. He thanked them for saving him from a long stay in the stockade. The way they had done it had surprised him. In fact, he found it slightly annoying to have been assumed to be an escapee from isolation.

"Really, Borter, I know it has been a long time since we've seen each other. However, I have a few things to say about the way in which this escape was made. There have been no recorded cases of insanity among my people, ever. Insanity is purely a humanoid affliction."

Borter traded sidelong glances with Helio. Parnak was allowed to ramble without interference.

"I know it was you who came up with this, Borter. Helio does not think in these devious ways. His race and mine seem to be left alone in not having to count insanity among their diseases." Parnak turned away for an instant, then back suddenly. "Not that I'm ungrateful for the save; however, there are some points of simple courtesy." The tirade went on and on as the two pilots worked to slot their flyer.

In the end, Borter turned to him. It was the nervous energy working itself off, he knew, but he had reached the end of his patience. "You ungrateful shell of guts," he shouted. "I had some amount of respect for you 'til now. I thought you were smart enough not to question the source of any aid. Especially from those who risked life and limb to do it. You damn near botched the whole thing getting mad."

Borter turned to Helio. "Hold 'er in orbit a few more minutes; I gotta get this off my chest."

"Menad Control is on," Helio said.

Borter thought for a moment, "Hold off for a few moments, pull out of the slot. Tell 'em anything." He returned to Parnak.

"By the way, you're slipping. You haven't even asked why we came. Do you think it was out of the kindness of our hearts? Two old space bums like us?"

Parnak pulled at an antenna vacantly, the equivalent among those of his kind of scratching his head.

"There's money in it somewhere. I knew it." Parnak sifted the sparse considerations that would motivate Borter.

The pilot smiled his wide smile. Parnak was all through preaching. "Do you remember a planet called Marcellus?" Borter continued smiling broadly.

Parnak stopped in his tracks. That name he had not heard for many years. In him, it stirred the invisible equivalent of a shudder down the spine, the same as the night before in the compound as he sensed Soarer in the sky. He shrugged. The hearing of that name had in it a sobering effect. The shudder reasserted itself.

"I remember," he said. "Lord Soal has called for me, has he?" His shoulders stooped visibly, giving note to an unexpected flexibility in the hard-shelled body. "Those people are not easily forgotten."

There were several moments of silence as they sat in the tube. Borter watched closely for the betrayal of any sentiment from his friend. He finally realized it had already come in silence. Parnak looked up, but Helio was the one who spoke. "Menad Control. They say right now or clear off. It'll take several hours to get back in the slot. I see no reason to wait."

Soarer slipped down easily to the surface of Menad, having circled its curious way safely. The runway screeched beneath Soarer's wheels. Borter wondered how Jibba had made out with the police. He was almost surely involved in something illegal on the planet. They settled the ship at a new berth, and Borter made his way from the spaceport, driving the car.

Had it not been for the fact that Menad belonged to both the Council and Federation of Planets, he would not have bothered to make good the return on his rental of the vehicle. It would have been much easier to dump it in the shipping lanes at the expense of some confused freighter pilot.

Short of cash, he'd picked up such space debris himself and turned it in for a finder's fee. It was an odd comment, left anonymously, on those times. Most often, the originator of such a message would not hear who found it unless, of course, it was something truly strange. It was an art.

On landing, Parnak, too, was off, collecting his equipment for the work on Marcellus. Borter dropped him off at his hotel and drove away with the car. Since returning to Tienan, his constitution had taken its regular, rigid, immobile state. He supposed it would be good to leave Menad and never return. Already, the dust of the city lay heavily on him. It bored him.

It had not lived up to expectations in the slightest. Leaving would feel good. In many ways, he dreaded the actions of a battlefield less than observing the quiet, cloaked existence in the city. This place, and others like it, were holding him back from newer things.

As he entered his hotel, the cool of the bar appealed to him. Borter may have already guessed that it would. Such away-from-it-all places held their charm, though he still had a reputation for endless hard work that would be sorely missed. There were none like it on Marcellus.

Marcellus itself represented newer things, perhaps the ultimate among them. Remembrance from that time there, long ago, tended to have a somewhat dreamlike quality. It had been many years. As he gathered his equipment, however, Lord Soal loomed highly in his mind; his craggy appearance beneath the battle mask remained vivid. Parnak supposed that, like himself, the Marcellean would not have aged much or really changed in attitude.

It was not long before he had finished and found himself still anxious to leave Menad. He pushed into the lobby, a two-man train of baggage carriers behind him. Stopping at the desk, he dashed off a message to the home office on the only place he would ever refer to as The Planet. Then, a second car and driver were hired, the luggage was loaded, and Parnak was on his way back to Soarer.

13

Parnak's Story

Borter turned, "Something wrong?"

Parnak looked beyond him at the small compartment hatch for a little longer. He smiled again at Borter, smugly. "Nothing is wrong as long as you intend going back to Marcellus, and spending some time."

"We're taking you back, but I don't know how much time we'll spend. Why, what's wrong?"

"Well, nothing really. Uh, did you know Marcellean currency is good only on Marcellus?" Parnak made a face equal to the smirk he read on the pilot's face. He laughed his best laugh in many days; that is, the translator laughed for him. To an angry Magnean, it was all the same.

Borter's face fell open. He went numb with shock. For a few minutes, he sat. Finally, he breathed out a long, resigned sigh and shifted his weight. Parnak relished every moment. He'd waited for a long time to see this Magnean pilot repaid for his glibness.

"You see, Borter, Marcellus has for quite some time, since long before you were born, been withdrawing its interests from the galaxy at large. The economy of the planet itself is stable in every respect. Your money is good – there!"

For all this, Marcellus rejoices. The planet, this planet, among planets, verges on becoming a rickety, old space legend, told about in wild stories by lonely and aged freighter pilots on long hauls through the emptiness of space only. No one goes there anymore.

He looked at Borter's expression of surrender, his dashed hopes of easy riches, and addressed the original question.

Stroking his chin thoughtfully, he said, "Lord Soal, you say?" In his insectoid way, the awe in which he held the Marcellean transcended even the circuits of the translator. He smiled at Borter who understood not at all. "It will be good to see him again. It has been too long." Parnak laughed, "I'll bet he gave those fools on Tyrus, you said it was, a real jolt."

Borter nodded suspiciously and Parnak went on enjoying other things than Borter's financial distress. They talked for a long time.

"Borter, you must remember, Lord Soal is like an old father trying to bring his children home," Parnak said to him. "You must know, too, that the Marcelleans are the earliest race yet known to the galaxy. Whether it escapes your notice or not, the galaxy bears their mark in a thousand ways. You must believe that, in a way, we are all their children."

"To Lord Soal, we are all children of The Heart, and like a good father, he loves his children. He will protect them with any means at his disposal, even if we dislike them. He listens only to The Heart. If he has called you, The Heart of Marcellus has called you, and that is that."

"I don't believe it," said an incredulous Borter. "No device can sense, much less control, a person's destiny across half a galaxy."

"The Heart can. Besides," Parnak confided sheepishly, "I might have mentioned you to him last time we met. It was a very long while ago, I first met Lord Soal very long ago. In all the years I have known of his existence, those I spent on the planet covering the eons of warfare between the Forest Spirit and The Heart, and those other more numerous years away from that planet, I have never been free of Lord Soal and The Heart of Marcellus. You and Helio are no longer free; neither of you were ever there. I always knew that one day, I would return. So, it is for you."

He stopped for a moment, frowned a little, twitching his antennae toward an obvious spot in the near bulkhead, and asked, "Can you hear me well enough, Helio?"

An embarrassed Helio answered from the bulkhead speaker, "Well enough, Parnak."

Parnak said no more to the eavesdropping Helio and returned to Borter, "I see your bad habits have rubbed off on the innocent Dillisome. Perhaps it's good that he listens. I do like a man who learns."

Parnak forced a squint from an accusing eye in Borter's direction. "In the beginning, I was sent to Marcellus to cover a planetary dispute. The Targan Wars, I called them in my reports. Of course, the wars were not news to anyone on the planet. They'd battled for eons already, as we were just hearing of it. Though, among so many other planetary conflicts, this stands far clear of all the rest in both ferocity and cause. The appearance of Modallas and The Helmsman lends far greater import to the battle and its eventual outcome."

"Yes," Borter interrupted thickly. "We've already run into a couple of Targans already, or Helio has, at least. From his account, they seem to be very good fighters."

"Absolutely savage, Borter, I assure you," declared Parnak. "I've seen their work. It is not in the least pleasant."

"They are involved, then, and off – planet? It has grown beyond all proportion. The Helmsman makes use of his servants. Over the thousand years, plus, that he has laid siege to the planet, he's had enough time to domesticate them, to train them. It helps him that Targans and Marcelleans are natural enemies.

Were it not for another force, a third force, in this conflict, the pressure brought to bear against Marcellus by The Helmsman, with his use of the Targan, the planet would have perished already. They are called Techno–Dwarves, another resource that comes forward at the call of The Heart, or such is the popular belief on the planet.

Only they, after The Helmsman proved himself a false friend, have made the difference between battle with honor and summary annihilation.

As the Targans poured from the forest with new and devastating Modallian weapons, the Techno – Dwarves filled the breach in this new war of attrition. Their technology is all that has allowed greatness to remain Marcellean. The Marcelleans are a race of warriors only. For all their prowess and valor, alone, they would have perished beneath the combined weight of Modallas and the Targans long ago.

The two races have a blind spot toward each other. Each is content, neither mistreated. They work together for each other's gain. I believe, that it is another contrivance of planetary biology like that between the Marcelleans and the Targans. In short, it is a case of one hand washing the other, but on a great scale. Strangely, indications are that in the most distant antiquity, the Techno – Dwarves are either forebears or brothers to the modern Marcelleans. At any rate, they are on a near branch of relation.

I'm sure Lord Soal would say it this way. Theirs is thinking beneath Marcellean understanding. In other words, it is knowledge that does not suit a warrior. Possession of the results of that knowledge is preferable. That is the explanation of The Heart, the only explanation that is suitable. Though the Techno – Dwarves accept them as the dominant race, it is truly a life equation canceling all other factors to the desired result, a reduction of all forces to unity.

Against Modallas and the Targan, the Techno – Dwarves present the completing prong of the Marcellean Trident. The Heart itself spells victory or defeat for more than one planet and one traveling world, Modallas. The future of the galaxy rests in the balance."

As Parnak was about to say more, Borter raised his hand and stopped him. "I think, Parnak, we have already seen one of your Techno – Dwarves. He called himself Old Face – If my translator is still working."

Parnak's antennae rose above his eyes. He smiled at the mention of a name he had not heard for so long. "Old Face, you say?"

"Yes, he checked us over before we came to Menad. Lord Soal's request."

"Well, Borter, you've taken your sweet time reviving my worries over the condition of this hulk you call a flyer. Parnak relented, "if you've got Old Face's approval, that's good enough for me. I'm sure your Soarer will get us to Marcellus."

Borter harrumphed at the words and gave a sour look to Parnak. In the cockpit, Helio, by himself, laughed quietly. Borter spoke, this time curious, eager for knowledge. "Just what is this Modallas?"

Parnak seemed not to hear him. He was looking down at the deck, seeing things long past and far distant. "You'd think they'd stop, but I'm afraid there's no reason to it." He sighed deeply as if breathing out his entire life. "It is most disappointing. The only escape available to them is to quit the planet completely, and I doubt they would do that." The sigh was a lament.

He looked up suddenly as if awakened rudely. "Modallas, Borter? Modallas is – I do not know what. Modallas is The Helmsman as The Helmsman is Modallas. It circles Marcellus and, through it, as his name implies – The Helmsman, directs his war on those below. The exact nature of either is unknown."

Parnak went on. "The Helmsman is not known, ever, to have set foot on the planet. He uses the Targan and a Marcellean traitor to do his work for him there. This may be to say that no loyal Marcellean has seen that and lived to tell about it only. It may also be noteworthy that the traitor is brother to Lord Soal."

Irony was not Borter's strong suit. He cared little for that sort of intricacy. His knowledge of Parnak told him that this might be important to remember. Parnak made no waste of speech.

"These two, Lords Markham and Soal, are two of the three remaining old Marcelleans. The other is their father, an old one called The Snow Beggar, who chooses a distant solitude for his final days. Only these three of all Marcelleans possess direct connections to The Marcellean Heart; they, alone, are capable of wearing The Heart. The Helmsman seeks The Heart's power through the insane Markham. A Wearer controls the power of The Heart.

Modallas is only a bright light in the sky at first glance. It may be called a station, a city in space if you wish. It is more. Modallas is a world, a power, unto itself."

Parnak stopped to organize his thoughts a little more. "So, it has been for just over a thousand years. The power of the Old Marcelleans is a match for Modallas thus far, though, now, it grows dangerously near fading for all time. That is the way of all living things, is it not? On occasion, The Helmsman has referred to himself as the servant of Modallas, not a Modallian or master of Modallas. Like some hulking, silvered giant, it circles Marcellus, with him in its belly, belching death and destruction on every orbit. More, I don't know. You will see Modallas soon enough itself; then you can make a judgment for yourself."

Borter listened to Parnak's words patiently but was not content to let go until he knew all there was to know, all about the danger he felt he was flying into. If nothing else was sacred to a flyer, a solemn contract to deliver cargo was. He would deliver Parnak to Lord Soal and make sure of the price when done. Nothing could break the contract outside of total destruction.

"What the Marcellean Heart is, I, also, do not know. It was created by the Marcelleans themselves in antiquity, to their detriment, in the greatest arrogance, or tragically, in the greatest innocence. In those days, they strode the galaxy as giants, with none to resist them.

Unlike Modallas, which suffers from the Targan as Sky God or the widely ranged forests of the planet that give them the cults of The Forest Spirit, The Marcellean Heart is not an object of primitive religion. In fact, it is the farthest thing from it.

The Marcellean Heart, gentlemen, while surrounded by the vagaries of fate, clouded by countless ages, is an object of great power. It is the single most powerful instrument in the galaxy.

I don't pretend to understand the order of succession in monarchies of any society, either petty or complex in design. This is, perhaps, a failing, perhaps, a strength.

Since Parnak stopped for a moment.

"Because Lord Soal and Lord Markham are, with the one called The Snow Beggar, the known, remaining Old Marcelleans. The Heart will pass among them. Most likely, it will pass from Lord Snow

Beggar to Lord Soal because Markham is insane and a traitor at the same time!

It will go to no other unless another Old Marcellean is found and one of greater rank. The Old apparently are some lost genetic strain of Marcellean, born to battle the Targans. Who knows how it came about, naturally or through the machinations of some older race predating them, equally troubled by the Targan or their forebears? Anyway, if there were any, they exist no longer. The new people are of the same mold, but not the same cast, if you get my meaning. The Old ones were a breed of their own, altogether extremely powerful.

When their end was apparent, the Marcellean Heart was conceived and built. Aptly named, it contains the life forces of those beings. That, gentlemen, is why The Helmsman wants it, precisely, the consequences, academic from that moment, if it is ever allowed to come."

Parnak gave a brief but embarrassed smile. "That is why I was called. It is a sort of permanent assignment for me, first, from my own people who have an insatiable want for such things, then by Lord Soal, I am his Recorder. Borter. Helio.?" Parnak's glance shot from Borter's intent face to the direction of the cockpit where Helio sat listening with rapt attention, "We may be about to witness the beginning of the first, true galactic conflict. It is, it must be, that things are at a crux, for both Marcellus and the galaxy at large, for Lord Soal to have called."

Eventually, all of the insectoid's descriptions led back to Lord Soal. Somehow, the warrior lord was everywhere at once, cropping up in the middle of situation after situation. The journalist recounted his exploits with enthusiasm, story after story of his daring in the face of the enemy and the utter devotion of his line troops to him.

Borter sat up straight with the sudden realization that Parnak's real preferences were coming out. Yes, here it was, at last, some sort of altered loyalty, unknown before in their old friend, this practical journalist who did his job with the single by word – objectivity. For the next hours, he sat speaking through the translator, his antennae bobbing rhythmically, up and down, the whole while.

Parnak went on with his stories until it was time for Borter to take his place in the cockpit. When Borter rose to his feet and stretched stiffly, he was grateful, at last, to stop Parnak.

"I appreciate your telling us all this, but I should tell you Helio and I are leaving the planet as soon as we drop you off and get a few more power dots from the Marcelleans."

"Borter?" Parnak was dismayed. Were these two giving up a chance to renew their friendship and the chance to do some of the usual revels in the bargain?

Borter turned around, halfway to his duties in the cockpit. "Yes, Parnak?"

"Borter, you would forego this, the last great battle on which the fate of the galaxy, on which all our fate rests, for what?"

Borter smiled, and the smile did not leave his lips, though at last, it curled at one corner of his mouth cruelly as he said, "For survival, Parnak, for our own well-being. We are not about to become involved in any galactic upheaval or any more desperate battles. We're taking ourselves and Soarer out." The pilot chuckled grimly, moving off toward the cockpit, shaking his head from side to side.

Parnak remained alone for a time in the tube, just sitting. Ready to argue the point, he stayed where he was. Maybe, things had changed. What was done was done, and what was left to be done would occur as ordained by The Heart. This, Parnak knew above all things.

14

Escape, The Helmsman, Markham and Sorel

During the next days, Parnak told them much more of the planet, though when they arrived it would not seem enough.

As always, one story led to another and another, until, at last, Marcellus came into view, a bright spot before them against the perpetual backdrop of near space.

"Shields coming on," Helio reported crisply. Borter rushed to his seat from the tube and wasting no time pushed all throttles forward full. "Three flyers," he spoke softly, betraying no excitement, "speed 4.4, gaining slightly."

"Engines coming on full," Borter announced.

"4.4 and holding steady."

By then, Parnak had joined them standing at the bulkhead.

"4.4? They're fast – let's see how fast?" Borter said.

A burst of energy smacked against the rear deflectors rattling the last words in his mouth.

"We're holding them off," he said relieved. He thanked the Marcellean power dots held in the propulsion tubes.

"Helio, let's get ready to drop our friends a few gifts, just in case."

Helio flipped three switches and spoke, "Mines armed –

three. 4.4 holding steady. Apparently, we're cooperating!"

The words came easily from his mouth, his voice unstrained.

The speeds matched, neither side gained on the other.

"They're holding back," Parnak announced pointing to the three blips on the distant sensor screen, "Modallian fighters are faster than your 4.4."

"It doesn't do much good to think about six Marcellean power dots, does it?" Borter watched the blips, eventually, the sensors make out the shapes of the individual ships

following them. They were swept wing craft, sleek and sharp-nosed, weapons pods appointed the undersides of their wings.

Borter watched them. They were playing a game and those aboard Soarer had no choice than to wait, the mouse in a cat's game. Borter had his throttles full out. Parnak seemed unruffled. "He's just a little curious about us - probably."

"They're ordering us over," said the Dillisome.

"Tell them, thanks — but, no thanks," cracked Borter.

"Where do they expect us to pull over? There's nothing here."

"There," Parnak pointed through the cockpit window.

"Modallas comes to us."

Borter followed the end of Parnak's finger to another growing bright spot far out in space. The spot seemed to rise from a place near the planet, as if it were a small moon rising. Neither Borter nor Helio had seen anything like it.

"Whatever it is," said Helio in that calm voice.

"It's big, cylinder shape, with symmetrical appendages on each end - it's coming our way very fast."

Borter tried to look unimpressed as the cylinder shape became evident to his eye though still far away. Parnak, for a while, kept silent. "Interceptors signaling again," said Helio.

Distant Modallas welled up below them dwarfing the flyer with its massive girth. Borter had already taken in its most prominent features. Hydroponics capped the ends like twin, revolving crowns. The exterior was louvered with bright panels of some reflecting material, opening and closing, each broad row in turn, against Marcellus' sun.

They watched as a bank of the giant reflectors opened wide before them.

Within, lay Modallas' interior, its center, and whatever that held. The material beneath the yawning reflectors was clear, like glass, but revealing nothing from that distance.

The cylinder rotated on its axis, its normal motion.

"It's on the order of a small planet," Helio spoke, amazed. "It's big."

The spectacle defied other description, beggaring even Parnak's gift for words. "This is no mere planet." His pause was dramatic. "Would that it were. Modallas is the death knell sounding for the galaxy as it is known. The dawn of a dark, new age is almost upon us."

It was Borter, as captain, a different Borter than the one they saw so often as friend and companion who acted swiftly, with decision, in the face of this danger. Soarer's nose swerved away from the oncoming Modallas. It followed, blocking his course, refilling the cockpit window with its bulk. The interceptors closed from behind. "They've ordered us over again," Borter heard Helio speak.

There was a third, sudden, jolt of energy against the rear shields. Borter snapped straight in his seat, "Tell them again – no thanks." He looked at Helio as if asking, in his expectant expression, why that wouldn't work?

Soarer raced head-long toward her unwanted rendezvous with approaching Modallas. Within her, Borter's mind worked to devise an effective means of escape. As the massive cylinder loomed closer, Helio and Parnak kept their silence.

Behind, the three interceptors dogged their trail, forcing them on, forward.

Then, as Modallas swept toward them, all but filling space before them with its steel cold, vastness, Borter spoke, "Remember what we did to that Imperial Scout on Forum IX two years ago?"

Helio remembered smiling a bare smile, Soarer went into a steep dive toward Modallas' louvered surface, no longer trying to avoid it.

There was a plan. The freighter's computer was readied to fire the engines against rear shields. Those to be reangled in a way that would blast Soarer away suddenly, at a sharp angle, from that of the original dive. Borter reangled the shields himself. As he did, Helio held the controls alone, then as Borter took over from him, mimicked his movements as a backup through the last crucial moments.

Pursuit from behind scattered as gun crews aboard Modallas opened fire to avoid the impact of Soarer's suicidal assault, too late. Energy burst behind them without effect; the last – minute defense was useless against them.

Both pilots handled the ship's controls surely.

Close, they could see into the clear spaces between the great rows of shutters into the depths of Modallas.

Directly ahead, they could see a great land mass and beyond it and part of another. Barely identifiable, on them, were fixed angles that zig-zagged and crisscrossed. Even to novice flyers that meant buildings and civilization. More, they could not see clearly enough to recognize through lazily floating clouds thickly, cluttering Modallas' empty, zero-gee center.

"Clouds," the Dillisome whispered to himself, astonished that the thing rising up toward them so quickly was so vast as to enclose a complete atmosphere of its own.

"I can see clouds in there."

"Forget them," Borter snapped, "this is going to be tight enough without sightseeing."

Aiming the ship between two rows of the opening louvers, they measured Modallas' rotation and matched it perfectly. At full speed they hurtled in, everything ready, Borter hoped. If not, this singularly unique view of Modallas would be their last, though he would not wish for another, even if they escaped.

The next instant would have been the last for two lesser flyers, Soarer's engines fired into the reset shields, jerking the freighter rudely sideways as if it were a child's toy on an invisible string. The computer leveled them off between gigantic, raised louvers while he and the others were helplessly pressed back into their seats by the gee force, allowing them to escape new detection by Modallas' sensors.

Behind them, a ball of flame shot into space from the Modallian hull, a lone explosion, supposed to be them, was a single space mine. Borter congratulated himself on the idea, his own final touch. The trailing interceptors, now far behind, had already let off their pursuit and headed home toward some unseen airlock on Modallas that would serve their fighters.

Indeed, within Modallas' Command Center, a Lord Markham was recalling his flyers from space. So low did Soarer fly against the hull of the giant structure and so convincing was the explosion against the hull that she went long moments undetected, speeding down nearly the entire length of the spinning cylinder before gun crews reported seeing an old target, one no longer supposed to exist, racing past them.

Markham angrily scrambled back to his scanner, ordering his pursuit ships to turn around and once again seek their old target. He would have this elusive quarry, if he had to chase it down to the planet's surface himself, all the way to Lord Soal if necessary. Markham roared commands from within his battle armor to subordinates, angry that they would let this one, small, freighter avoid them.

Scanners reported nothing. Soarer flew too low between the louvers for them to be of any use. The sighting was visual only. Borter watched carefully as the louvers yawned at them, peaking, they began to close-down. He counted the seconds. Modallas would soon face the Marcellean sun straight on and Soarer would have to leave the closing pathway to escape. Tense moments passed in the small cockpit as the two friends gauged their futures heartbeat by heartbeat. Markham raved madly, thrashing around the Command Center as Soarer rolled out of the nearly closed bank of louvers.

They struck for Marcellus having to make no more than minor adjustments in course. The maneuver was brilliant, consummate, deceptive with ease. Their exit, though dangerously near disaster, was a desperate gamble that had paid off.

"Commander," bellowed Markham to his interceptors.

"Where are you? I want them back – I want them back alive – Commander?"

Nearby, trying to control his fear, a voice sounded, shakily, with more bad news, "I regret they have reached the planet's atmosphere. Do you wish to continue the pursuit, sir?"

"Markham snarled, "Yes. To the surface." He stalked out of the control center without another word.

After a few steps Markham drew to a quick halt. He stiffened noticeably as another, darker, more foreboding figure loomed in his path. The Helmsman stood suddenly before him.

"Your results, Markham?" The voice boomed at him, a hint of disfavor flared in it. Markham found it difficult to speak. "Has your primary pursuit failed?" Markham grasped at words. His greatness led as his throat dried and tightened. "Words, Markham, words, tell me you have not failed at this easy task. Quickly – no dawdling."

"Yes." Markham managed finally.

"You have launched a secondary pursuit, I assume, or was that too difficult as well?" Markham nodded once again that he had. However, by that time, The Helmsman was already on his way into the control center. "I think it is wise that I supervise our on-planet offensive, don't you, Markham?"

The Helmsman taunted him, reaching deep within the sealed Marcellean armor, stripping him bare of all self-respect.

Markham shivered involuntarily in dread.

Modallas hurtled through the dusk of orbital space, high above the rim of Marcellus. The gargantuan cylinder glittered brightly, reflecting sunlight. Along the immense hull, one long row of shutters opened in its turn after those before it and before those behind it. The effect was that of ocean waves, each breaking in turn endlessly against a shoreline, graduating those within the artificial world from light to dark with its rotation from day to night and back again, unless the massive bulk of the thing passed on the backside of the planet there was always sunlight in its interior.

Frantic activity boomed at one end of the spinning giant. A huge airlock admitted returning Modallian fighters from their latest sortie on the planet below. All were piloted by Targan whose forebears came from the planet, removed from the Marcellean forests, standard following a mission.

Beyond the airlock the great panorama Modallas opened. The cylinder stretched out wide, as far as the eye could see. Its width was all the more impressive given the knowledge that it was only one-fifth of the length.

At regular intervals, three large land tracts appeared. On them, the housing for the inhabitants of Modallas and their life support. One could not see the growing pods that supplied the food at either end of Modallas, but they were there with everything else that would make life in space comfortable.

Two of the land strips always appeared overhead from the view of any other, clinging to the interior walls of the cylinder. Save the constantly changing light caused by the Modallas' rotation and the unending opening and closing of the giant louvers, they never seemed to move. Occasionally, actually a time or two during the day, there would be a glimpse of the planet, large enough though the view of the enclosure, but still far away. It would quickly pass, sometimes beneath, sometimes above and present its curious appearance and disappear behind the louvers or a land strip.

Looking up and toward the middle of the hollow central shaft, at zero gravity, a white cloud hung the length of Modallas. Transport tubes crisscrossed reaching out into each of the land strips and beyond, to each other. Most were underground, leaving the surface areas open for the tremendous array of massive buildings, streets and parks on all three of the plains. Targans paced the streets and rode the fast transit tubes, no one could be seen who was remotely describable as a Modallian.

More ships were put into readiness at the vast airlock and others like it along the outer hull. Preparations were underway for the final assault against the once great planet

below. The Marcellean Heart was the object of conquest as ever. How many lives had been paid out in the effort to possess it? The Helmsman himself did not know.

"Helmsman," the smooth and featureless armored head did not turn to acknowledge the arrival of this subordinate, "Squadron Four reports readiness, Stage Three. Squadron Ten, also, reports readiness Stage Three. Squadron Six has returned from their mission and is debriefing, preliminary report is, all objectives successful. End report, Sir."

There was no response. The Lieutenant took a single step back, turned and left The Helmsman's presence. In the nerve center controlling all of Modallas, The Helmsman watched a large screen from which he could see any point on or in the huge cylinder. The control center was spacious and well lit. Targans worked all around him at a variety of consoles.

All wore the standard green uniforms of Modallas and insignia denoting rank and unit. Markham and The Helmsman alone wore complete battle armor. He was never seen without it. No one around him dared take eyes away from the duty at hand. On this bridge, he alone was supreme. The Lieutenant returned. "Helmsman," he paused cautiously, "Lord Markham."

Before Markham could fully step up to be noticed, from one of the nearby consoles more information came in. "Launch coordinates, fifteen minutes." The battle mask remained implacable, The Helmsman within his armor studied other information. He spoke to Markham. For the moment his report complete, the Lieutenant again turned and went to other duties.

"Your contact with the Targan, Sorel, on the planet, is satisfactory?"

"In all ways," Markham answered from within his own battle armor. "He moves to the designated area. The necessary weaponry has been delivered and the Targan tutored in their use."

"You will be present on the planet?"

"Of course, Helmsman."

"You have no reservations on strategy? The Targan, you are sure, will perform well?"

"Your strategy, as always, is flawless. As for the Targan," Markham glanced at them around the control center contemptuously, "They will always be the Targan and nothing more." Markham looked back at The Helmsman, at the place on the opaque battle mask where eyes should have been and spoke, "The company of equals is always preferable." Markham saw no immediate reaction from the awesome presence before him.

It remained the same, unbendable, unyielding, unreachable. The Helmsman pointed a finger at him accusingly and spoke harshly, "Have care, Markham, Lord of Marcellus – you are not among equals, especially now." Markham shrank.

"It is time you took your place at the head of your troops. The hour draws near."

Dismissed, Markham turned quickly and left the command center without speaking. Equals – indeed. The thought burned him. This small raid would be preliminary. He would lead two squadrons of fighters to the surface of Marcellus and destroy installations there. In all the times he'd fought his own people, it never struck him more than, now, curious that no Modallian had ever joined him in battle on the planet.

15

The Trench

He did not bother to enter the atmosphere in the approved manner, angling the shields forward instead to absorb the heat of an accelerated reentry. Modallian pursuit had not again caught up to them. They could not see it, and on the rear-turned sensors, it did not exist, but it was there all the same. Soarer dived blindly into the atmosphere.

"Coming fast," Helio pointed suddenly to his screen.

"Company?" Borter, in turn, muttered over his shoulder to Parnak.

"Three interceptors – same as before," Helio announced. Soarer raced them down through the clouds of Marcellus. Thinner than those they'd plowed through leaving Tyrus, they gave no cover. The trio of interceptors was almost on them.

Energy exploded all around them. Borter replaced his shields behind. Parnak leaned over Helio's shoulder, looking at the terrain far below. The three smaller ships were heavily armed. Soarer dipped lower toward the ground.

"Along the right wing. That wide trench." Parnak pointed to the right, "Go toward that."

Borter wheeled over, rolling Soarer down. In doing so, he caught his first sight of the Modallians. They were sleek vessels shaped like arrowheads, a design he'd seen before.

They came on hard, flying together as if flown by a single hand. He pushed Soarer all the more, for all she was worth. "Say, I'm getting good at this!"

Finally, the trench swallowed them. Borter looked up and saw the Modallians pass above from one side of the trench to the other. They had overshot. His attention turned to the yawning canyon before them. Most of it was between sheer, high, palisading walls.

"Slow your speed," Helio ordered.

Borter reached for the throttle. "High rocks ahead. You'll have to fly between them."

As Soarer slowed, long, delicate wings stretched out on either side of her fuselage. Behind them, the Modallian interceptors entered the trench, some distance behind, bent on overtaking the fleeing trio. "Behind us again."

Helio nodded toward his screen.

The first tendrils of rock edged just into view. Borter estimated their height to be even with the rest of the planet's surface. He angled Soarer's shields to better advantage and, once again, the ship's computer began ticking off new information.

Soarer rolled up with its wings vertical, going between the first two of the pillars. Just behind them, a blast of energy caused a rockslide.

"Behind," Helio updated their position succinctly – "Closer."

The interceptors drew up steadily on the fleeing Soarer. All three passed the first obstacle intact.

"There is another, larger ship tracking us from above," said Helio. "I can't quite make out its configuration."

More energy snapped around them as Borter rolled the ship from one wing to the other rapidly, zigzagging between other colossal pillars. Their pursuers began to have difficulty with the same test. "How much farther?" Borter barked the question at Helio.

"The trench goes on indefinitely, a few twists and turns here and there, but it goes on – it is a planetary trench," answered Helio in a disarmingly calm voice. "You are doing well. I now have only two Modallians on the screen." Helio looked over at the overworked Borter with little relief.

The missing interceptor had destroyed himself, a negotiation missed, among the rocks. The others came on. The shape of Soarer served the situation well. Able to drop speed, she moved with comparative ease through all obstacles.

There was a hard jolt from behind. "We're hit." It was Borter of the three who shouted. Soarer lurched heavily. "She's not going to be so graceful anymore.

Controls grew heavy in their hands. A shield at the end of one wing skimmed a rock. Soarer groaned and rebounded into the air, then down. Parnak braced himself where he stood, expecting a sudden crash. Borter shouted. The Dillisome merely looked back at him.

"Can't you get more power out of her? We're losing altitude!"

"We're going down. Helio, you and Parnak, get in the Gotha-Kite," Borter shot a grim look at the insectoid who was not used to taking orders. Helio was on his feet as Borter tried to steady the ship.

"Come," Helio motioned back into the cargo tube. To the surprise of the pilot, Parnak followed.

"Get out," Borter shouted into the tube. "I'll use the other kite. I'll be right behind you."

He waved the pair into the cargo tube and waited for Helio's signal to release the hatch. Air rushed in from the open pod. Helio and Parnak were nowhere to be seen; they were already gone. There was enough thrust left to allow Borter time to get back in the tube himself.

Pushing a second manual release, he went nowhere. Beneath him, in his pod, was a hopelessly mangled Goth – Kite. Parnak and Helio had already ejected safely, he hoped. Indeed, that kite had been packed a separate compartment and had launched without a problem. His was too mangled to drop from the pod. Escape cut short he closed the hatch and went forward quickly. The Modallians had managed to put them out of the air completely. His only chance was to bring Soarer down.

The way ahead had cleared, at least. Soarer lumbered heavily on autopilot, just as he had left her. He reached his seat in the cockpit. Lowering the landing gear, he readied for impact.

Another of the Modallians found trouble coming through the last set of pillars. Glancing from one pillar, he careened into his companion flyer. Both went down in a hail of flaming metal. Somewhere beyond, Borter brought Soarer down as gently as he could.

Helio's Gotha-kite had dropped from Soarer, plummeting into the yawning trench. He waited, waited, and waited until the darkened hull of Soarer was well away with its Modallian pursuers in tow. Then, Helio tripped the release, holding the kite in its tight cocoon.

Wings spread around them, though they hardly looked worth the trouble. A thin frame was covered by a thinner fabric and looked as if it would not hold one passenger in the air alone, much less the two of them at once. Helio turned to Parnak and told him to pedal.

Surprised, Parnak looked down at his feet and, indeed, there was a set of pedals. They were already in motion. Helio worked another pair in front. He looked back at the swishing sound behind a propeller turned, moving them forward.

Matching the rotation of the pedals with his feet, he began. "Pedal," the blue man shouted. Struggling to turn the kite in a wide, agonizing arc, they turned to face around in the trench. It would require both their efforts to keep themselves aloft. Borter and his pursuers were far out of sight. They would be fortunate to remain in the air.

Still, they were high above the trench floor. Helio leaned over dangerously, taking the kite off balance. He leaned back, having quickly gotten his bearings.

Parnak nudged his shoulder. He indicated a pall of smoke rising in the distance from the trench floor. "Was it Borter?"

Helio nodded without speaking and brought the nose of the kite in that direction. The last set of pillars rising out of the trench blocked the path towering above them.

The Modallians had been good, tough flyers; there had been no outrunning them. Borter, he thought, must be dead or, at least, downed, awaiting capture. The second kite was nowhere to be seen. No chance of getting to him first existed, he thought. If they could have managed it, there was room on the kite for two only.

Minutes later, Helio steered into the pass. It took all the skill he possessed to keep them from being swept against the steep rocks by the wind. The terrain beneath was flat, they. They could have made a landing anywhere. Helio worried more, though, about finding Borter alive. Looking down, he saw the wreckage of the two last Modallian fighters. Soarer, expected to be there, was nowhere to be seen.

The co-pilot was not much relieved. It could only be farther on. Straining his eyes to the fullest, he searched again for the second Gotha-kite. He turned to Parnak who was of no help. Parnak motioned, waggling his hand, though he could have spoken that he, too, saw nothing.

Borter had certainly gone down with Soarer. He reasoned that the second kite was defective. Borter was not so attached to Soarer that he would have lost his life for its sentimentality.

One thing about the pilot was there was a reason for everything, even if that reason appeared totally insane to everyone else. He would have tried to get out.

Several kilometers above them, the fourth Modallian ship hovered. Borter had become lost to them, but they did have Helio's Gotha-kite. Those aboard were ordered to wait to see where this plodding vehicle would lead them.

A landing party was prepared and stood ready for the call to descend to the planet. The Modallian transported assault troops meant to venture on the Marcellean surface. It was intended that they land quickly and bring a swift end to this mission on the planet.

Parnak, looking down as they passed the wreckage below, said the Modallians were not such good pilots as thought. Helio said nothing. He was instead wondering where Borter had gotten to. Soarer had gone down; he had seen the freighter's instruments himself and, from outside, had seen the damage to the ship.

She must have crashed farther on than expected. The trench split the ground very far ahead of them. He leaned backward and looked up into the hazy sky. It would be better to find Borter one way or another soon. It would be dark soon in the trench.

The two added to their efforts on the kite, speeding it along. No other pillars rose in their path. The trench became a flat plain between its canyon walls, very flat.

Then, Helio pointed ahead, still kilometers away, toward the middle of the flat. It looked like a huge plume of red dust. That had to be Borter, he was sure. They redoubled their efforts. The kite moved ahead obediently as the propeller throbbed more loudly behind. Helio looked intently at the red cloud trying to make out something familiar in it.

16

Gotha – Kites – The Trench Continues

The Gotha – Kite spread a broad shadow deep in the empty bottom wastes of the trench. They jogged on doggedly at its rear, slicing steadily through the air. Helio was glad they had picked the kites up last trip to Magnus, giving in to Borter's whim. One, at least, was proving its worth.

They closed the distance between themselves and the slow – moving dust cloud. Helio was surer than ever it marked the spot where Soarer had gone down. The cloud was thinning, no longer as thick as when first seen. It had been a long way in the trench's middle, far away, and it had moved only a little since then. They pedaled for two hours and appeared to be only a little closer than they had been when they started.

Parnak became more silent than usual behind Helio. He watched the sky above for any sign of the remaining Modallian he was sure must still be there. The fact they had not been bothered told him they'd been content to sit and watch for a while. There was something aboard Soarer they wanted. It was unlike Targans, even those from Modallas, to leave survivors.

Borter pulled himself, meanwhile, from the wreckage of Soarer. His landing had dug a long, deep furrow in the ground. He'd managed to slow his airspeed, level off, and bring her in, still hard.

With contact, the landing gear had collapsed, throwing the nose into the ground. The freighter was no longer as pretty. After one bounce and long skid covering several hundred meters, Soarer came to a very ugly halt.

The clear shield of his hastily donned helmet was broken, but he was unhurt. Borter stood beside the wreckage, shaking, not quite believing he had survived the remains of this battered hulk. 'Marcellus' sun looked near to setting at the rim of the trench. He, too, remembered the Modallian ship above somewhere, lurking. It was safer, he decided, to leave the wreckage than to invite an easy capture.

Modallians? He didn't know what one looked like. Humanoid, he supposed, like most of the galaxy. Even on this far rock, there would be humanoids. He did hope they were not all copies of Lord Soal, as Parnak had said. The Marcellean by himself had been enough.

Borter had not really had time to get at him properly for their illegal Tyrean launch. With Soarer all around him in pieces, he wondered flatly if it mattered any more. It was incredible; the man had come aboard half paralyzed and had then been able to launch the ship without clearance – mentally. That had lost them a good port – of – call.

Then, he had become comatose – or seemed to – for the remainder of that trip to Marcellean space. The physical and mental power of the Marcellean made him uneasy; how many more like him were on the planet? Borter did not like nearness to any being more powerful than himself. He did not trust other humanoids – none at all. He theorized that Lord Soal was more asleep than comatose on the journey back. How would he be able to thank him properly for the loss of his ship?

Helio and Parnak had gotten away from the ship for sure, but did they escape the waiting fourth Modallian? It could have scooped them up easily, a Gotha – Kite made an easy target, come to think of it. In that case, he was stranded alone on a strange planet. No help would come nor was there any hope, after all.

From Soarer came an array of survival gear. It was a haphazard collection centered around temporary shelter, energy, food concentrate, and his blaster. The package itself did not come too much. The prospect of walking a long distance, to who-knows-where, just to get out of this trench did not appeal. He decided to give the remaining Gotha – Kite a try.

The left wing had warped and some of the fabric covering it was torn. There was a repair kit – the three-year maintenance contract he'd bought did not include house calls. The lines used to control its flight were torn loose and badly snarled. It would be better than walking, he supposed, and began getting the light flyer airworthy. From Soarer came the mangled cocoon that was to get him to safety.

Borter had no idea where on Marcellus was or what the Marcellean idea of that safety might be. The sun faded over the rim of the trench, casting deep shadows. It looked as if he would have to work into the night. Except for darkness, the work would not be difficult; Gotha-Kites were made from very light materials. The real problem facing him was to sort – his complex web of cables that steered and held the craft together. All of it was a mess.

In the fading light, Helio brought his kite to the ground slowly and gently. The thin, brittle film covering the wings rattled as the wheels touched the red soil. The two slowed it to a stop. They could not fly at night. There was no place in the spare frame for navigational equipment of any description.

How would they get off the ground the next day – he did not know. Test flights under better conditions and with no passenger, besides a pilot, had gotten one into the air with no trouble. Later, standing beside it, he began to realize what an insane thing it was to have ejected with Parnak in a collapsed, man – powered vehicle.

Helio folded the long wings of the Gotha – Kite neatly – and tied down the fuselage. They were ready to spend the night. Helio asked Parnak how long the Marcellean night was. The reply was that night would last fifteen hours.

They shared food concentrate. Surprisingly, the Dillisome found more need for nourishment than Parnak. They sat beneath a wing left partially extended, on second thought, for shelter. Neither slept nor talked for a long time.

The Dillisome realized there was little he could not do, at that instant for Borter or against the tracking Modallians. The Modallians, if there, they were truly there, and he had no reason to believe they were not, would come when they were ready. Helio was very tired from the effort necessary to keep the kite airborne. So, he did not want to talk, but sleep. Parnak did not move as Helio at last drifted from consciousness.

Hours later, new light struck the far rim of the trench. Had they waited for full daylight in the canyon, they would have waited far into the morning and into the heat of the day to take off. Parnak woke him early.

After a breakfast of – tasteless concentrate, they extended the wings of the kite. Helio did not untie its ground moorings. He was afraid it would lift away in the morning breeze. The wind, they hoped, would help them get into the air more easily.

Finally, Helio pulled loose the mooring lines. The delicate flyer rolled backward before they could begin pedaling. A short distance down the canyon, the Gotha – Kite lifted her straining cargo into the morning air. With more effort and more wind, they reached the altitude they had the day before. Again, they were on their way.

That morning, Borter, too, had already raced his newly repaired craft into that same wind. He left the ground more rapidly and climbed higher into the air. Soarer lay behind in the red dust, a broken, useless hulk.

He wondered what scrap sold for on the planet. It would take a long time to raise the money for another flyer. He remembered the promise he'd made to himself to search for Helio and Parnak.

His kite, he finally found some flying room. But, heading in that direction would mean another wide turn for the return trip.

The final pillars he'd passed trying to steady Soarer for her landing could not be far off, he thought, or could they? He couldn't find them anywhere. At the bottom, from his altitude, the canyon appeared to be no more than a wide bowl. The walls now looked the same everywhere. The angry furrow made in the red ground by Soarer's crash was his only point of reference.

Still, the task began to appear more and more impossible. The ejection point was not near. If Soarer had been traveling at a high speed, leaving it to reason, then the two parts were farther between than Borter cared to travel under his own power, airborne or not.

For the better part of the morning, he logged useless kilometers. No matter how noble his intention was, the Gotha – Kite was not a search vehicle.

Into the afternoon hours, he pedaled, watching on all sides, when possible, but the trench did not yield his friends. His speed and his distance kept him from seeing Helio and Parnak when he passed over them, far to one side and below. Finally, the afternoon burned into twilight.

Borter munched on concentrate and took water through a flexible tube. No longer searching for the two, Borter had no real plan. He had no map, nor did he know where the Marcellean civilization was, or any other for that matter. He'd decided to go back down the trench from where he'd come. Perhaps, if the wind continued, he would be able to raise himself above the rim of the canyon. There could be something there.

The propeller churned, cutting the air with a dull, monotonous whoosh. Several times, he gained enough altitude to see a little over the rim, but that was all. There was nothing to be seen before his legs gave out, and he had to glide down.

He'd fully expected to go on into the night. There was a moon circling Marcellus, in fact, there were nine. One, however, gave more light than the others. He could not see Modallas in the night sky. It was very far out just then.

If closer, he supposed, it would reflect light enough to be seen. He knew it did – he had been there and had seen it. More amazing than any supposition that the half – world reflected enough light to be visible in the night sky was the sheer size and mobility of the thing, and more, what sort of people had built it in the first place.

Never could Borter remember having seen anything that had astonished him more. Too tired to go on, he landed the craft and got ready for a night in the Trench.

That morning, the moment Borter had left the ground on Marcellus that morning, he raised a signal aboard the Modallian ship hovering in near space.

"Commander, I have a contact leaving the planet's surface."

"Has Modallas been alerted?"

"Yes, Sir. Very well, alert assault squads. Troops alerted and stationed."

Sensors had located its second object in less than one hour. It was an easy detection that neither object was the small space freighter that had cost them three interceptor-scout ships the day before, but something closely related. Given the amount of traffic in the trench, ordinarily, there could be nothing else.

17

More Trench

"Alert, Lord Markham," the Commander ordered.

"Yes, sir," his subordinate answered instantly.

Elsewhere, Targans boarded attack transports bound for the surface of the planet. The mother ship hovered at the edge of Marcellus' atmosphere. They wore Modallian blasters in the rifle form and the side arm, pistol version as well.

With the same primitive, animal quickness common to the forests, they moved into the holds of the transports and filled them quickly. In two neat rows, battle helmets lined both sides of the bay shinning with reflected light from above. It was silent. They were ready. Modallas had trained them well.

Aboard Modallas itself, Lord Markham watched the preparation calmly. The opaque, featureless mask was over his face and sealed, his own ever – present Shoulder Falcon, eyes blinking, peered down on alert. It was almost always the case. The Helmsman was said to be the only one aboard the cylinder world who knew his face. It was in itself a queer trade, for the truth of the matter was Markham did not know The Helmsman's. He alerted the Launch Room. No one knew the face of The Helmsman.

Modallian technology had long had teleportation and lord Markham made good use of it. He, for many years as Modallas, had marauded the Varian System, slipping in and out of the troubles made across the planets.

As for the Forest People, the Targans, of the vast Marcellean forests, they assumed Markham's sudden appearances and disappearances were the will of the Sky God.

Targans were finally beginning to make themselves useful to The Helmsman's plans, he thought. Troops were always assaulted by transports, saving teleports for Modallas' elite. Markham stood for some minutes, quietly going over the new information.

At first, the slow movements of the two Gotha-Kites confused him. Then, the patterns they took independently of each other, at last, made sense – each searched for the other. At the end of the great ravine lay the city of Toth.

Both, now, appeared to be headed there either by intent or chance. He and his Targans had ravaged the place weeks before. Deserted, it stood an empty reminder of things to come. He and his Targans could catch them easily enough there. It would be hours before the slow flyers would reach the city.

Markham signaled the Launch Room for transport a second time, "Launch." He gave the coordinates for the abandoned city to them. They would be there, on planet, waiting for him when he arrived.

Helio flared back the nose of his Gotha – Kite just after dusk that second day, beside the wrecked hulk of Soarer, slowing it enough to gently land. Leaping through the tube hatch, he examined the fuselage completely from the cargo ramp at the tail through the cargo tube to the cockpit.

Borter left no conscious sign of his direction in leaving the place. It was difficult to say immediately whether or not Borter had brought the ship down or ejected in the second Gotha – Kite. The kite was gone. If Borter had ejected, where was he?

Parnak, however, was the more complete investigator. Calling Helio to him outside the ship, he showed the marks left by Borter assembling the Gotha-Kite. Farther away, Parnak showed him where he had begun his takeoff run. Helio could hardly believe his eyes.

"Borter is hard to kill," Parnak combined his thoughts into a summation.

"A Waugreb tried once on my frozen planet," Helio said proudly, reaching his side, "it died."

Neither lay praise lightly. His planet was a test of endurance in itself, even for its natives. Borter was a successful off – worlder, something rare on Dillisome. Helio did wonder if Borter had gone back, looking for them. He should have stayed with the ship.

"Yes." Parnak muttered beside him, "Our Borter is something very special, indeed."

Several hard hours of pedaling, later brought Borter to an unexpected sight – the conquered city of Toth.

Unseen in his labors, he was almost over it before he saw it. It loomed near, still graceful and elegant in defeat and ruin. Its several spires reached from the sky, austerely set, simple, enshrouded by the early dusk in the trench.

They soared like jagged spikes above the deeply lengthening shadows and failing sunlight. Later, even in the fragile light of all Marcellus' moons, he would be able to make them out as they seemed to float lightly in the breezes above the ground.

Wearily, Borter brought the Gotha-Kite to a landing some distance from where, in the pitch – black darkness, he judged the city's first access to begin. Staking the delicate flyer to the ground, he again crept beneath the protective wing to sleep until morning. His sleep went undisturbed for many hours until, at last, he awoke to the fresh light of a new day.

Light touched him early in the morning. Surely, there must be a way out. Whatever this place holds, he thought, there must be a way out. It was only a matter of finding it. Borter scrambled through a quick, almost tasteless liquid nutrient breakfast while gazing vacantly across the brief expanse of red desert that was between himself and Toth.

In the sharp new light of day, he examined the city once more from the ground. He toyed with the idea of launching himself in the Gotha-Kite to reconnoiter before actually setting foot inside. However, a certain characteristic residue of fatigue stifled the demanding adventure, so the Magnean would walk instead.

The spires were the skyline of Toth. There were no other buildings of such size, only the tall, massive spires rising before him. On the ground, as hard as Borter tried to make them out, yet, far in the distance, he could not see their bases. He supposed, without really thinking, that other, smaller buildings dotted the surrounding area, leading to the great spires.

Borter was caught in the wonder of them. as they magnificently punctuated the width of the trench they were built within. Just beyond the end of the arid, red earth, a new sensation of color took his eye. Grass, pale green in color, greeted him pleasantly. It did not grow very tall, as some grasses he'd known were given to do, and seemed to lead the way into the city. Other things received his notice, as well.

A road sprung up. It glistened with the hard look of pure, polished silver in the sunlight. Borter trod the distance to the grass, now eager to test it beneath his feet as he journeyed to the heavens, reaching spires. Roads like this crisscrossed Toth in winding curves and long uniform thoroughfares with much built alongside them as they led to the city's center.

Nearer to the heart of the city, even before he reached the sight of the smaller structures, there were signs of a recent battle. Among the grass, too, there stood out the mangled wreckage of war's machinery. Even in this most burned – out and crumpled state, the universal designs of death-wielding designs were clear. Going further, the remains of mechanically driven carnage gave further testimony.

There was no obvious system of mass transportation. There were no signs marking the streets or any of the buildings. Borter wondered how they found their way around. Sidewalks were similarly in short supply. Was it that no one walked? Borter was, at the same time, both interested and confused.

Wandering the streets for some minutes to ease his curiosity and to find help, he crossed the greater part of the city. His feet began to ache. He supposed, though, that he would have no trouble finding his way back to the landed Gotha – Kite. He only had to count backward. All the buildings of one kind stood in rows together neatly.

Turning any corner could show him something altogether different. It was the architecture that caught his eye. He couldn't imagine what might happen in a long row of buildings that seemed based on one idea, like a cube or a sphere, then others that were pyramids. Some seemed to tumble up from the streets, one shape built on top of another.

He found some of it stunning because he couldn't see exactly how they stayed up. Nothing looked like private or individual residences. He wondered if the inhabitants had lived together in the deserted buildings, one like the other, all their individuality surrendered. There was no one to answer his questions. Helio would have been a help, he thought. The Marcellean, Lord Soal would be, certainly. If only they were here.

18

The Spires of Toth

He sat for a few moments beneath a gnarled old tree and looked around, considering his situation. Warfare had indeed been waged in the city. It could return at any time to him, and it could be going on elsewhere, soon to return to this place. He could not imagine the population leaving the city of their own free will, not a city so well put together it appeared to be the work of a single hand for a single purpose.

He wondered sourly if the builders of the place had also been carried away by their attackers. Remembering his experience with Modallas and its interceptors, it did take much time adding two and two to come up with four. Rising slowly, he started back toward the Gotha-Kite. With no one aid him in the city, prospects were not good, maybe even dangerous. It would be better to go on.

Everything was as he left it at the Gotha-Kite. But something was wrong. He could feel it in the small hairs on the back of his neck. He could not see it or hear it, but something was different. Borter took a suspicious turn around the Gotha-Kite. At first, there was nothing. Then there was a scuff mark in the dust, then a footprint, not his own. He studied the bottom of his boot. He needed new boots.

Drawing his blaster, he knelt beside the light flyer. Only the wind moved in the narrow pass outside the city. Flying out, if there was danger, would not be an answer. A Gotha-Kite was far too slow. Anything competent to catch him on foot was competent enough to be feared, competent enough to overtake the plodding Gotha-Kite as he urged it into the sky.

In other words, if they had blasters and were intelligent, the sky would be no haven. He decided to retreat to the dead city. It would provide him with cover, at least. He never counted it as impossible that help would arrive in time. Taking careful steps, again, trying to act normally, unconcerned.

Behind him, Targans crept silently down the sheer canyon walls. They came in full Modallian gear, creeping upside down as if gravity had no meaning for them. Their transport was far above them on some impossible ledge. Their dusky faces stared out intently beneath the visors of their battle helmets. This mission was important. Lord Markham himself had ordered it.

As he reached the city, the tiny hairs on the back of his neck, again, stood out straight. The danger was near, but he couldn't spot it. The intuition that raised the hair on his neck had saved him before, and it would again. He would not turn against it now. At the first corner, he broke into a run.

Before he reached the next corner, Targans blocked his way. Diving to one side, he hugged the walls. Other Targan ran up from behind, exchanging inaccurate blaster fire with him. Borter ran for his life into the wide doorway of the nearest building. Across the vast lobby, he found narrow stairs winding upward. Not wanting to be trapped, he looked for another way out. There was none. The staircase became his only option.

The Modallian blasters became more accurate. Struggling up the steps, he exchanged more fire with the dogging Targans. To him, they looked mean and moved like thugs in the worst of the Bouley bars. They moved quickly, covering one another as they came. Borter, at the first full turn on the staircase, leaned over the rail and downed the leading Targan as he reached the first stair.

The second, just behind him, came on as if nothing had happened. Borter scrambled higher. He looked ahead for a place to hold them off. They took the staircase. Borter took the first landing, finding cover in a doorway. Anything out of the line of fire would be fine. From such a place, he could pick away at them for a long time. The second Targan crumpled on the stairs. Others came.

Borter resolved to make a good fight of it, to go down gallantly in the face of greater odds, that is, if he had no other choice. Keeping up a constant stream of fire, he climbed higher up the stairs. On signal, the Targans rushed forward. He crept higher, and it became difficult for him to miss any target.

Silently, behind him, a dark form began to materialize. First, there was the vague inference of a shape, and then the full form appeared. Lord Markham stepped forward. Borter heard nothing until Markham's ion blade left its scabbard with a zing. He turned to the grim, terrifying visage as the pommel of the blade heavily crashed down on the side of his head. It was the last Borter remembered until much later.

Markham motioned two of his Targans up the stairs. He said nothing, letting his gesture command. Borter was lifted up and carried away. Materializing behind an unsuspecting man may have seemed cowardly to a Targan who did not possess teleportation, but none would not have said so. For Lord Markham, it had been a matter of necessity.

There were more things to be done with Borter than watching him slaughtered at the cost of many valuable Targans. Markham simply had the means to end the battle, expediting the inevitable in a manner that suited him and saved all possible resources available to him on a hostile planet. Besides, dealing with Borter in any other way was far beneath his station.

Targans scattered as Markham gave new orders. It would not be long before the two others fell into his trap.

Once again, Targans surrounded the lone Gotha-Kite on the outskirts of the city.

Markham was relieved of the task of having to find another way to carry out The Helmsman's command. The city had too recently been taken for any off-worlder to have heard. Therefore, Toth made the perfect trap, and it was necessary that these men be taken alive. Reports from Soarer's crash site indicated the wanted object was not in the wreckage. The Magnean did not have it. It had to be with the others.

Eight other vessels attempted to enter the system had been stopped and boarded, then destroyed. Of them, only this one possessed the necessary speed and skill to reach the planet. It cost the Helmsman much in trained Targans and material to find nothing. Lord Soal, the Earer, would return eventually. When he did, he, Lord Markham, The Wearer, would be waiting. The Heart of Marcellus would turn to him. Then, victory would be academic.

Beside Soarer's wreckage, far from Toth, Parnak lectured Helio on planetary geography as well as the situations they were liable to encounter before getting out

of the trench. Helio found they were not out of the woods yet, at least as far as Parnak could tell. That Modallas did not send more interceptors told him Lord Markham's hands were in the finer workings of things.

The Modallian method of dealing with the problem of a simple blockade running freighter was somewhat more direct and final - much more direct and final. Lord Markham, on behalf of his Modallian employers, would be heard from again.

Helio took stock of their total weaponry, only two handheld blasters. He hoped they would not prove necessary in their search for Borter. Parnak said that was a good possibility, but this confidence in saying so was not pressing. Beside the wreck of Soarer, Helio fell asleep.

For a while, Parnak stared down at him, unable to sleep, envious of the Dillisome's ability to do so, for two reasons. First, he concerned himself with the thoughts he'd not discussed with Helio, and second, the fact that his insectoid body required less sleep.

In the morning, early as before, Parnak awakened Helio to begin the day's journey. It felt as if he hadn't slept at all. To him, Parnak seemed to be standing as he had when he'd closed his eyes. Grudgingly, he moved stiff muscles.

Parnak already had the kite prepared for the day's journey. He said Toth, a city of some size, was not a full day's flight ahead. The news served to strengthen Helio's resolve to get on the kite and pedal on and leave behind the remains of Soarer, his only home.

Borter also woke. This time, Groggy, with a pain in his head, was in a dusty room between two unpleasant – looking Targans. At the other end of the chamber waited for Lord Markham. The same twin dots of light blinked on his shoulder as had Lord Soal's. There was, however, an undeniable difference in their carriage.

Borter called out, or almost did, suddenly catching himself, holding back, quickly realizing him not the same man.

Markham paced heavily across the room. Borter struggled to rise, but the Targans held him down. First, he demanded loudly the meaning of the attack on his freighter while insistently trying to shrug off the heavy Targan hands on him. Describing himself as a simple freighter pilot brought only laughter from the renegade Marcellean lord.

"Possibly, you are what you appear," Markham said softly. "Possibly, you and your companions are enemies of The Helmsman." The Marcellean toyed with him. "Why else would you refuse our orders to stop and be boarded?"

Borter countered that, perhaps. The Helmsman, whoever that was, thought he owned all of space and that, perhaps, he'd, whoever he was, never heard of The Free Space Act. Borter pretense of innocence and arrogance failed to impress the rogue Marcellean.

"You have cost us a squadron of interceptors and several well – trained soldiers of Modallas." Markham glared as he spoke the words.

"It's not my fault," Borter answered, continuing defiance.

Markham cuffed him with an armored hand. "Ok, you can bill me," he gasped. The Targans' grasp became heavier.

"Hey. I am the offended party here - and I demand to be freed immediately." He struggled against the combined weight of the Targans, this time for dramatic effect. "And, compensation for my freighter."

"You demand?" Markham's calm returned. "My friend," the Marcellean counseled amiably, "how are you able to demand from - such a *demanding* position?"

Markham enjoyed his little joke at Borter's expense. Borter wriggled uncomfortably. "It is I who demand here and you who shall answer with all that is required of you." Markham rose to his full height, glaring down at the pilot. "Your cargo bay was empty. What was your cargo to the planet?"

Borter hesitated. "Electronic navigational equipment, we jettisoned for speed. It's probably all ashes now."

Borter had not imagined being interrogated but thought the lie believable; it sounded at least as good as anything else. "We were bringing sales samples from the inner galaxy from one of the big corporations on Forum 9. My passenger was a sales representative."

"Impossible," Markham shot back. "Marcellus does no business off-world." Marcellean Techno Dwarf fabricate their own equipment, equipment superior to any in the galaxy. Marcellus is self-sufficient in all technologies.

Well, my sales rep did say they hadn't heard from you in quite some time." Borter smirked.

"Your ship was powered by Marcellean power dots," Markham was not put off by the Magnean's glibness. He countered again smoothly. "It is also known that this type of power dot is only available to high-ranking Marcelleans — very high-ranking Marcelleans."

Markham scowled behind the sealed battle mask, sensing an end to his little chase. "Come, now, make it easy on yourself — you are enemies of The Helmsman, aren't you? Out with it," Markham's manner went from calm to angry in an instant, "Perhaps we will be merciful and spare your miserable lives!"

Borter asked, choosing this time to be silent.

"Your cargo should arrive soon. Shortly, we will know all there is to know about you." Markham said nothing more. Markham turned, leaving the room. His Targan guards remained.

His orders to the Targans awaiting Parnak and Helio had been curt, simple, "Wait!" He went to reset the trap that had snared Borter. The penetration of this single ship had been exceptional. Lord Soal would make use of such beings in his long-awaited return to the planet.

It could signal the time of triumph that was long — awaited by Markham. Marcellus would be his after the proposed defeat of his brother, Lord Soal. It had been assured him. The planet would be his, The Helmsman had said so. Yes, these were the types Lord Soal would use, he was sure. There was a plan, and he would discover it.

103

19

Escape

Long ago, in a time long past, a star had blinked and then dimmed in a far part of another, an unknown galaxy. Circling it, a planet grown nearly cold and barren. In those final years, Modallas was built to serve its few last beings. The mammoth structure was more than a satellite and more than the planet that spawned it.

Both refuge and ship, Modallas left its dying star. Of the number beginning the journey, it was said few remained. Even Markham, who had served them and their Helmsman those long years, did not know how many. He was forbidden entry into the White City of the Modallian Third Plain.

Later, after entering the Varian subsystems, Modallas orbited Marcellus and The Helmsman made his evil pact with Lord Markham for possession of the Marcellean Heart. That had been a little more than twelve hundred years before. Since that time, the planet had been torn by warfare, other than the biological sort that was normal for that world. The leading race of Marcelleans was systematically reduced in number at, both, the hands of the Targan and their new masters Markham and The Helmsman.

Helio, and now Borter, had already seen first-hand the race of forest people. On Marcellus, The Helmsman found his key to galactic conquest, the last of the necessary links, The Marcellean Heart. An instrument of most unique qualities, when joined with a wearer it became the most powerful of objects. It was the most sought after of objects in the view of Modallas. Of the wearers, two survived the turmoil of a millennium and two hundred years, the Lords Markham and Soal.

Seducing Markham quickly, to his will, with the promise of a conquered Marcellus for his own, The Helmsman was near the final key to galactic conquest. Lord Soal was not so easy. Lord Soal figured, then, to be the only obstacle between the Modallians and their goal, therefore, his elimination became most desirable. Numerous battles were fought for just that purpose, with interposed cunning and intrigue, all played with no clear success for either side.

The holdover Markham was indefinable. The promise alone of ultimate lordship over Marcellus drew him irresistibly, true. But, Markham as wearer, could demand his own price and thus far he was necessary to the plan.

As he regarded Borter under close guard, he realized that day, his suspicions had been true, his long apprenticeship would end.

Years before, he had begun to think of the galactic campaign as necessary, though, at the beginning, it was something The Helmsman alone wanted. The reasoning for such a scheme had also long passed by him. He followed blindly, this also being a necessity. The wait had been long. He hoped that when the day ended, with all his being, he would be the only Marcellean wearer.

Borter's head ached terribly. The Targans released their hold allowing him to sit up. The two looked implacable. They stood away, facing him. The future held little for him if he did not escape soon. He thought twice about attempting anything against their blasters — unarmed, at least. The capabilities of the Marcellean were unknown.

Since he looked like Lord Soal, he expected him to be equally formidable.

Nothing could be done with Markham and his Targans in the room. Borter correctly suspected that he was in the same the building where he had made his stand. He knew nothing of why he had been spared, or for how long.

The eyes of his Shoulder Falcon blinked. Markham nearly came to attention as it spoke its message to him, a message only he could hear. Something was about to happen. Markham finally left the room.

Borter began to think over methods of escape. The Targans would have to be put out of action. And, back on the staircase, how many more would be waiting for him? It stood to reason that many Targans or few, he would stand a better chance of survival by fighting.

Markham, expected Parnak and Helio to fall into his trap. If he could get free, he knew where that trap waited. He wondered, by the way, how it was he had managed to get so many hours ahead of them by doubling back all that way. He would have to ask if he lived long enough to ask the question. He moaned.

The heads of both guards nodded more his way. He toppled over and seemed to stop breathing. One guard mumbled something to the other and glanced at him.

There was concern he might die in their care. Lord Markham ordered that the off – worlder should live, for the present, at least. If he died before he was supposed to, they would suffer.

Elsewhere, the Shoulder Falcon updated the position of the approaching Gotha – Kite. The news excited him, the promise of battle always did, even one so small an occasion as this. He hurried. The city's edge was not far. His Targans had been in position for hours, the trap was set.

Markham took his place in the center of the hidden perimeter, waiting. The crossfire would be inescapable. Once the location of the Heart was known, he would have the pleasure of seeing all three executed.

The propeller plodded behind the man – driven Gotha-Kite. The sound of it had become reassuring and friendly during the new day's flying. Not exactly the in – atmosphere roar of Soarer's engines, but enough, suitable. It saved them a longer, more uncomfortable walk.

The climate did not much please Helio. The thought of trekking across this semi-arid land did not appeal to him above the prospect of covering the same distance on his native ice planet.

Nothing on Dillisome seemed attractive to any off – worlder except the view from orbit, outbound, of course. Few Dillisome left the place and those who did, did not come back.

Caring little for things from outside had gotten them their racial name and the name of the planet, too. The first explorers to the planet had named it, finding the natives, dilettantes, sometimes in things of critical trust. That there was nothing desirable on the planet and the Dillisome, in fact, knew it. They didn't change and they wouldn't. They worked as hard as they had to and no further. They simply did not know ambition.

Stumbling on the truth did not change the opinions of several galactic scholars and did nothing about the name of the planet or the way others thought of the population of the planet. Helio, like most Dillisome, would never ask why Borter had come to the planet? Borter, in turn, had never asked why he left? If he had, Helio would have had no answer for him. Borter would have claimed to have lost his way and ended up there accidentally. Helio might have said nothing, but that would have meant he'd found a way off the planet.

Helio's thinking frightened Borter at times. The broadness of it was startling. He had never used such a variety of thoughts or new ideas. The Dillisome, singly or as a people, thought as they lived, without complication. Intelligence was not the problem. Helio had learned to pilot Soarer in just three short weeks.

Toth came into sight. To Helio it appeared quite unlike Bouley, unlike anything he and Borter had ever seen before. The clean silver streets and the distant shapes of the tall spires were distinct in the bright sunlight of the day. Always, Helio was awed by architecture. As the kite made a graceful peak, both Parnak and Helio leaned back pedaling hard for more altitude.

The kite, ungainly at best, lifted its nose a little more trying to obey, if slowly, the panting demands made by its passengers on its limited aerodynamics. Then, Helio turned to Parnak and said, "Now – let it go."

As they glided easily forward to a place selected for landing, between two – yet, somewhat distant buildings. Helio took the few moments to rest. Parnak noted with interest the lack of movement in Toth's symmetrically drawn streets. In the back of his mind, the sensation that warned of danger began to ache. For a moment longer, there was nothing – then Borter let himself out of the room. Looking into the corridor for more Targan. The first pair lay back in the room. As they had come closer, leaning forward, dangerously so, Borter grabbed a blaster from one of his Targan's belt and used it.

He peered out into the corridor, left then right, slowly. It proved empty. The sound of blaster fire from the room had not drawn more Targans. Down the stairway, his own blaster recovered and in hand, there were none. The building seemed deserted, except for him. Opening the main doors, he let himself out into the street. A great and suspicious quiet greeted him.

20

Helio and Parnak

Energy burst all around them from hidden Targan positions below. Feet leapt to pedals, once again, Helio and Parnak worked furiously. Helio pushed the lumbering Gotha- Kite into the steepest dive he could manage. It made the way to their landing site quicker, supposing they could get to it. The long wings moaned like specters disturbed at midnight, beneath the new force placed upon them by the dive angle, the flyers would be fortunate to make a landing at all.

The nose of the fragile craft leveled off just enough for Helio to see light over the horizon and escape total disaster. He pulled back on the control stick as straining metal groaned, accepting its tortures. The light landing gear splayed and struck off as it met the ground.

He lurched heavily against his back, unable to control himself against the force of the crash. Parnak fared little better though with his natural strength he kept himself in the cockpit, bracing until it came loose in his hands.

Upright, they skidded, tipping from wing to wing out of control slipping on the hard, silver pavement. Helio thought that if they lived through the crash they might, indeed, skid to some position of advantage behind their attackers. That is, if they still had any luck.

Trailing a chorus of shattered metal struts, garlanded in torn fabric from the wings, the kite came to a rude halt and leaned over heavily on the stub of one wing. Parnak tumbled out following Helio.

"Quickly, ready your weapon," the Dillisome ordered calmly in the clamor, the sound of heavily shod and running feet came to them.

Parnak adjusted the power indicator on his blaster to full and slipped the safety off. "Targan," whispered Parnak. Helio, beside him, panted heavily from the quick sprints. There was a silence in the street where they had run for shelter. He tried to remember the number of Targan he'd seen as they'd rushed from cover to fire at them as the Gotha-Kite flew over their position and then crashed into the street. He couldn't remember.

Blaster aimed, Helio leaned around the corner of a building. Parnak joined him quickly. They darted across the street. They drew no fire.

Another street of identical buildings, these shaped like cylinders and rounded at the end suspended on small tubular uprights on both ends. More of the identical buildings and streets later, they rested, seeing no Targan. They tried to relax, to catch their breath, to gather themselves and to think.

There was the sound of a footstep behind them. Instantly, Helio crouched low, spun on one knee, coming around to fire. Parnak bumped him knocking him off balance, spoiling his aim. The shot went wild among the buildings. The armored figure made no effort to move.

"Lord Soal," gasped Parnak. "How nice to see you." The Marcellean moved forward acknowledging the greeting. Lowering his blaster Helio tried to make amends.

"Your shot went wild, but it will bring the Targan to us. My Shoulder Falcon tells me they are coming, now." Lord Soal nodded in their direction. The eyes on his shoulder blinked. Helio and Parnak turned to face the enemy.

"Too bad we have no help," said Helio.

"Reinforcements are nearby – should they be needed," the Marcellean assured them calmly. "I'm sure their services will not be required."

Helio was amazed at the Marcellean's confidence. The sound of running feet, the same sound and the same feet that foretold of

Targans coming. They rounded the corner. Helio went flat, ready to fire, as the Targans themselves dived to one knee or sprawled flat out to fire.

"Surrender," the Marcellean demanded, "and live."

Behind the Targan, another Marcellean strode into view, one looking strikingly like Lord Soal himself. Helio had to turn and make sure Lord Soal was still behind him.

"We were about to make you that offer," Markham countered, his voice loud, above the clatter in the street.

"Only you would have the monumental conceit to make such a – request, in your situation."

"And you, the colossal evil, Brother. Let us make it single combat." Lord Soal offered.

Markham declined. "You are to be captured alive - if possible." He added the condition of life grudgingly.

"You serve a master, Brother. I could not serve that master nor could I surrender to his underling – a hired dog."

The remark galled the traitor. "Very well, Soal. See how well I have trained the Targan to serve my ends."

Markham gestured grandly to his Targans. "Enemies of The Helmsman and The Sky God - take them," he ordered.

A Targan moved to fire his blaster. Helio dropped him.

Without warning, Lord Soal moved forward as did the Targan themselves. Markham kept his position. The brothers' ion blades snapped from their scabbards with amazing speed.

Lord Soal, among the Targan, moved swiftly, throwing himself at their center. The blue edged ion blade moved from one to another with ease as it had in the street fight at Bouley. Helio could not target Markham standing behind his fighters. Nor could he fire into the center of the fight without hitting Lord Soal as he moved among his enemies. The ion blade took a toll, in and around them touching each like a licking tongue of fire taking first one, then another, almost a living thing among them. It fanned the entire area, crumbling any in its path. Finally, Helio managed to squeeze off shots at a few Targan who managed to outflank Lord Soal and attack him from behind.

Markham watched without surprise as his Targan were cut down before his brother's charge. The ranks thinned, an enemy falling like stalks of wheat before a reaper. Soal was irresistible in battle, more and more of the Targans fell around him. He edged ever closer to his renegade brother.

Several broke away and stumbled into each other, trying to avoid the cutting blade. Ranks bowed backward. At such close range they found it impossible to aim their weapons. Those unfortunate enough to escape were cut down by Markham himself in their attempt to flee. For a moment, the carnage seemed directed at the Targan alone by the feuding Marcelleans.

In the thick of battle, Lord Soal's features seemed fused into a mask resembling the hardness of the of his body armor. The Shoulder Falcon blinked continuously, one second on and the next off, faithfully. Like some protean force, the Targan in their primitive minds once might have worshipped, Lord Soal moved among them delivering quick death this way and that, unstoppable in his drive forward.

Those near were swept off like chaff in the wind. The great beast he had become was loose among them, cutting them to ribbons as he passed. Targan were on all sides at the battle pressed along. Helio and Parnak found themselves unable to keep pressure on the flanks. For each one cut down another took his place. Others came at Helio and Parnak.

Borter, at last, made an appearance. "Borter!"

Helio smiled a rare smile. "It's about time," Parnak entered a view! The Magnean slipped up, taking cover next to them. The three off-worlders edged forward from their places aiding him in the remainder of the battle. Lord Soal kept an eye on his traitorous brother, not wanting to lose him.

To the Targan, he hardly paid attention at all, except to kill them. The freighter pilots took their chance to avenge Soarer. With Parnak, all firing, they cut down the number of Targan beginning to encircle Lord Soal.

As the Targan fell away, Markham could be seen just a few meters away. The distance separating the brothers became insignificant. The bodies of the dead lay in heaps. The last fell, slowly, like a tall tree. Markham, his blade still drawn, made a mawkish salute to his brother and disappeared, dematerialized, transported back to Modallas.

Reaching the spot, Lord Soal passed his blade through the vanishing specter doing no good. Markham's dark form gone, he returned to Parnak and his pilots. Borter wiped his brow of sweat. Helio stood calmly beside him showing no outer effects of the action.

"Nice party," he quipped, unable to release his grip on the favored Reggian blaster. "Sorry, I'm late." Lord Soal sheathed the deadly ion blade. "I must thank you for the support," he said reaching them. "A ship is on the way and will be here soon."

Without another word, he turned toward the city's edge where Borter's Gotha – Kite was moored. Parnak glanced toward his friends, the flyers, and fell into line behind the Marcellean Lord. Borter and Helio looked to each other, each noting the surprised look on the other's face and followed with resignation. What now? They had made a powerful enemy and had nothing to show for it and a single Gotha-Kite would not get them off the planet or back into the freight business.

One useless, lifeless, heap of bodies among all the deserted buildings of Toth, seemed something of a monument. Borter had wished the same fate on the Reggian pirates after dumping his cargo there. It looked different when he could see it with his own eyes.

Something was in this. They had not seen before in all their years spent shifting from planet to planet carrying in the cargo tube who knew what? Magnus and Dillisome were not planets of wholesale killing.

Reggian pirates killed easily, they destroyed what they could not take. An energy blast here or there, somewhere amidships was something more anonymous and more calculated than what had happened to the Markham's Targan, something that felt cleaner.

Lord Soal went out to await his ship. The cold matter-of-factness of it stunned them. Borter was the first to speak, "Let's go," he muttered. "There's nothing more for us here."

Toth was no longer a place of curious excitement for them. It looked empty and old to them. The galaxy would seem older to them, infinitely so, and colder after that day.

A short time later, Lord Soal would amaze them with accounts of ancient fighting, real fighting. Then, a shiny object appeared in the sky and came nearer, growing larger as it did. They felt a surprising lack of elation at the sight of their own approaching rescue.

The engines of the Marcellean ship droned into silence. Men came out, men like Lord Soal, armed and armored. They recognized the Marcellean overlord greeting him formally.

Everything was calm, efficient and official. Shoulder Falcons exchanged information - the numbers of Targans killed and so forth.

"The pilot is ready to takeoff." Lord Soal moved toward the rescue ship. Borter, Helio and Parnak followed quickly. It was a rare occasion for them to take a seat in someone else's flyer. As he boarded, Borter took a look toward the cockpit and then around the cabin in which he sat, that he would have called the tube on Soarer.

21

Enemies of The Helmsman

The flyer had no graceful, extensible, long wings like Soarer, to help her sail in the atmosphere. Wings, in fact, were almost nonexistent, short and stubby and inextensible. Borter guessed the ship was designed for orbital and suborbital missions. A small cubicle was set aside for passengers. All took seats there, Lord Soal, Borter, Parnak, Helio and their rescuers.

Borter had time to reflect upon the day's events. Events, though recent, were only a blur in his mind. He'd ordered them to surrender, thought Borter, there must have been fifty – plus Targan and the other Marcellean. Were they all like that?

Parnak remained silent, glancing from time to time at Lord Soal. Helio wondered what was going on in Borter's mind. One man often knew the other's thoughts with a startling regularity, now there was little room for doubt.

Leaving the planet was their best option. Nothing they had done, seen or heard, inclined them in the slightest to stay on. Violence was the watchword of the Marcelleans and their activities. Both flyers felt fortunate to have survived. The rear hatch slammed shut and the Marcellean vessel taxied onto the open floor of the trench for takeoff. All remained silent as the reddish terrain blurred by outside.

The new ship leapt into the sky pushing them back into the soft seats. The blunt craft tilted back steeply and sped toward suborbit.

"Well, she was a good ship," muttered Borter to Helio.

"A very good ship." His voice was soft. He spoke sadly.

"Helio, Parnak, we'll have to get something to drink when we get wherever we're going." He turned aside to Lord Soal and asked, "You do have alcohol on this planet, don't you?" The overlord of Marcellus nodded affirmatively.

"You will join us, of course?" Invited Borter. Lord Soal looked forward without answering for a moment. Marcellean finally nodded that he would attend.

 At length. Lord Soal half smiled, "You are correct, Borter. The enemies of The Helmsman should take their leisure together in memory of the battles fought and in

anticipation - of those to come." Borter sucked in his breath at Lord Soal's words. In his seat, he began to wonder who was kidding whom. To date, the pilot had given no better performance.

Talk continued for some time. Parnak kept an eye on the two as only Helio looked from the portal onto the vast planet hurtling beneath. Borter revealed the untrue story of his short and unfortunate life and all the circumstances having brought him to the loss of his flyer.

Lord Soal countered with an equally false story of his long and, also, unfortunate life that had seen little other than battling with Modallas to no end. Borter, putoff, by the Marcellean's unexpected ability to lie, at least to fabricate, broke first and asked for a new flyer.

Lord Soal eyed, first Borter, then Helio, and finally Parnak. "Have you seen much fighting, Borter?" He waited for an answer.

"I've seen fighting, sure," came the answer, "but not quite that close."

There was the sound of the Marcellean's laughter. "My friend, war is hazard," he said. "War is all enemy and grunts. Living is neology for dog-soldier. You have lost a flyer, not your life."

Borter laughed, "When we ran supplies in the Jinzikan Wars, Parnak said the same thing. I'm afraid I've heard this one before."

Lord Soal raised his eyebrows, "You are surprised that I have read the works of Parnak the Jillian? My dear friend, they are indispensable. Is it any wonder I repeat them?" He gave a second burst of laughter.

"Warfare was thrust upon us, thrust on us by Modallas and by our own bones." He paused looking at each one in turn. "Very well, we accept it," he spoke loudly. "Modallas has threatened us and when the time is right, we will destroy it." There was a stunning silence.

"And, we will destroy it." The booming voice sounded again.

"*And, we will destroy it?*" Borter repeated the words limply. "We? What do you mean we – us?"

Borter did not relish the thought of more Targans or another encounter with the artificial Modallian world. The memory of his running battle on the staircase in Toth till shook him. He eyed Lord Soal carefully, "Just where are – we going?"

"Why, my dear Borter, we are going to your ship." Lord Soal looked away from Borter and his surprised face and then back. "Do you remember the power dots I paid you with at Bouley?" The Marcellean smiled, enjoying Borter's discomfort.

Borter nodded, not forgetting the game, "The best we ever had."

"We are going, very soon, to the place where they are made," said the Marcellean. Something nudged Borter's memory to recall an old gripe. "What are we going to do about Bouley? Granted you had to get out of there, but couldn't you let the authorities on Tyrus know what happened? After all, we did not launch the flyer, you did."

Lord Soal gave another laugh. "A billion stars to lose in the galaxy and you are worried about one planet?"

"Fifty," Helio spoke up.

"I don't understand?" The overlord turned to him.

"Fifty. Tyrus holds strong trade alliances with fifty planets in four systems."

Helio explained what he meant. "What offends one of them, offends all of them."

"I understand," said Lord Soal. "This problem will be remembered. Worry about it no further. Your – flyer will be repaired, also, at no expense to you or Helio." He looked to Borter and Helio. "You have rendered excellent services." A bell sounded, announcing a flashing red light in the compartment. Borter and Helio started though the sound was soft.

"Modallians?"

"No," Lord Soal spoke. "Look." He pointed through the portal. Against the backdrop of the planet another ship crossed not far beneath them. It was much larger than the sub-orbital vehicle in which they traveled and larger than Soarer, too.

"What is it?" Borter asked.

"A transport. It carries your flyer to repair. Don't worry, you will like the improvements we make," Lord Soal smiled broadly at the flyers.

Borter objected, gasping weakly. "Better? Improvements? I made several advanced improvements myself."

"You will enjoy a new high in performance when my Techno – Dwarves have completed their task," he added confidently.

"Techno – Dwarves?" It was Borter who then raised his eyebrows in surprise.

"Of course," replied the Marcellean loudly, "Who else would do it? We are warriors, are we not? Enemies of The Helmsman." There was a deafening cheer from the Red Warriors in the bay. Borter did not quite know what to do.

22

Marcellus

The first night in Marcellus, the city, found the promised one drink turned into a celebration.

Marcelleans, curious at the off – worlders, joined the party in large numbers. Helio and Borter, for the first time in many days, had a chance to relax. Marcelleans wanted to know everything about them.

"What is your taste in our world's art," the tall, elegantly dressed woman asked matter – of – factly, "Do you prefer Varian Normal or Hyper Revisionist?"

"Well, I don't know much about art," Borter insisted. "However, I am partial to *Pittean Slan*," he said.

Helio had found little in the Galactic Atlas. The woman excused herself and turned away, her dress of some material, finer and thinner than the wing fabric of a Gotha – Kite, rustling a little as she went. Borter had been something of a disappointment to her, and he sensed it.

To others, Helio was introducing himself by his specialty title, "Grade 5, Subworld Specialist. Proper greetings were given and received all around. Heads nodded, his hands shook. The Dillisome was in his element, impressive.

"Then, you are familiar with our world?" One asked.

"Not extensively," the Dillisome explained, "Though your

ancient art has reached the main planetary systems of the galaxy, not much is known about the planet itself.

Knowledge of modern Marcellus is especially rare. The antiquities of the planet come down to us as legends. We lack the critical knowledge of facts to make them a history." Before their party, Helio had just enough time for a little research on the planet.

Borter stumbled through his conversations, finding it difficult to put his thoughts together.

Helio had more grace, "Coming here has been *a great experience* for us both. We consider ourselves most fortunate."

The two flyers stood close together, Borter, thankful for a lull in his own part of the conversation, paid attention to what Helio was saying. The woman who asked him for his artistic preferences now addressed her question, the same question, to Helio. "While Pittean Slan is my favorite for effect, *Morrean Blue*, the more ancient form, though rough, has greater stability and shall be the historically lasting example of the Slan school. I find besides their high standard, forms such as Porcean Blue and other imitators are mere pretenders."

"I had to ship out with a sub-world genius," mumbled Borter to himself.

"I beg your pardon?" A soft voice spoke beside him. Borter turned.

"What?" Then. "I – beg your pardon, what did you say?"

The voice and question belonged to a young woman, as beautiful a young woman as he'd seen before, anywhere. Women of such quality did not, nor had they ever, come up to Borter, especially, not at a party. "Uh – ," the pilot begged off. He smiled. The smile was returned to him.

Julia laughed quietly, without concern. Borter kept an ironically childish way about himself for odd occasions, especially the socially unknown. He found it pleased women who often wanted to mother him just a little. Borter had nothing else.

They connected. He was able to observe the city in daylight, with her, he strolled the broad thoroughfares much of the early morning. The buildings were as magnificent as their builders, stretching identically in even spaced rows as far as one might see. Something in them was indescribably more grand than those he'd seen in Toth.

Civilization, here, was older than anywhere else in the known galaxy. The very antiquity of the place was stunning. Julia happily told him nothing had changed in the city's structure for several hundred years, the buildings, were as they had always been.

Borter saw no one working, he gathered from his conversation with Lord Soal that mere work was beneath Marcelleans, that their only expertise was war. Julia said as much, all other work had been done.

Many years later, an historian would tell him that all humanoid life in the greater galaxy originated in the Varian Subsystem, specifically ancient Marcellus. Regarding the confidence, that borne of vast numbers, he was amazed when told there were only a few million of them on the whole planet. Julia walked beside him that night, until dawn and into the morning.

There were no outward signs of the warrior culture in the city and no signs of government, or any enforced order.

Although, there was an order. It was almost as if the city and its people had been and always would be just this way. She felt as if that behavior held a norm of acceptance, voluntarily, with nothing needed, at all, to enforce it. Strangely, the same odd intuition that led him throughout the galaxy told him such things were not even thought of.

As Borter observed, once again Helio researched. Lord Soal left all doors open to them in the city. Before long, Helio had introduced himself to the Public Information Bank. He found an empathy cubicle where he was able to watch the condensed history of the planet. There, he spent many hours over the next day's cross — referencing subjects at random in the memory banks.

Following a brief geographical orientation, the ancient history of the planet began. The first permanently recorded histories appeared visually of a technological civilization of some sophistication, Helio could only wonder how many years, millennia preceded other epochs he viewed more haphazardly.

Almost immediately, there were the references to war. The Marcelleans had, apparently, fought enemies both on and off the planet many times. The pilot envisioned them marching across great savannahs, the lush savannahs that led to the Targan Forest, it must have been. A voice narration described the fighting and the campaigns scene by scene.

So, it went for hours, Helio had become comfortable in the private cubicle feeling secure there, sure that ensuing histories held many curiosities, answers perhaps. Most surprising, he found Lord Soal, or another Marcellean who looked like him, in the tapes, long before modern times.

Twelve hundred years on, it looked like Soal, but Helio was not sure. He again ran the recording, but it was just as blurred the second time as the first and as brief. The mammoth military parade through history went on.

There were other, more repeated references to Lord Soal. Helio supposed, in the end, that they referenced some other member of the same family, an ancestor, a prominent family beginning its emergence in that distant antiquity.

Within that another brace of years there were references, also, to a Lord Markham, Modallas and The Helmsman, more ancestors, more coincidences? Helio had great difficulty believing his eyes. No being in the galaxy lived twelve hundred years. Modallas, itself could have existed easily for that long and warfare was an easy certitude always - but no humanoids.

There was a large gap in planetary history. Several references were found to other sources. Helio turned through several, but they were of little value. When the histories rejoined, times were modern. The recording quality was nearly perfect. A familiar face appeared – Parnak's. The insectoid was there on the tape, right in front of him, buzzing in his peculiar language spoken above the familiar subtitle translation into Universal.

The recording must have been made sometime before they'd flown him in the Jinzikan War. Parnak had never mentioned Marcellus to them. That was strange, given he was an earnest and incessant talker.

For many hours, for hours and hours on end, they'd listened to his stories. Surely, a place like this would have would have been worth a mention.

The Jinzikan War had been good for them all, in a manner of speaking. Parnak paid in hard cash and was more than satisfied with the quality of their service. It had been a time they would fly anything anywhere, for money, on instant notice. Several times, they'd almost been killed, getting Parnak to the fighting. Those experiences made fast friends of them all, a camaraderie born of facing mutual danger. Helio would make it a point to ask Parnak about this.

Following in the same record was a dazzling array of battles fought against Modallas. Peripheral information fed in by the Marcellean narrator clued him to the date of each event. Lord Soal's face was clearly seen when he was mentioned in the later recordings, especially those done by Parnak. This Marcellean was too much a man of mystery.

Beneath that shell of superb armor, there was a great void that demanded answers. The two flyers did not know enough about their present employer. "Where have you been keeping yourself," the Magnean asked a day or two later, smiling affably, though knowing full well where Helio had been. Borter looked good and relaxed, more so than at any time he could remember.

"The library," Helio replied, "as you know." He then encapsulated the planet's recent history for his partner in two words, "*Very interesting.*"

Then, turning quietly Borter *sniffed*, "Right – a culture this old and they still use *taped media.*"

he walked toward the large window of the apartment they shared as the Marcellean overlord's guests. The window was large and held a commanding view of Marcellus, the city. Borter knew it was more than his imagination when he felt something was wrong.

Helio had joined him in Julia's apartments. Borter had been rarely out of her company, except at night when Marcellean propriety demanded they separate – that and a healthy respect for Lord Soal, her father.

That afternoon, Borter was in a mood that, for the time being, outweighed any misgivings held by the venerable Dillisome, his partner. "She's beautiful, isn't she?" Borter said, beaming, just behind Helio's turned back. Julia had gone out of the spacious room just before Helio had arrived. "I – I'm thinking of settling down," he spoke finally.

The Dillisome turned slowly, his jaw set firmly. His eyes looked straight into Borter's, their grasp more inviting than all of Marcellus' stretched out beneath the window. Helio might have known to expect something of the sort.

In the brief space before Helio spoke, it seemed to Borter, an eternity had passed. In his partner's mind, he knew, whirled only the thoughts that would serve the flyers best. Before them lay Marcellus. Through infinitely more grand than Toth, it reminded him of that deserted place. Helio thought, too, that Marcellus was doomed to that same fate.

The same pale green grasses grew there as had grown between the silver ribbons of pavement in Toth. The buildings were a little different, though there were more of them. In the streets, busy Marcelleans without battle armor walked back and forth about their business without giving a second thought to any whom they passed, not even one whose skin was a light blue.

He did not know when it would come, but to his senses, this sweet place of great parties and other magnificent gatherings, and even of children, the generations to come, had the same lank air as had Toth, the bitterness native to an old battlefield's memory of death and destruction.

Helio spoke slowly with deference, with a consul of one many years his senior. Borter was told all the things, both thought and felt, the Dillisome had found. It took only moments to say.

At first, there was disbelief, then acceptance.

Even though Parnak was not present to confirm or deny, Borter soon found himself with no choice but to believe, compelled not only by words but by knowledge of his partner as well.

"You are thinking of staying here – on the planet?"

Borter became thoughtful, "Perhaps." He said, stroking his smooth chin. "There may be something to be had for us - in a local run."

"I think not," Helio said with finality.

"You mean you don't want to stay?" Helio, too, took a thoughtful mien, "No, and I think you will not want to when you hear the things I have found."

"Well?" Borter turned, arms folded across his chest, impatiently waiting for information he did not want to hear.

"There are several points. If you'll allow me the chance, I'll explain things to you," said the Dillisome. His voice was calm, though its intonation was grave as he went on. "Firstly, Marcellus is the only city presently inhabited on the entire planet, save, of course, the Targan villages, towns, and, if you will – cities. Between those cities and towns, there will be no transportation, at least as far as we are concerned. Since warfare is the leading industry, I think it will be a while before there is any viable alternative."

"Marcellus is the only populated city left on a planet this size?" Borter's imagination staggered at the thought of such a thing. Helio went on.

"Modallas has been systematically destroying everything Marcellean for just under twelve hundred years. That is to say since Modallas appeared in the sky above the planet, many other cities, both larger and smaller than Toth, lay in ruins attesting to this. Marcellus and a few beleaguered outposts on the frontier guarding the edges of the Targan Forest are all that are left.

I doubt The Helmsman means to let these final remnants last much longer in his questing after The Heart. We already participate in this world's principal industry. When that is done, so are we. Nothing, after that, will remain for us on this planet."

"Then, Julia will come away with us," said a determined Borter.

"Ah," smiled Helio, waggling an admonishing finger. "But, will she?"

Borter stopped. "I – don't know. I'll ask her."

Helio nodded seriously without looking at Borter. "I have some suspicions," he began once again most slowly, "Julia may be other than she appears."

The statement hung in the air briefly until Borter lashed out at it as if to grasp and wring from it only the truth he desired. "Meaning?" He sneered.

"You are in love with her," observed Helio calmly without giving the look of one making some great deduction, "already?"

Borter stammered. "Y – yes." Then catching himself, he stood bolt upright, staunchly as if receiving unheard orders, defending the emotion he had not yet named himself, that Helio had, until that moment.

"I – I am. Does it worry you that it may prove to be the end of our partnership?"

With that outburst, Borter felt his face redden, and his anger and confidence waned. He looked for a long moment into Helio's dark eyes, sensing a great emptiness in himself – an emptiness that, for an instant, rivaled the emptiness of space.

His space brother looked back for a time, also in silence. Helio's regular features were somber. Now, they, too, had a look of worry and distaste at what must be said.

Borter denied a second, weaker urge to get himself clear by lashing out at Helio. He shrugged instead, turning his gaze once more to the view of the city. It would be useless to deny the findings of Helio's natural intelligence. The Dillisome was too efficient, too exact to be denied. Trying to disprove him would be futile and a waste of time.

"Not bad, " Borter spoke, "for a guy from an Ice world."

"Borter?" Helio began once again in a softer, more soothing voice. "There is more," he said and waited for Borter's signal to continue. The pilot glanced back with a quick nod to him. Helio began. "There is good reason to believe Marcelleans live a life span far exceeding our own or any others we have known in the galaxy. Only the one known as The Helmsman seems to have lived as long – and his origins are unknown."

Helio paused dramatically, giving note to the silence of the very air in the room. "I believe Lord Soal, for one example, to be, in age, more than twelve hundred years old. That is in our years, Borter. This may have significance for you regarding Julia." Helio, again, waited unmoving, silent. "It means that she could be many times your age now, and when you are an old man ready to breathe your last, she may not seem to have aged at all." A third silence imposed itself. "Borter, do you hear?" Helio's voice held calm and steady as Borter found the strength only to nod that he had.

"I will leave you now," said the Dillisome, knowing he had done what he had come to do. "Any decision you make will be fine with me – concerning both Julia and our partnership."

He had never challenged Borter's leadership. The man, though sometimes erratic, was a superior pilot and friend and possessed a formidable intelligence of his own. The Dillisome quietly turned and left him alone. In the next room, Julia heard all. As Helio closed the door behind him, she walked toward a silent Borter who brooded at the big window. Though Helio had been more polite than usual, from the time he'd come, she'd sensed something amiss between the two and planned her discrete exit. At last, Borter faced her, acknowledging her presence, but it was she who spoke first.

Nearing him, that beauty unknown to him elsewhere. A beauty Borter felt was somehow doomed and forever beyond his grasp. She asked, "Helio has said something to upset you?"

"Yes," he said at last, "he has. It appears I've just been told the facts of the universe – for the second time."

Beneath his cocked eyebrow, the taste of sarcasm was bitter. Borter's face reflected the appropriate sensation.

"I'm afraid I overheard," she said plainly. These rooms are not large, and one grows accustomed to the usual sounds. It is not difficult to hear things.

Borter went to her. Taking her hands gently, he spoke, "If what Helio said is true, there is no point in asking you to come away with me."

"If it were not, I could not leave Marcellus. The duty of all Marcelleans is here, even though we perish." Borter said nothing. He looked aside, not wanting to catch her eye.

"If it is any consolation," she replied softly, "the difference between our life spans would make any relationship questionable, at best. Borter that we are linked in this manner is not the will of The Heart.

However small your knowledge is of *The Heart*, you must know that. With that, too, take the knowledge of my true sorrow that it is not."

An hour later, Borter requested his flyer. For days, it had been undergoing repair, but neither Helio nor he knew where it was. The last they'd seen Soarer had been as they had neared the city, carried from Toth beneath them in the belly of the other Marcellean ship. Julia nodded saying transportation would be made available for them to the repair station. The manner of it all was business – like and efficient.

23

Night

Above, the stars of the galaxy twinkled across the sky. The day had become night. One of the planet's fast – orbiting moons rose dimly over a darkened horizon. Modallas and its terror were nowhere to be seen.

The summer months of Marcellus warmed the air and kept it laden with the heavy fragrances of new flowers. Borter walked for a long time in this early evening air before turning back toward his apartment near Julia's. In her apartment, Lord Soal glowered at his daughter.

"He walked out into the courtyard," she said, most careful of her father's feelings, "as if burdened by some – great weight."

"He doesn't yet have his ship or his friend and most of all you have his heart," said the Marcellean overlord, "He will be back."

Below them, in the vast courtyard of the living complex, the center of Marcellus', the city's, daily life, was lighted with dim globes of artificial light, augmented only slightly by a second of the planet's fast moons reaching, now, just above the horizon. No guards were to be seen, though they were surely there.

"It is good we continue this no further. It is not the intention of The Heart." Lord Soal spoke beneath his own burden, his own sadness. His voiced was solemn, his words paced slowly. "Not only is he a good flyer, but he has some wisdom of things beyond his years."

"He has Helio who is most loyal." Julia added softly. "It is not good to be in the galaxy alone. It is good he has a friend."

He watched her with an unfamiliar coolness, it seemed as if he looked at her for the first time. Then, he looked from the big window out onto the courtyard as if the entire vista of the planet lay below. One as great as the other, he supposed.

Beyond the city lay the grass savannahs and beyond them, the Targan Forests. Only a small rim of protectors ringed in that, saved, last vestige of their civilization from an eternal enemy. Julia went to the couch across the room and sat, waiting, without looking at her father, instead looking down at the thick, plush carpet at her feet. Soal felt her loneliness.

Much had been demanded of her. Times were hard for all and the most noble paid the highest price. This had been her lot. Everyone had lost something. He would not lose this daughter, he swore to himself, his gaze lost out the broad window on the broad expanse below.

The second moon of Marcellus' night dawdled, over the courtyard, a wandering, too slow, a pale eye, blind in the night, indifferent to the trouble beneath. Both father and daughter knew the terrible loneliness of the galaxy. Julia was in love with the Magnean, he knew. It had been the same with Rand Sabbling, her husband, dead, lost, a hero, at Duranas.

Tears welled in Julia's eyes, bitter, sprung from the depths of her being. "My place, I know, is here," she said haltingly. Her fists clenched at the soft fabric of the couch, "I will not run away." She stifled several wet sobs.

"You have done your duty to Marcellus and The Heart," he said turning curtly, noticing, at last, the silent tears that wet her cheeks. He regained his usual manner against her tears.

Julia looked up angrily, her streaming eyes and spoke through clenched teeth, "Had he less wisdom and had asked me to leave with him, and had I not my loyalty to our cause, if he'd asked, I would not have gone." She dabbed a kerchief at the tears coursing her cheeks. "I know my duty too well."

"You grieve for Rand Sabbling on your own account." He spoke in a low, half voice, his anger halved by sheer amazement.

"You would not have gone with this Borter in any event, not given the terrible proof of Sabbling's torn body on your doorstep." He looked toward Julia who wept more bitterly on the couch.

"I remember that day. The Red Flag, their final effort, raised above his position at Duranas. We were too distant from them to be of any help. It was the last of them. He died there that day with his men, who followed him, like the gallant warriors they were. Many witnessed the final struggle. Against them, that last time, the Targan hurled all they had, less had been repulsed several times that last hour alone.

The Forest Spirit paid dearly to take the Companion Blades that day. There was nothing left. Accept that fact, that Sabbling met the redemption of The Heart as all must. That was duty."

As for Borter and his loyal friend, this Helio, the Dillisome, they serve the will of The Heart though they know little and believe none of it. "No," he muttered half to himself, turning, "in the end, you are Marcellean, you will remain and serve The Heart. As for them, they are, again, excellent pilots, better than any we have."

Lord Soal towered above her even from across the room, "This infatuated flyer and his partner, these babes in the woods, serve well. The Heart has predicted their arrival here and that is enough. Parnak has asked for them as his pilots, they will not be quitting the planet just yet. We follow The Heart, all of us — we have no choice. In all the galaxy - that destiny is ours. Their destiny, too, is of The Heart."

He stalked toward the door, his long strides devouring the space in an instant. The door opened and the Marcellean was quickly through it, his mind already on other matters. His heavy steps sounded in the plush carpet of the corridor. His personal guard, close behind. On her couch, Julia spoke quietly to no one.

"If they refuse to serve, these two off-worlders, though they are unforgiven by The Heart, they are only denied the planet. Theirs is not the hatred of lost love between brothers. Markham's punishment is many times greater, his is to be the unforgiven hound of Marcellus forever, the only of that kind."

The walls of the apartment gave no answers, but rang with silence instead. Later, by only moments, Julia, feeling the warmth of the night closing on her, started out for a walk in the cooler night air in the courtyard below her own windows. She was in love with the Magnean, she knew.

There were scattered trees across the vast courtyard though none were thickly enough grown to obscure vision. Borter scuffed his booted feet at the minute cracks between the neatly sunken stones that covered the ground. The air had cleared his mind and now, he wanted to get back to his rooms.

The courtyard was still, and though it was not late no one was about. Nothing stirred, except Borter and an occasional breath of warm air. There was that same bleak emptiness he experienced at times on long missions. He almost always chose to sleep it off. This time it was no different.

24

The Battle in the Courtyard

Some distance away, dim figures left the portico of the building. As she stepped forward, he recognized Julia. The other figures were members of her guard, silent men, large and armed with Marcellean blasters, standard issue, and ion blades.

Borter stopped in his tracks. He had no stomach for another meeting with Julia, at least not so soon. His emotional wounds were quickly opened and then slowly closed. The guard, through their Shoulder Falcons, he was sure, knew already he was there and who he was.

The scanning distance of an individual unit was immense. They moved from the portico into near darkness, into the courtyard itself. Julia walked some distance in the lead. The guard properly paced a few steps behind.

Fresh air pressed by slowly, a welcome stranger passing after the warmth of her apartment. Somehow, it pleased Borter's mood. Julia's sudden appearance in his life and, equally, her sudden loss made the whole experience distant and unreal, as if in a painful dream from which he only slowly awakened.

There was a great deal about Marcellus that he liked. The nights reminded him of Magnus – home. He wondered what he would do if the situation was reversed, and it was Magnus and not Marcellus if it were himself and not Soal.

Much came to mind, very much that he had not thought of or

even remembered for quite a time. Magnus was a distant orb shining elsewhere in the galaxy, one bright spot among many others. Borter had been to many of them in his time in Soarer – the lights in the sky. None pleased him so much as those seen from his world.

The cool air of Marcellus' night bathed him, at once relieving him of the day's cares and reminding him that he was also very tired. As the first moon lowered itself beneath the rim of the trailing horizon, Borter wished he was on Magnus, peaceful Magnus, once again, as a young boy.

Julia was, meanwhile, having thoughts of her own. Profound sadness had touched her life as it had no other on the planet with the possible exception of her father. Fate played her a cruel trick, perhaps, even, The Heart had.

The constant battle for survival against The Helmsman toiled at her, chipping away at that controlled exterior others saw as a serene beauty. The thought of the dead Rand Sabbling repelled her. Only Borter's presence allowed her to consider it.

Perhaps because he was an off-worlder and because he had seen so much of the galaxy, she found him so attractive. To her, he had already described so much that was strange and beautiful.

Marcellus seemed only a dark pit beside his words. As Helio had done for many long hours in the years before the two had come, she, too, scanned the records in the Public Information Center.

Somehow, they did not say enough. The galaxy Magnus, which Borter had talked of most, seemed especially wonderful, in ideas – larger.

These things were far distant, now, unreachable. Her duty to The Heart, to Marcellus, was strong and undeniable. That must come first as they had to her father and the lost husband, Rand Sabbling.

Borter helped her forget for a while. Though she slipped for a moment, she never let go. The Plan, the will of The Heart, was their last hope. She would not go against it. She'd stumbled and let Borter lips touch hers and more. For a moment, though, in that moment, they touched each other deeply.

Markham turned quickly in Julia's apartment, as one of his tireless android lieutenants returned from another room to report her missing and the remaining guards neutralized. He asked if they should enter the other apartments. Markham would have enjoyed the destruction of all those in the building, but there was no time.

"No," he said coolly. "Prepare to move the search out of doors. Our prime objective remains the abduction of my niece." The armored android lieutenant showed no disappointment as his heels clicked together. He saluted, acknowledging the order. His emotionless forest eyes reflected only the sensor displays that flashed across the inner visor of his helmet.

Silent data reached Markham, from Modallean sensors and matched with information he'd gathered on planet, that from sensors of his own.

"She is in the courtyard. Lieutenant, Two guards with her — medium armament. Remember, my niece must not be harmed," he ordered.

"Yes, Lord Markham." There was a redundant click of heels with an accompanying salute, and the android was away again, issuing orders efficiently to his subordinates. In the corridor, their feet went quickly and quietly, especially for their armor and numbers. Moments later, they emerged into the courtyard.

The androids left the portico even more silently than they had moved through the corridor of the building. Holding to the shadows, they were not close enough. They advanced along the side of the building. In the dim lights, meant only to save the occasional night walk, a barked shin on unfamiliar ground, they closed on Julia and her guards.

Markham's lieutenant led the party of raiders. He had his orders and the signal to begin when it was given. The two guards were not as attentive as he'd expected. They walked along quietly, some paces behind Julia, looking neither left nor right. They held no caution for anything coming from behind. This mission would be easy. Imagine Marcelleans, such easy prey in their strongest stronghold.

Julia stopped short as the air in front of her tingled with energy, then glowed up to the height of a tall man. It sparkled briefly, and there was a brighter flash as Markham made a spectacular appearance. Her two guards stumbled forward, already dead, coming to her aid before they knew it. Julia was surrounded by the silent, well armed – androids before the two were on the ground.

"Coward," she hissed at Markham, ignoring the androids completely as inferiors when he'd transported.

Their eyes showed dully in the reflected lights of the courtyard. Markham stood gloating, making no answer. The lieutenant spread his men in a defensive perimeter around them. Markham looked straight into her eyes. She was not fearful as he'd expected she would be. Finally, he spoke.

His tone of voice, saved for such occasions, mocked her.

In a moment," he said, "a large teleportation tube will appear - for your convenience. You will be safe aboard Modallas within moments. Please do not bother yourself by screaming for help. It is too far away to do anything good. All the help that is alive, that is." He chuckled behind his mask.

Borter saw the flash of Markham's teleportation tube, and then the cluster of defending androids gathered around Julia. His blaster was in hand before he'd really had a chance to think about it, and he was crouched over, low, moving toward the tight circle of soldiers from Modallas.

Had they sensed him? Borter did not know. Nothing came in his direction. He was still a long way out. The hairs on the back of his neck stretched angrily. Reaching a small bench of stone, he knelt, adjusted the indicator of the blaster's butt to full, and took careful aim.

Energy exploded against one of the androids, who was knocked backward by the force of it and bounced heavily in his shattered armor as he came to a rest.

With an equal crash of metal armor against stone, another and another android came to the same end as the first. The recoil of their own heavy blasters echoed in the courtyard. A window flung open quickly, and the alarm was raised. Borter worked his way forward carefully, firing each time from a new place and from a different angle to conceal himself.

Markham barked quick orders at the androids, but did not move away from Julia himself. His ion blade remained sheathed. He pointed toward Borter, and as he did so, Their blasters ripped the stones from beneath the pilot's feet.

So fast was the action, Julia had not yet thought to move. Markham grabbed her small wrist in an iron grip as she became aware of her mistake. "Not so fast. You will be visiting me aboard Modallas, won't you? It has been some time since I've had the pleasure of your company."

Androids were not falling fast for Borter any longer. The surprise had worn thin. He dared not let them get away with her. His hearing rang with close blasts, and heat reached him from the still — hot stones nearby, which were hot from near misses.

25

The Attack

Borter spoke in awe, "A whatever – that – is."

The dangerous hair on the back of his neck stood straight out. They crept toward him. Where was help? Where was Lord Soal and the rest of his guard, the Red Warriors? He wanted to know. He demanded to know. The Targan were invisible to him, blending suddenly into the stone with all their killing craft learned from eons in the Forest. A white-hot flash struck just behind him. He whirled and caught an unlucky Targan with a better – placed blast of his own.

He rose from cover and retreated, firing. Markham looked, for the first time, realizing he'd seen him before. "That man." He gestured to his lieutenant. "It's the flyer – get him."

More androids leapt forward at the command. Headlong, they dashed after Borter. Firing wildly over his shoulder, he ran. At a dead run, he was still no match for the androids. The best he could hope for was to find cover before they killed him and held them off waiting for help.

Markham was content to watch the contest progress from a distance while keeping his hold on Julia. His androids ran, but all did not fire their weapons or let the threat of Borter's hold them back. While one or two stopped to steady their aim and take a shot at Borter, the others came on.

Then, two more dropped by from the pursuit and fired, and the first two ran to catch up. Others trailing the Magnean coming closer, waiting for their turns to drop and fire. The pilot would be taken over with just a little more effort, and they would be snatched safely back to Modallas with their prize in a fresh teleportation tube.

"Borter?" Said Julia, just realizing who it was. "Borter."

"So," the disgraced Marcellean ventured a guess, "this one is special to you? Well," he continued darkly, "He is a dead man. Mourn him aboard Modallas."

Markham's androids lunged savagely for Borter. A single blast from behind felled one but did nothing to stop the others. Though, it did give Markham a start. He turned to catch sight of the blue man from Dillisome running up at full speed.

"The other. I will rid us of this one myself." Julia still in hand, he drew a Modallian blaster from his hip and raised it to the level of his shoulder, taking careful aim as the battle raged on in the distance. The androids chased after Borter.

Helio was swift enough to dodge the first two or three of Markham's blasts, no matter how well aimed. The quality of the Dillisome's movement and the quickness of his reflexes had taken his enemy unaware.

Julia shook free of his grasp and ran for her fallen guards and their blasters. Her uncle was as quickly after her.

Like Borter, Helio found little cover. Doing the best he could, he began firing. Julia reached the blasters and reached for the nearest one when Markham again had her, holding her arm more tightly than before. Helio's fire was dangerously close, but only close, fearing for Julia.

"Lieutenant," Markham called for help, unable to handle both the struggling Julia and the new threat posed by the Dillisome behind him. "Recall your men." Before the androids could respond to his new orders, something new, something else, happened. One of his androids screamed out in the stark terror of someone, knowing he was about to meet his end.

Borter went to the ground in a deep crouch, and there he remained. Standing directly in front of the android charge was 5D. In his powerful maw was another screaming android. The rest suddenly held back.

He shook the tightly held body once more and tossed it aside, giving up his fatal grip at last. Android legend has been passed down for many generations, stories of these half-mythical beasts that roamed the tall grass savannas in the past.

They shrank back fearfully, then turned and ran. 5D regarded them with angry, twisting, coal black and pure white squares receding, bending into its single orifice, deeply set in the center of is form. Then, he charged after them.

Helio ignored Markham, firing swiftly into the running androids and dropping two quickly as 5D claimed more victims of his own. Borter continued to add what he could now that the fight was more equal.

In the shadows, Julia struggled against Markham's fierce grip. Markham, himself, fought her, at the same instant, trying to draw a bead on Helio without success. The two pilots brought down a constant hail of fire until Markham's teleportation tube appeared. He ran to it. Those of his androids still able followed hastily and disappeared. Julia slowed her uncle. The tube shimmered, flickered, power waning, Markham, Julia, the prisoner within, closing, in the darkness, disappearing, a second hail of fire following him from the teleportation chamber, aboard Modallas safely, doing no harm whatever.

Lord Soal, arriving, ran into the courtyard ahead of his arriving reinforcements. Helio and Borter kept their distance from the strange 5D.

"5D, old friend," he said, "5D. Where have you been?"

Lord Soal walked up and stroked the 5D on its wet nose, or where its nose might have been if he'd been another sort of animal. The beast trembled with delight as his young master petted him.

"Boy?" Borter looked wide – eyed at Helio, who went on ignoring his partner's query.

Lord Soal approached Helio who by then stood alone in the courtyard. "I wish to thank you, Borter – and you, Helio," he said.

"This little adventure will cost Modallas dear. They won't be back soon. You may rest well with my thanks and that of Marcellus and

The Heart of Marcellus, my friend." With this, Lord Soal walked away, his guard of Reds following.

Aboard Modallas, the Helmsman stalked the chamber in his dark, faceless armor. Markham stood before him in silence.

"The Modallians send their greetings from the White City on the Third Plain," he said evenly in a deep, pleasant voice.

"They, in their wisdom, have taken into account – gratitude."

26

Old Face

The car slipped forward to the center of the street. On all sides, Marcelleans went about their daily business.

No one took special notice of a rare vehicle in their midst.

Minutes later, they were past the last of the identical pyramids that made up the edge of the city and onto the Red Plain beyond.

Helio wondered obliquely at the distance to the hidden repair facility. Borter wondered, in the back of his mind, at the decision they'd made to refuse any further Marcellean hospitality.

After all, they could point out nothing to complain about. They had been well treated and given freedom in the city. Yet, they had been offered nothing of the real story of Marcellus. Instinct had saved them before, rather than any hard evidence gleaned from firsthand situations. Both decided to depend exclusively on their feelings.

Borter considered it too pat. They were being sheltered like children, told nothing, but provided with everything almost before they could ask for it. That anticipation finally dawned on them. He felt that beneath the outer facade put on by the Marcelleans, there was a lot of manic activity they were not privy to.

Helio, meanwhile, kept his thoughts on the horizon, hardly daring to reason why the departure had, so far, been easy. Some distance from the city, the car increased speed. There was no real driver - that is, it was driven by computer. The plain whisked away beneath them. Borter tried to decide, unsuccessfully, whether they rode on wheels or skimmed the ground, actually airborne. Both men seemed to notice, very little, the vehicle in which they traveled.

Borter asked himself what control they had over their own departure from the planet. Certainly, this also fit some Marcellean design. They had not seen the more and more mysterious Lord Soal since their first night on the planet, except briefly in the courtyard at the end of the battle with Markham. Other contact was nil. He had stumbled in, near unconsciousness, as they made their escape from Tyrus to the rendezvous with his own ship.

He awakened just in time to turn them around sending them off to Menad and collect Parnak. Ever so cleverly, the wrong pieces to the puzzle were laid out before them, a solution was impossible. The hand they'd been dealt was too pat, they had to make a move on their own behalf.

The battle fought in deserted Toth taught them again the Marcellean was an adept warrior who killed with startling rapidity, efficiently, but without celebration.

If personal enemies were any indication of his importance, he was, indeed, a man of reckoning. What was he, then, to his equals, if such there were. The history of the planet which Helio related briefly was inconclusive in learning his true identity. Instead, it served to fuel suspicions that they were about to be used in some way they normally refuse. Certainly, now, it might never be found out. Possibly, there would always be a doubt as to his true intentions. It would be, no doubt, a knowledge held by men still alive and far from Marcellus. From time to time, the two scanned the sky, perhaps expecting a Modallian attack, perhaps Marcelleans. They would demand Soarer upon arrival at the underground installation, though neither spoke of using his blaster to regain their ship. Quietly, each to himself, they resolved not to come away without the flyer, no matter what it might take.

Borter suddenly ordered the speeding car to stop. Helio looked at him curiously for an instant, surprised at being shaken from his thoughts. The car slowed and stopped. Borter returned the blank stare from Helio with a stranger look of his own. Realization came to them, the ability to choose their own destiny was theirs, as always.

With no other word, Borter sent the car forward. "No sense in coming out this far without seeing what we've come for." Helio, breathing easier, had to agree – no sense, at all.

Three hours later, they dipped into a steep ramp leading beneath the desert surface. The two were startled by the suddenness of it. The swift loss of light blinded them temporarily. Gradually, a little illumination spread through the car. Their eyes adjusted. They sped through the tunnel as they had the desert above, computers did not need to see. Several minutes longer, they traveled until the car began to slow, this time on its own.

On both sides, docks appeared, the door latches clicked, and the car doors opened. The car stopped at one of the docks. "This must be the place."

Borter faced Helio, a stupid smile across his face. He wiggled his eyebrows up and down. Helio followed his lead. Having seen enough of the tunnel, they walked toward a doorway nearby. The dock was little more than a brief dot of light along the length of the tunnel. As they walked through the door, the car doors breathed out with a hiss and closed with a thump. Moments later, it slipped away into the tunnel and its gathered darkness.

Footsteps echoing Borter and Helio took the stairs up one level. Borter stopped on the first landing, waiting for the sound of other feet. Nothing came. Knowing what it took to repair a flyer like Soarer, he fully expected the sounds of heavy machinery. Nothing.

Climbing flight after flight, they wondered how far beneath the surface they had come. The walls were red like the surface, but they were finished, glazed. Borter realized that they were not made of any manufactured material, rather they had been cut by something very hot.

They continued quietly, trying not to make noise. Neither could figure out why. Suddenly, there were other steps heard coming down to them from above. Both men pressed themselves to the wall. The steps were quick and uneven as they came closer.

Whoever it was made no attempt at stealth, a good sign. One flight above the feet stopped. For an instant, there was no sound at all.

"Hello?" A raspy voice called out in recognizable Marcellean.

Borter shrugged at Helio. Poking his head around a corner, he called back in freshly learned Marcellean, "Hello, we speak Universal better than Marcellean." The pilots held up their translators.

"Universal? Universal what?" The cranky voice replied, again in Marcellean, from its place in the darkness.

"Come up here so I can see you." Translators translated appropriately. "There are stairs right in front of you - hurry, you're wasting my time." The two obediently marched upstairs.

"How'd you get to the lower level? Shouldn't work that way." The translators did their jobs again. The speaker sounded more thoughtful.

Borter and Helio could not see the speaker as they advanced. Neither was sure to whom he spoke or what they walked into. Helio felt his feet scrape slowly upward on the stairs. The next landing was reached, and side by side, they rounded its banister for the next flight up. Both stopped short. Above them stood a tiny being, a small, thick man-shaped creature. An aged, wrinkled face greeted them with a smile, looking ever upward as they gained the advantage of his height step by step coming finally to the landing.

They stood motionless for a moment, looking, "Well?" The dwarf demanded. "Haven't you two spent enough time down here?"

The small figure turned reckoning with a crooked finger and a broad, sarcastic smile and ever impatient manner. He turned and walked the few steps toward a door. Borter turned his head for a moment to glance at Helio, "Old Face?" Asked Helio.

Shortly, they followed the little man's bobbing gait through the rambling underground structure. "We're like moles here," chirped the Techno – Dwarf, "underground here one day, there, the next. Those Modallians, they're bad ones. If we launch from here, next thing you know, we've got Targans crawling out all our orifices, if you get my meaning."

Old Face went on, "Not here, though. Gone." Many ships dotted the vast space of – an astrodome. That was the only word for it. Other Techno – Dwarves worked on them and around them, climbing through moveable scaffoldings to work on the hulls.

"We'll mass-out tonight – a little something in your honor, you might say."

"Do you remember us?" Helio made his approach carefully.

"I remember you," Old Face chirped. "You belong to that winged beastie we brought in a few days back. Yeah. How did you make 4.4 in that? No wonder you got chewed up. Lucky you got away at all."

That was enough for Borter. "What do you mean *winged – beastie?* I made several very special modifications in that ship myself."

"What – the automatic hand washer? Was that yours? You really are a genius – *all they say about you* – I am impressed."

"Maybe he has a daughter?" Helio, smirked, leaning in. Borter charged around front of the Techno-Dwarf who neither stopped nor seemed in the least concerned.

Borter railed on at the particularly touchy point. "Sure, she would do 3.2 with the old power dots, but my circuits held up very well under the new ones. She did 4.4 without an overhaul and only half a load of our dots. You should see her handle in a medium atmosphere with those long wings. Those Modallians were the only ships fast enough to catch her in the whole galaxy."

Old Face stopped suddenly and, with hands on hips, turned his face. "You send me that wreck for fixing and tell me you can make it fly better. Then you should have been here to fix it." He said something else to the effect that Borter should have his head examined, but the dwarf's Marcellean was so garbled in his anger and Borter's translator's command of the language so shaky that he did not get it all. Instead, he seemed to agree with what was said to him.

Reeling off in his uneven gait, with Borter and Helio in tow, the Techno-Dwarf pointed in a ship surrounded by scaffolding in a bay not far from them. "That's it. Go look at it. Your precious darling will do something over 8.0.

Don't touch the new controls until I've had a chance to clear both of you on them."

"New controls?" Borter stood rooted for an instant, dumbfounded. "8.0?" The little man went straight over to another flyer.

He called back over his shoulder, "Remember, now, you can look all you want - but don't touch. We might as well let the Targan have the pleasure of destroying the place. You can give us a head start, can't you?"

Helio waited as Borter swung himself up on the scaffolding around the new Soarer. Well, the outside was still the same. Nothing new or radical looking. Helio climbed up. "Do you see anything different about her?"

Borter looked around for any mark or injury left unattended.

Helio shook his head, not.

The landing gear was supporting the ship again, looking as it had. Borter remembered it as it had looked, ripped from the hull, splayed off, and sitting in a heap some meters from the wreck in the Trench. The wings were extended partially, back in place. One wing was all that he could find at the wreck.

27

The Reason

There was a gentle light flooding the cargo tube as they entered. Borter did not remember the light at first. He decided, after a moment, that it had always been there. Helio wandered toward the cockpit. Neither had any idea what had been done to Soarer.

Borter prepared to complain, long and loud, if things were wrong. He trekked through the tube to the cockpit after his partner. New console lights flashed. In fact, it was a whole new console, different, changed. More switches had been added to the overhead stabilization controls. Helio thought they would make flying easier, However, Borter was not yet prepared to give in.

Window space was improved. They had not seen the cockpit from the outside. Helio, now, could see the ground beneath them and the landing gear beneath the partially extended wing on his side of the cockpit. "Let's see what's in the power pods," Borter sharply jerked a thumb back toward the freighter's stern.

Aft, in the double system of energy pods, there were shining, through the heavily shielded glass observer ports, six Marcellean power dots. Helio said nothing as Borter sighed heavily. "It appears they are many years ahead of the Inner Galaxy in propulsion technology." Borter finally admitted to second place. "I wonder why the galaxy hasn't beaten a path to their door? These power dots, alone, are fantastic."

Helio nodded. "I have a feeling if the Marcellus wanted to

advertise, they would. Their history is long and rife with warring, perhaps their wealth tempted others to try to conquer them.

They could be tired of fighting and the problems brought from contact with the inner worlds."

"Riches, is that what brought the Modallians here?"

"I doubt it," Helio said thoughtfully. "I think The Helmsman stumbled on the place by accident. He's unknown in any other part of the galaxy. I think the Marcelleans do have something he needs to have the rest of the galaxy. Heroes they are, they will not give it up, nor will they call for help.

Why, indeed, would a being as obviously powerful as The Helmsman delay his conquest of the galaxy to subdue one reticent planet? The possibility is easy to see when one comes from a planet as inhospitable as Dillisome, that no one wants anything there. Something here is very important to Modallian plans for the galaxy."

"That or he's insane," Borter added his own thoughts. "Fighting a powerful enemy for no reason is insanity. The Helmsman would be utterly irresistible here if he had the rest of the galaxy behind him. Coming here is like going to Dillisome.

Nobody goes to Dillisome – it's crazy. What's - here – that's – not – only – for – Marcelleans?" Borter's words rolled to a stop.

Helio eyed him curiously with a wry smile creeping across his face, stopping him midsentence. "You did. In fact, you've come to both worlds, Dillisome and Marcellus."

He had no reply. Borter knew it was time to say something, anything to save face, but nothing came. Three days, he thought - in three days something, some smashing, devastating, verbal retort would spring to his mind that would crush his co-pilot's intellect and ego and vindicate himself, all at once.

However, at the moment, facing the Dillisome, he could think of nothing. It was likely that when he thought of it, in three days - and he would, Helio would not be nearby. His luck. "The Heart of Marcellus itself, of course," Helio injected himself into the silence.

"Possibly," Borter agreed dumbly. "We don't know anything about it for sure, not even if it really exists – has anybody ever seen it?"

The Dillisome thought for a moment. "An object of faith, in truth, is a deceptively existential thing." Helio went ahead calmly.

"I believe in those footsteps taken by the Old Marcelleans across the galaxy eons ago. They are to be seen if one only knows how to look. "Imagine," he said, "being in touch with the knowledge and wisdom of the very beings who made the first strides across the stars, who made them their own and gave them up, both before either of our peoples took notice."

Borter still had nothing to say, at least temporarily. He was content, for the moment, to stare at Helio without comment.

"You must think I'm half crazy," a rare grin set on Helio's face. "Fair is fair. I have wondered about your sanity from time to time, as well. I wondered once *whether or not*, again, at your own sanity in coming to Dillisome."

"You mean before I came here and clinched the deal?" Borter tried not to laugh at his own words.

The Dillisome smiled again, going on, "You never told me why you came in the first place or why, once there, you insisted on stalking the most dangerous snow beast on the planet, with no more to kill it than some – primitive weapon?

Actually, I decided you were insane long ago. You very nearly died then and there for no good reason that I could see. That's twice insane on Dillisome."

Borter replied with a grin of his own, but a faint one to be sure. "For that matter, you've never told me why you agreed to guide me out on the ice or why you dragged me, half – dead, from beneath that monster, then sledded me two days back to medical aid, or why you insisted on leaving Dillisome and learning to fly freight across the stars. I do what I was born to do."

28

The Deal

Borter walked the scaffolding surrounding the ship. Taking advantage of that height above the hanger floor, he scanned the area for Old Face. "Where do you suppose the little guy is?" He turned to Helio finally.

"You know what I was just thinking?" Borter groaned miserably, letting himself down from the scaffold onto the floor of the giant structure.

Helio, at last, joined him. "He was talking about help. You don't suppose that help could be us, do you? Remember the way Lord Soal was talking to us before we transferred him to the Marcellean ship? I'd almost forgotten. He's got us mixed up in this, I know it. He said chosen well."

Helio replied slowly, choosing his words carefully.

"We have only random words and a few vague suspicions. Though we have encountered no restrictions of any kind, we may have been lied to – and deceived. What is he not telling us? That's still a possibility."

"You appeal to my most cautious nature – we have not been told enough," the Dillisome went on.

On the big floor, the Techno Dwarf was nowhere to be seen. "I think he wandered off this way," said Borter, moving in that direction. They turned once, looking back to see the new hull from more of a distance. "I hope they paint her for us," he said, viewing the fuselage at full length.

"That's the flat black you like so much," Helio spoke as Borter went on, giving him a hard look. "I thought we were leaving soon?"

Borter looked at him, wondering what it was that he had just said. They continued walking. The sound of heavy tools closed in on them from every side. There were many Techno Dwarves working across the vast floor, but not the one for whom they searched.

Borter stopped one, with some difficulty, from the completion of his task and asked for Old Face, the Marcellean language spoken through his Universal translator.

The tech answered in a stream of gibberish and impatience even the translator couldn't handle. In the end, the Techno – Dwarf pointed in the opposite direction from which they'd come. Before they had quite turned away, he was deafening them with his power tool.

Borter could no longer see the repaired hull of Soarer.

Helio walked beside him casually. Where they were, that was not known except in the most general terms. A dozen places seemed familiar as they passed by them, whether for the first or the fourth time. The entirety of the hanger was spare, even Spartan, each new section a repetition of the last.

A sharp voice sounded behind them.

"There they are!" It sounded above the mechanical din. "Can't stay put. We'll leave you here for the Targans."

The old Techno-Dwarf walked up to them, scolding, "You'll listen to Old Face one day. Come!" Old Face turned, walking away.

"Yes, Grandfather," said Borter, just out of earshot.

Borter and Helio caught up easily.

"I have a visitor for you."

"Who?" Borter asked a great wariness in his voice.

Old Face did not answer directly. "I don't know why such an important man would come all the way out here just to see you two."

Borter stopped short. Helio followed the lead and stood with him. Old Face turned and stood silently. His lip wrinkled in disgust at the two. "Well, what is it, now?"

"We've come for our ship, that's all," Borter said. "We don't want any visitors."

Both fully knew the visitor they had was Lord Soal.

Soarer was still out of sight, hidden from them by their own carelessness, somewhere in the girth of the astrodome, in plain sight. Borter gave the little man a hard look to match his own.

"Can't find it, can you?" The Techno – Dwarf laughed.

"Too bad," he sniggered. "You'll have to come along if you want it. Come along. There's nothing to be afraid of."

Helio gave a confused, resigned, look and moved ahead. Borter came along after him, more reluctantly.

For several minutes they moved steadily, everything looked familiar, as before, but they knew nothing they passed.

Ships of Marcellean design were around them as far as they could see. Somewhere out there Soarer was parked, ready to take them away, anywhere away, if they could just get back to her.

Then, Old Face stood proudly beside an open, unremarkable doorway letting them enter first. Inside, Lord Soal stood waiting. He waved them forward. "I see you've found your way here. That's good, very good. Only days on a new planet and you already find your way around."

Old Face asked them to sit, chuckling, a wry smile on his face. The Marcellean overlord stood before them, not ready to say more. Borter and Helio, both, sat heavily, then, without moving, sensing they should, at least, be polite. Borter would verge on civility, Helio could keep the superfluous amenities all for himself, for all he cared.

Old face stood away from them silently, to one side.

"I'm sorry, I could not stay to thank you properly for your quick action in the courtyard last night," Lord Soal spoke. "I was forced to leave suddenly. Our troubles with the Targan and Modallas escalate in other areas and demand my attention. I'm sure you already know this."

Borter stared at him without a word and made no attempt to look over and see what Helio was doing beside him.

"What is it you want?" Lord Soal said nothing further, realizing his failure at cordiality. Borter decided it self-defeating to delay the real issue. He jumped in where the Marcellean had merely hinted, hoping to find some advantage in the action. There was a silence. Lord Soal looked ill at ease.

Old Face seemed so stunned by Borter's directness that Helio, seeing a little of his own reaction in the Techno – Dwarf's reddened face almost laughed in spite of himself. Borter continued.

"Soarer is what we want," Borter rejoined his own question. "We have done our job, our mission is complete. Where is our ship?" Borter, growing angry, left a large silence to be filled in the small room that seemed to be getting smaller.

Lord Soal looked at him intently, with genuine admiration. "I see our adventures together have not made us the friends I'd hoped." Pausing a moment, he said, "Very well, your ship is yours – as it has always been." He turned. to the Techno-Dwarf, "Old Face – if you please?"

Old Face straightened respectfully at the overlord's call.

"Prepare Soarer for Borter and Helio. We will not hold them where they are not willing."

Old Face, without a word, left them in the room. Both Borter and Helio retained their silence expecting one word from either to make their good fortune too good to be true and thus jinxed, evaporating before their eyes. "Word that you had left the city came unexpectedly, but it was not surprising," Lord Soal commented. "In fact, it was pleasant news, in a way. He smiled.

I thought you had no more mysteries for us to discover. However, this one has made me think more highly of you." Borter wondered whether Lord Soal was trying to anger them or not, using that to wheedle them into doing more of his bidding.

He thought that would work. What reason could they possibly have given any Marcellean to think any less of them?

"Was the work of my Techno Dwarves satisfactory?"

"More than satisfactory," chirped a relieved Helio. Borter gave him a replay of the look he'd given Old Face as he'd chided them earlier, unable to find Soarer, on the vast aerodrome floor. Helio was talking. To an old wheeler – dealer like Borter that meant he was coming around, wrecking the solitary of their combined front. He hated it when Helio bubbled enthusiasm.

"No," Borter broke in.

"Yes," said the Dillisome.

"No," Borter repeated. There was a pause. The flyers regarded each other and the Marcellean standing before them.

"How about if I talk for a minute? We haven't seen her fly yet. That's our proof."

Borter tried to discourage any sudden feelings of camaraderie Helio might be having in the Marcellean. He was the same sword-bearing gallant with the same sullen, blinking Shoulder Falcon as before. Helio remained silent.

Borter saw no reason to change his first opinion.

Helio should be more reserved. It was disturbing, the stoic Dillisome's show of rare enthusiasm to this off-worlder.

"I'm sure, once you're used to the new controls, you will find them sufficient for your needs." The Marcellean spoke politely, in the same friendly, affable manner, though Borter made repeated attacks on his credibility.

"Old Face is particularly proud of the dual systemization in the power pods, would you please congratulate him on it. I would consider it a personal favor.

I think you'll find it will add much extra power to your shields, as well. The Modallians will not be able to catch you again, much less put another proton explosive into your hull. It will, also, prevent another burn out. And, we offer a *thirty – day* guarantee!" Borter did not laugh at the Marcellean's suddenly salesman's jest. Lord Soal on his own account grinned broadly.

The mention of Modallians prompted Borter to have another look at Helio. "I don't think we'll have much more to do with Modallians after leaving this planet. I trust that will be soon," he continued. Helio made no gesture, one way or the other.

"I see," Lord Soal seemed to back down. "You are in a hurry. You have another cargo to carry? Of course," He smiled in a fatherly, most understanding and loving way.

"You know we have nothing. Have you kept your promise and straightened us out with Tyrus Control yet?"

Borter felt an anger rising within him.

"We have taken steps. However, you do understand that we have no embassy on Tyrus, and to discuss anything with them must be done through a third party, and discussions become somewhat - lengthy?"

Borter felt sure he should have expected as much.

"Every opportunity is being used to expedite matters on your behalf." Helio nodded, but Borter did not acknowledge the statement.

"Since you have nothing, really, no place to go, so to speak. You could be of some other assistance to us here."

Borter turned, looking at Helio.

"C'mon," he motioned, getting up, "let's get out of here. I don't think we can afford any more of these favors."

Helio got to his feet. He took a step forward.

"It is not without its dangers," continued the Marcellean lord, speaking nearly to their backs, nonplused, "but it pays well.

Through no fault of your own, you have no place else to go. Real pay is offered for this new mission. I will add, from my knowledge of you, this mission will prove quite enjoyable."

Helio stopped short, taking hold of Borter's arm. "You know he's right. He is offering cargo and pay."

"Wait a minute." Borter grated. "Just before we came in here, you were full of suspicion about all of this. Are you telling me all that's forgotten now?

C'mon, we can find a cargo somewhere – else." He cast a grim look back at the Marcellean.

Lord Soal had not moved from where he stood in the small room. "I will tell you who your cargo is and where you will be taking him."

Borter turned. He faced Lord Soal, and his body turned halfway sideways as if ready to run away at any second. His expression was one of anger and defiance.

He felt trapped. If the Marcellean did not prevent them from leaving the planet for good, circumstance did.

29

Mass Out

"Him?" Borter asked wearily.

"Parnak-the-Jillian," Lord Soal answered.

"Who pays?" Borter turned quickly and stood, waiting for his answer.

"Parnak," Lord Soal answered again. "Your terms, I believe. You'll pick him up soon. All information and coordinates are in your on-board computer. All you have to do is mass – out with my flyers from this installation. From here, you may set course for the Inner Galaxy or fly for Parnak."

"Where, exactly, is Parnak?" Helio asked.

"With certain of my troops doing his job on the Frontier.

Parnak and I are old friends. He asked me to see you since he could not be here himself. For you, this is the least I could do in repayment for last night and our previous misunderstandings.

"Which is it to be, gentlemen?"

Helio nodded. Borter muttered his agreement, "All right," he said.

Old Face reappeared and led them, this time, to Soarer. Passing several Marcellean flyers in various states of readiness, they found their freighter. The scaffolding around her had gone. Other Techno-Dwarves, all around the path to Soarer, stopped work to stand silently as Lord Soal and his company came by. It was a rare occasion that the Marcellean Lord appeared at such a facility. A fact of which Borter, at least, was unaware. Management of the astrodome was Old Face's alone.

"You're going to leave it that flat black color?"

Old Face smiled, "That's a flat black frictionless coating you got there, mister. Not that stuff you had on it before. I'm not running beauty contests here. She'll go, that's enough."

A thin stairs led them into the freshly blackened hull. Lord Soal tramped in behind them. Old Face himself led this procession, and proudly.

"Well, how do you like it?" Old Face gestured hugely to the entire interior of Soarer, which all stood moments later.

Helio nodded toward the propulsion units aft, "I'm sure there are many improvements. Before you acquaint us with those, we were most impressed by your work on the dual propulsion units."

Old Face gazed about, from face to face, beaming more proudly, looking quite as if he could radiate sunlight himself. "Oh," feigning something like a schoolgirl's shy embarrassment, "it was just a little idea of mine. Do you really like it?" He was in a better mood now that Lord Soal seemed to have gotten his way. Borter and Helio were bending to the will of the great Marcellean.

"Come right this way, let me show you – " his voice trailed off toward the cockpit. "You'll think you're in a new flyer." All plodded obediently through the cargo tube into the cockpit.

The new console blinked pleasantly at them with a reassuring regularity. Borter slid into his seat. The Techno – Dwarf allowed Helio to seat himself and then stood between the two. Going from point to point, the little man explained the deeper workings of their new equipment.

Borter stopped him when a new word was added to Soarer's compliment of terms. "Armament?" It was Borter's turn to wear a surprised look on his face. "What do we need armament for? Space mines have been enough until the – present. Sorry," he backpedaled, remembering to be nice. "Uh – thanks."

Old Face clicked his tongue against the roof of his mouth, "Yes — " his voice saddened appreciably, "We heard you dropped one on, on — that large piece of space trash circling our fair planet." Old Face smiled a sickly little smile at them as if he'd rather spit out a rat than say the word Modallas. "Space mines are not effective against a *serious* Modallian pursuit.

Face it — it was just a little skill and a little luck that brought you through at all. Besides, we thought you might like to get even."

Borter's shallow enthusiasm faltered quickly towards the new weaponry as Old Face's increased. His own pet projects had been removed altogether. There were no traces of any. Old Face went happily on, showing where on the newly elegant, retractable wings the new weapons pods had been installed.

"In either position, extended or retracted, you have six heavy, rapid — fire photon guns. With your new speed, I doubt you'll have much use for them — unless you get really angry with someone."

Borter looked narrowly at Helio, who kept his polite smile. "Personally," said Old Face, "I hope you have a strong dislike for Modallas growing. Yes, sir, very strong." He gave Borter a rascally wink and reached up, managing to pat both flyers on the shoulder. Borter was loath to return the gesture but did so. He felt uncomfortable with Old Face's sudden fatherly concern.

"Look," Borter said, "uh — we don't usually travel this heavy. Soarer is not a fighting ship."

"Well," the old Techno Dwarf grinned broadly, "you do, now, and she is. If you weren't fighters, I'd be breathing your ashes from The Trench to here.

Old Face nodded bowing his head deeply to the Marcellean lord and left the ship having completed his instruction to Borter and Helio.

"Well, you always talked about getting more armament. Helio looked at the agonized Borter. "You don't have to use them, you know?"

"You'd best call yourselves into Control for takeoff instructions." Lord Soal moved away. "It will be a few hours before we see one another again — fly safely, gentlemen.

Modallian pursuit will be insignificant this evening, their top speed is 6.0," he added. The Marcellean tipped his hand to his brow and walked after Old Face.

The partners, left alone, faced each other across the cockpit at first silently, then, "At least we've got the ship back," said the Magnean. Helio nodded. They did have the ship back.

"I thought we were just going to get the flyer and leave?" Helio was amused at their sudden change in plan.

Borter began reluctantly to explain, "I must admit, it seemed to be a good idea at the time."

Helio did not bother to answer. Instead, he was openly amused at Borter, he opened a channel to Control.

Borter toyed with the controls on his side of the console like a small boy at dinner, half-heartedly examining unwanted vegetables on his plate. Everything lit up obediently. "It still seems to be the best idea."

Helio turned from monitoring the Control frequency. "At least, there's pay. Tyrus is jailed for certain and confiscation of Soarer as well. On several of the other planets in that sector, too. No shipping, at any rate."

"Is that the bright side?" Borter asked.

"We'll get to see Parnak again," the Dillisome said, that hope sounding in his voice.

"Right!" Borter listened as instructions came from Control, spoken in clear Universal.

His new controls proved to be no problem. In minutes, Borter knew where everything was. This, after all, was his element. They would probably not have to use all of them. He hoped they would have no use for the new offensive weapons.

Both knew if they did, things would be bad, their backs against the wall. A policy they had always preferred was to turn tail and run.

The new computer gave them a course. Helio confirmed it. Control rattled off a familiar take-off procedure. Every one of them would leave at the same time. The astrodome would be left suddenly, conspicuously empty. With instructions given, he expected to take off with nearly one hundred other ships.

Abruptly a great slit opened in the rock ahead of them, the heat that made it let steam pour out of the fissure into the atmosphere. Engines whined across the cavernous expanse. They joined theirs with everyone else's. There would be a short runway, and then they would be airborne, Control said. Soarer rolled forward behind the Marcellean leaders. They were quickly gone.

Marcellean pilots thrust their flyers into the darkened night sky. One rank after another lifted off taillights and afterburn glowing behind them, lingering in the memory for an instant longer than the actual sight. Borter's rank shot out of the slit and banked right. Others came after them, and more after them. It was a sight to behold.

Sensors picked up incoming ships. These could be none other than the promised Modallian interceptors. Helio commented that there were certainly a lot of them. Borter, in the meantime, decided to see what 8.0 felt like. As he accelerated, those flying with him did so, too.

"Do you think they're protection for us?" He glanced toward Helio.

"Could be. In case you haven't noticed, we've been getting very special treatment through all of this," Borter harrumphed loudly as Helio finished his statement. The stars were coming closer. More lights began to streak the sky, the afterburn of the closing interceptors. The rank began to break apart as opponents chose opponents. Helio checked their weapons, just in case.

"We have company," Helio announced at length. Borter looked. Sure enough, a dot followed them on the screen.

"6.0," said the Dillisome co – pilot calmly, "Shields are at maximum. Are we still accelerating?" Borter nodded that they were.

"7.1, he's fading. They must have to make their attacks just so, before the Marcellean accelerates beyond intercept capability." Together, they counted off altitude to the edge of the atmosphere. Suddenly, they were alone in the sky.

Modallas would have to have been on top of the Red Desert base to launch a strike so quickly. They expected to see its massive shape once more very soon. No more Marcelleans were near them. Soarer flew a straight course. "Modallas."

Helio pointed at three o'clock from the cockpit. "What a hulk. I'll bet our space mine didn't even dent it."

"But it did what we wanted it to. It bought us time and covered our escape."

The new power dots did as promised, hurling them forward at 8.0. Helio could not believe it until they saw, with their own eyes, the distance they were putting between themselves and Modallas. Hundreds of kilometers away, the massive cylinder still had the same awesome appearance as they remembered.

"Remember what you said? Why you lived among the stars?"

Borter stopped. For a second, he thought back to his words. Then, it came. *"Fly freight across the stars. I do what I was born to do."*

"There," Helio brightened noticeably, "that's it – the poetry."

"The poetry?" The Magnean was incredulous.

"Fly freight across the stars. I do what I was born to do - quoth the pilot," Helio laughed.

Borter reddened. "I'm the one who's insane, and you, then, are the model for sanity?" He complained.

"My dear, Borter, all my poets are madmen — all of them - be calm. You are in good company!"

The Magnean sputtered. "Be calm? What does that mean? Just what do you believe in?"

Helio smiled again, more grandly announcing himself, "I believe in Parnak!"

PART TWO

30

The Targan Forest

Sorel moved among his men. They had not yet broken forest cover. Thousands waited hidden in the deep gullies for his signal.

He looked past the cover at the Ranger camp beyond. Night would be on them soon, the Marcellean night with only the meager light of its fast moons. This camp would be no more difficult than the others. It would fall to him. It would be done that night as were the others, always at night.

This Ranger camp would be his sixth. It was no stronger despite the soldiers and supplies that had been diverted from the other fallen camps. All glory due to the Sky God, who armed them and gave them strength.

The edge of the forest seemed to tremble with anticipation. Sorel found his way to the front. All of his Targans pressed forward. Blasters had turned the tide against the outnumbered Rangers before. When the time came, Sorel would leap in and kill them all.

Beyond the scattered outposts lay the Red Desert and then the green savannahs separating them from the conquest of the remaining Marcellean city. Targans had no use for cities, nor did they know their reward for service to the Sky God, if any. Perhaps serving the Sky God a single day longer would be all, or the knowledge that a fatal twilight drew down upon their Marcellean betters. Targans could think of no greater joy than destroying all things Marcellean. Perhaps they already had their reward.

At the Ranger fortification, all things lingered at the edge of existence. Not much changed. Marcelleans came and went. Only a few stayed longer than they had to. There were frequent convoys to and from the outpost.

Targans, themselves, rarely ventured beyond the confines of the vast forests. They waited for the signal to rush again on a natural enemy who must have certainly known they were there and waiting. The deep green forest turned an inky black as night fell. No Targans moved or made a sound, waiting.

Only Sorel moved about freely. He did so with an animal grace, the fluid motions of one long accustomed to keeping the silence of the forest. He was feared by all in the dim Targan Forests. Marcelleans had come to know him, too. The pouch tucked in his broad belt contained the ears of those slain by him.

He would have liked one of their ion blades. As if the life spirit suddenly went out of them, the blades inexplicably died in Targan's hands in just a short while. Sorel knew nothing of power supplies. But did the Sky God not give them all they needed?

The coming of the Sky God had changed all. Their destiny had been placed before them. The enlightened Lord Markham brought it to them, and it was brought to him by the Sky God. Markham, though he found it distasteful that a Marcellean looked down into that mass of seamy faces gathered around his presence and informed them of a new destiny.

When the time was right Markham had been teleported into their midst. Both the medium and its message were a success instantly. The enlistment of the primitive Targan people began.

Then, Markham appeared in one of those brilliant flashes of light only in the presence of Sorel, the chosen.

The hulking, thick-browed Targan was a ferocious fighter, irresistible to all before him in battle. He was their acclaimed leader at Markham's nomination.

The Targan, at best, was only a rabble army, fading in and out of the brush, carrying all the needed with them. They called themselves the Forest Spirit, Brother to the Sky God. Under Markham's careful direction, they became near gods themselves.

The way was clear. The Sky God's Markham had chosen their leader. He was just the type needed to forge the savage thrusts against the Marcellean outposts and cities. An obedient army was created that struck over many kilometers, swiftly and savagely, whose real strength was in its endless numbers.

No lights showed from within. The earthen embankments stood firmly around a central dome. Walkways filled as Rangers took their rampart positions. The battle would involve more than the small fortification.

Both sides possessed weapons that far outmoded their use. It would serve, instead, as a magnet drawing the Targan primitives, a magnet for their hatred. Three sides of the firebase would feel the hot breath of the Forest Spirit crush down on them.

"The will of the Sky God," The Helmsman's words reached Sorel through Markham. Through him, The Helmsman rained terror and death across the planet, on Marcelleans, on the rim of forests and cities alike. Sorel raised the, leader symbol aloft, the sign from above.

A patch in the clearing glowed eerily in the night. It shimmered for a second and Markham took form. His features showed up in stark contrast between light and dark shades from the glare of his transmission.

Sorel turned so that all could hear. "The Sky God calls his Forest Spirit, his Forest Brother - to the attack." The horde rushed the clearing. The space around Markham was filled with shrieking savages. The Marcellean himself walked forward calmly, undisturbed by the commotion. Targans reached the first barrier of the fort's embankment. The gap bridged, and they rushed the embankment itself. Few wore any heavy covering on their feet. A dew had set, making the grass covering the incline slick.

The leaders found themselves faltering, sliding back into those who followed. As some tumbled, others replaced them. Brandishing Modallian weaponry, they, the mass of savages, crested the embankment, finding no resistance.

Those reaching the top of the embankment were killed instantly by a great blaze of defender fire. Rockets dipped into the charging

Targans, exploding with deadly effect. Lord Markham watched carefully the strategy for defending Marcelleans.

The Marcellean defenders, having waited for the Targans to be drawn out of the forest as far as possible, then laid down their most ferocious barrage. Sorel pointed to his right, where dark eyes watched his every move, a new wave of Targans rushed from that direction to try the steep bank. There the same determined defense met them, with the same effect.

Rockets again fell among them. The closely packed horde became easy prey to this manner of counterattack. Many died, but many others poured from the darkened forest.

The Marcellean traitor had not come without a plan for himself. The Targans could advance no farther so long as the Marcelleans were in place on the other side of the embankment. Again, the signal came. Rockets burst across the embankment, this time from the forest. The steady *crump-ing* sound of exploding rockets across the Marcellean compound. The Targans fared better under the cover of their own fire.

Defenders were forced to take cover. Sorel mounted the top of the embankment with many attackers close behind. The rocket attack lit the interior of the camp. The dome could be seen in the center of the enclosure. Charging down the steep incline, they were met by the recovering Marcelleans, who at once exacted a heavy toll.

By the time Markham reached the crest, the first of their positions had been taken. But, Marcellean rockets still struck among them. Markham had succeeded with his first strategy, having gotten the Forest people into the field and the camp without being stopped.

Loss was heavy, fearful. But it was not his concern, their lives were meaningless to him, except for this important, temporary service. They'd won battles, now they must win a war.

They fought hand – to – hand, struggling over individual weapons. Often, as they became harder pressed by lack of space, Marcelleans resorted to their ion blades. They cut into the oncoming savages.

All over the fortress, down into the flat toward the enclosed dome, Marcelleans and Targans fought.

A rocket hit the dome. Shattered material showered down from the sky. The explosion lit the enclosure for a few seconds before burning itself out. The Marcelleans pulled back toward the center, their backs kept together, one against the other.

During the blast, a Marcellean unwittingly set in motion Markham's final ploy to massacre them all. As the explosion lit the darkness from day to night, the Marcellean commander pointed his ion blade straight at Markham.

Though he was still far away on the embankment. "Markham, the traitor – Markham," the shout alerted the Marcelleans on all sides to his presence.

The glare faded. As it did so, Markham drew his ion blade and held it high above his head. The defenders, seeing this, charged him as a body. At the cost of their own lives, they would attack only him. It would be Markham's end. More rockets fell behind them. For a long way in front of Markham were Sorel's picked men, those who fought best and without fear.

The Marcelleans defeated themselves by exposing flanks to the enemy and moving toward the embankment. The rockets drove them forward. Isolated pockets were cut off and quickly taken. Driving toward the upheld blade, the Marcelleans cut a path into the heart of the resistance, to no avail, for every Targan that fell, another took his place with equal ferocity. Blasters fired at them from all sides. Their numbers thinned quickly.

Markham himself moved forward, the Targans quickly making way. In the conflict's center, he met the Marcellean commander.

"Traitor." The man cried out bringing his ion blade up, ready. "This is the proper way for Marcelleans to fight, not with these animals," he shouted.

Markham answered the challenge and the concept, "Fool," he charged the man, matching the position of the sword. The two blades met with a loud snap. The Marcelleans circled each other, looking for openings.

Markham feinted left, as his challenger went to meet the attack whirled his blade to the right. The trick was barely met. The powerful blades came together once more.

The Marcellean challenger cut at Markham's armored head, hoping for a quick kill. Markham dodged skillfully, making the man look amateurish. Off balance, the officer staggered.

Markham came around viscously, cutting back. His challenger collapsed to the ground, dead. A small pocket of defenders remained a short distance ahead. Markham turned on his heel, leaving them to the Targan.

Again, back to back, one defending the other, they cut their way with an undiminished fury at the enemy. By the time Markham reached the place he had first come down the embankment, they were gone. It was over.

31

Foreboding

Sorel walked beside the Marcellean lord. Markham could not stand his presence. The Targan, beside him, offered the trophies of battle. Sorel bowed to Markham politely, "Ears, Lord? For the Sky God."

Marcellean traitor stood repulsed at the sight. "See?"

The Targan smiled broadly, his white teeth standing out in the darkness. "No blood. The Sky God will not be offended by the sight. Removed with his own ion blade. No blood."

"Very well," Markham snapped impatiently, "But bring them in a covering, your best." Sorel snarled, turning to those behind him. Lesser Targans scattered to obey his commands. "The Sky God will accept nothing less," he growled.

It would do no good to insult Targan institutions, few that were. He needed them for much more. The severed ears would be discarded upon Modallas arrival. The savagery of the practice sickened him.

"We did well." Sorel tried to make conversation.

Another Targan brought him the battle mask of the Marcellean Commander. Markham took that more readily.

This was a Marcellean trophy. He had a wall full of them.

He saw no Targan dead, they were beneath his notice, there were many. The Targan believed he simply was too good to walk across carcasses and recover them for himself.

That he was also too good to get away without accepting the trophies due to him for slaying the Marcellean commander was beyond them.

Aside from the fact it was an institution among Targans to take ears, it was a mark of a respected leader to have trophies of battle. Since the Targan thought of him in a mystical way, as a part of their Sky God, he was sometimes called Sky God, but not to his face.

A brilliantly encrusted pouch was brought to him. For the second time, Sorel bowed, presenting the trophy to Markham, who accepted it with only passing grace. The primitive stood before him, as straight and tall as he could manage. "Are there more instructions, Lord?" He asked in a deep, gravelly voice.

Markham waited making his answer seem as if a decision had not already been made. "The Sky God will be in touch when all is in readiness. Keep your people ready."

They reentered the forest, Sorel's men disbursing among the trees and thick growths quickly. They were with a party of Targans, smaller by far than the original party used to attack the encampment. The ragged march from beneath the trees was decisive, a conscious movement with a single, definite goal in mind. Never had that been accomplished in the forest. By the thousand, from the barefoot to those heavily shod, Targans merged in an unending stream of dingy bodies beneath the trees.

The night forest rippled with the wind. Markham could, he thought, smell the trudging, unwashed Targan as they filed by, not far away. His battle mask was still shut, airtight. Sorel, several paces downwind from him, stood watching.

From time to time, Markham snapped questions at him. Each was answered quickly, dutifully. One of the Targan, one constantly with Sorel, lit a cooking fire. Several men scuffed around it, bringing wood to keep it burning for a while. They were far from their women, who kept their loose camps for them. Soon, meat roasted over the flames.

Markham soon longed for his solitude aboard Modallas. Business was tedious with the simple-minded, he thought. Things lasted longer than they should. It was never done soon enough.

At other times, he thought the Targans were looking at him with a different kind of curiosity than he thought healthy. Among them, with so little else to occupy their minds, curiosity was a dangerous thing.

But their interests were too far flung to be simple. Sorel was not satisfied with the supplies coming from Modallas. He demanded more. Superstition ended with weapons, things primitive did not. For their planned attack on Marcellus, he wanted heavier weapons. Markham took note but was slow to answer, telling him the Sky God would supply suitable weapons for that campaign at a time of his own choosing.

Food stuffs that came from Markham were not trusted. Everything came in a manufactured, prepackaged state, Targans had never seen such a thing. They refused to eat it, this food of the gods. Sorel, and the others, assumed it was consumed with the container that it arrived in and ate those, too. Markham had been forced to explain things.

Sorel's demands, he guessed, were to placate members of his party in the flickering half – darkness around the fire more than to gain reassurances from Modallas. He was in constant danger of assassination from those beneath him. He had to show a strong connection with the Sky God to remain in power or even alive.

Markham looked warily at Sorel through the battle mask, wondering what the man really knew and what he was trying to find out. His distrust of Targans was inherited from birth. His true feelings had not been much abated by time. It was difficult to control the old feelings, especially when the reasons for them could no longer be remembered.

He would not fully approach the primitive security the campfire offered. Sorel's wishes would be considered, he said, as for several other problems of minor concern, he made amendments in orders or gave new ones.

However, the basic design of the operation was unchanged.

Far away, Lord Soal reflected on the rebellious nature of his own children. His family had its share for sure.

Recalling the wild moments of his own youth, he thought of the one who pleased his heart most, Julia. Gaining her own way, she almost always managed to ease his mind as well.

At any rate, she was no child and not property. Any decision on how she would lead her life would rest with her.

Brother Lord Markham, on the other hand, was different. If possible, he would be made to pay for his treachery. Lord Soal intended to see it become possible. The power of The Helmsman, so far, kept him safe to lead raids all across the face of Marcellus. It would not be much longer, one way or the other, and it would be finished.

A force would be led to deal with the main gathering of Targans. He fully expected Markham to appear during the course of the battle. The initial segments of battle would be joined by the Targan leader, Sorel. He could expect certain things from the Targan and Markham as they doubtless would from him.

The Marcellean idea of honor demanded a specific type of behavior from him on the battlefield. Probably, he would not be reduced to the use of his blaster, though he certainly kept on with him and fully charged for the times he wanted it.

He was powerful enough to press battle with the traditional Marcellean ion blade. If he died, it would cost both Forest Spirit and Targan dearly to take his ears.

Julia would have to be left alone in the city. Though the city would contain many others, he would think of her as alone without him. She was, at times, wearing on his remaining hold on sanity.

Revolving on a schedule, as he did, given to duty and counterplot, there was very little time to pursue peace for himself. She was the single pleasing island in a vast, turbulent sea. Circumstances permitting, he would speak to her again, this time more gently, against selecting Borter as a life companion.

Through no real fault of his own, Borter would have trouble enough surviving the next few days. It stood to reason that sooner or later, The Helmsman and events set in motion that day would cost the two flyers their lives before there was any chance to speak with her further.

32

Nine

Outpost Nine was several hours drive from Marcellus itself. A car chauffeured by a Techno Dwarf stood waiting to take him.

It served him well to travel on the surface. At times, the air was full of Modallian fighters searching for an easy target that a lone flyer might provide. The sweeping low profile of the car, by comparison, offered less of a target to enemy tracking systems.

The way from the city was clear, with no other traffic. Lord Soal settled down in his seat and was fully relaxed. His mind was completely involved with plans for the campaign to come. Memories from the old wars fought against the Targan came flooding back to him across countless years, in contemplating those strategies that had worked and those that had not.

But it seemed so much the same. The wars, more or less, continuously intervened in the peaceful course of his life. He could say that his life and the lives of all Marcelleans had traveled down the same bumpy road of violent intervention and the interventions of fate as well.

First came the Targan, then Modallas and The Helmsman. The new Marcelleans, in particular, led lives more shrouded in battle. His life had been longer by far than theirs, the last of a very special kind that they were not and could not become. Lord Soal was a Wearer like his discredited brother, Markham. The Snow Beggar was a Wearer and a Keeper as well. His duty was to keep, then pass on,

The Marcellean Heart. All Marcellus depended on was this: the situation was critical, and there would be no other moment than this.

By his right of succession, Lord Markham should have been the first Wearer and Lord Soal the second. But, in the fortieth century of their modern civilization, Lord Markham had chosen a path of rebellion. The result was the ultimate devastation of the inner-lying planets of the old empire.

For that act, he was unforgiven and totally disowned. The Marcellean Heart was never to be his. Lord Markham became a man without a home. No planet in the inner systems would knowingly allow him refuge, those few that could offer refuge to anyone. He was truly alone - alone until The Helmsman appeared. With the coming of Modallas, a new in Marcellus' history was written.

Lord Markham found The Helmsman his only possible ally in the known galaxy. From where his sinister presence had guided Modallas was unknown. One day, Modallas simply came and began to orbit the planet. At first, there were open, friendly overtures, and those on the planet who would throw wide open their arms in welcome, as well as those of a more cautious nature demanding references of the home-seeking Modallians.

So went the dialogue. Each had something to offer the other, so it was said. Modallas would have a home, and Marcellus would have a peaceful, humane solution to the eternal problem of the Targan. This, The Helmsman promised all the while wanting the Marcellean Heart. All occurred without any exchanges of official envoys. In fact, no Marcellean, save Markham, had ever been to Modallas. There was only the constantly reassuring voice of The Helmsman.

At last, the temptation of peace became too great for them, and those who jumped to meet it overrode all caution until the point of no return had been passed. Entire regions had fallen to annihilation. Modallas quickly swept up the Targan to do its fighting against their age-old enemy. Destruction of natural resources became calculated and systematic. In their reduced state, without allies in the galaxy, Marcellus fell back in a valiant defense until they could return blow for blow what Modallas handed out.

Wholesale destruction of the planet was stopped. Marcellus had lost the best of her warriors in the effort. Many of her great cities were reduced to rubble beyond any hope of repair. Modallas, yet, circled their planet unscathed, counting its losses only in Targans and material.

The force that ran the place was beyond comprehension. Still, though, there was the need for the Marcellean Heart.

Warfare fell to attrition, random attacks here and there at odd intervals. Marcellus adopted a system of outpost fortresses at the edge of the Targan Forest, a large number, in fact, to contain the Targan who always struck from the forest. Now, in this modern time, only one remains.

Superiority in the air swung back and forth for some time until Marcellus again conquered her own sky, sweeping Modallas' Targan pilots from the air. Marcellus came in time to despise the Targan flyers who opposed them. Their blockade of the planet, however, was only broken with great difficulty. No matter what, feelings about their most ancient adversary prevailed.

Landmarks in the dusty plain bled away behind the car. It grew dark. No lights showed it the way to the outpost, instead the cockpit instruments in front of the Techno Dwarf showed the way. A distance from the forests they dipped into a deep, man-made tunnel for the remainder of the journey to Outpost Nine.

On the surface above him, thousands of Marcelleans moved into a well-described position over a great area. From such places, they would attempt to stem the tide from the forest. The mass of Targan outnumbered them greatly.

When Sorel appeared at the head of the throng, finally, and led them out, neither Targan nor Marcellean would avoid one another.

The forest was full of Targan that night in the area near Nine. It was silent, unlit, and dark. Even the normal light breezes that came every other night did not come that night to rustle through the trees. Instead, a wet heat pervaded everywhere, and there was no relief. That day, the entire sky was overcast, well suited to be called a shroud foretelling a time of trial at hand.

Nothing broke the solidity of the sky's beak depths. No flyers landed. They appeared, in fact, to be avoiding the sky. Air traffic was brisk at any other time. Modallian fighters hovered far above, out of sensor range. One could almost feel them. Somewhere above, the clouds blinding the eye of the galaxy to what was about to happen, they remained just out of reach. Safe from Marcelleans below, they waited for the unwary or for those who had the poor luck to draw a mission to the place.

In that dark silence, many others waited with a single mind, they crouched low in the dense undergrowth. An order from Sorel would bring them screaming from the ravines and the shallower depths behind the rolling hillocks leading toward the fortifications of Nine. The slaughter would begin suddenly and go on and on until Targan no longer came or Marcelleans no longer lived. It had always been so and it always would be that way.

Still, nothing moved. Nothing seemed to breathe. There were no sounds, not even those that were supposed to have heard. Truly, it was as if the two great beings faced each other across the wide clearing, The Forest Sprit faced the Heart of Marcellus, awaiting the signal for combat. The shadow of the Sky God cast itself across them both. They watched cautiously as night wore on beneath the fleeting faces of Marcellus' pale moons.

Inside the domed citadel at Nine, the faces were steadfast and alert, reflecting the faces of other Marcelleans deployed thinly over the vast area protected by the fortification. All were practiced warriors able to defend themselves in the forest. The battle would be in the old form, the Marcellean form. The enemy would be fought face to face.

No historical precedent would be set to make it otherwise. Marcelleans believed themselves superior to any opponent and would accept nothing more than an equal hold. The Targan held no such scruple.

They did not know how many Targan lay in the forest waiting for the attack signal. They could each remember the statistics, though, one after another, telling how many, but not who among them, would die that night, however. The results of old battles had become the fact and prediction of others.

Each held a particular bravery and duty to himself that day. Each would move forward with a resolve that was purely Marcellean, purely his own, less savage, yet as determined as that of the Targan who would rush on them.

No matter what horror from Modallas, no matter what The Helmsman had prepared for them, the attack would be theirs. The urge to make it so was not from any false sense of heroism but from duty and the necessity of survival of the Marcellean people.

There was no restlessness among them. No looks were exchanged between worried men about to die. Each held a promise to make the enemy pay dearly for his life, to make him pay dearly for Marcellus itself. The city waited behind them this time, clearly the prize of the victor. The people there waited, too, to learn the fate of the last real force between themselves and the forest.

At last, the sky darkened. In the long minutes, the Marcelleans drew themselves up. Weapons were checked and held ready. They waited for the first sounds of battle to reach them, for the Targan to come rushing at them across the plain.

33

A Narrow Escape

Helio piloted Soarer. Borter was manning the co – pilot's console beside him. Parnak stood in the cockpit hatchway.

Modallas was nowhere in sight. Control came on with instructions. "That's not Marcellus," said Borter, looking at the coordinates they were given, "this will land us about an hour out of the city."

"Correct," Parnak spoke through the translator. "We would only be going to the city if it was – too late." Borter returned the words as a curious glance at the insectoid.

"The city is not our prime concern," Parnak went on, barely allowing Borter's quandary to interrupt him, " – at this time. All goes according to plan. Do not be concerned with these coordinates, I recognize them, Borter," he added. "Instead, continue scanning for Modallian fighters."

The Magnean grimaced once again and returned to his scanner. Parnak's argument was well taken, he decided at length. For the time being, at least, no fighters blocked their way. He expected full attendance, but the Helmsman issued no free passes. It was simply a matter of time, like everything else that had happened to them in the last days. It was expected, and there was nothing anyone could do about it.

"Heavy clouds," Helio noted. "I –"

Borter interrupted, mocking concern, "It's not going to rain on us, too, is it?"

"Maybe," Helio answered. "I hope there's a clear — runway — down there, somewhere."

Borter looked up from his screen at him sourly.

"The Modallians will be somewhere in the clouds."

Soarer had just left the weightlessness of orbit. Borter peered out the cockpit windshield, "Let's go in." He said.

Looking around at Helio, he asked, "What have we got for covering terrain?"

The computer flashed the information onto the main screen. There was flat plain and then forest. They searched for some feature that would shield them from Modallian fighters. At the speeds they would be forced to use, the Modallians would be on them all the way and wouldn't need sensors to do it.

"Here," he plunged a finger at the screen. "This range of hills. It leads in the back way, nearly where we're going."

Helio agreed silently, nodding his head.

"Four minutes," he added at last. "Braking action, now."

Helio slowed Soarer to reentry speed. They skimmed the edge of the outer atmosphere. Reaching speed and the proper altitude, Helio extended Soarer's broad wings, and once more, Soarer soared.

Beneath them, closer, thick, gray, billowing clouds rose toward them. "I guess we'd better get down there before we're spotted." Borter nodded to Helio, who made for the clouds immediately.

"Entering planetary terminator into night," Helio noted. Screens hung in the darkness, pools of light written over by the computer, as they overtook night on the planet. "We're going to lose cloud cover in one minute."

Borter noted the information without comment. From above, the planet looked peaceful, but all three, Borter, Helio, and Parnak, knew the facts to be different.

Each of the three handled the idea of their continued association with the planet differently than they had only days before. Each was more heavily invested in the Marcellean struggle in ways that gave new dimensions to the planet's existence.

"How far above the surface is this cloud layer?"

"Around a half kilometer," Helio spoke. "It's uniform all the way down to our hills. Cloud cover dips almost to this ridge." The Dillisome pointed. "It's our best chance."

Borter turned to Parnak, who was still watching from the bulkhead hatch. "I hope you like sightseeing. We're going in fast and low."

"Of course," Parnak answered, the translator pressing his sarcasm into Universal. "My people have always been close to the ground – you might say."

"Your people have been," Borter made a diving gesture, "down, under the ground."

Helio seemed to enjoy the levity despite being heavily occupied. Unless it was his own, he ignored it. Borter ignored Parnak. Returning to the business at hand, "It will do. We should be in good shape if we reach it."

He took control of Helio. The more experienced of the two pilots, he would take Soarer through the most difficult moments of the flight.

It took no time at all for five dots to appear and grow on the screen, all rising toward Soarer. It was Helio who announced that fact. It was Borter who took action quickly. More dots joined the chase on the screen.

"I wish we had tried Old Face's armament. At least, we'd know it works," Borter moaned.

Parnak spoke from the bulkhead, "Don't worry, if Old Face installed it, it works. I only hope you know how to use it."

"Interceptors should be coming visual, now." Borter looked and, indeed, could see them coming. "Ten o'clock, five, coming in tight." The Targans had not bothered breaking their formation. "Gimme forward guns. Coming at ten o'clock," he echoed himself!

"Forward guns," Helio announced.

"We go directly for cloud cover and hope they can't track through it," The five Modallians came on, meaning to force them away from cover, "They get in our way. Too bad for them."

"Parnak buzzed something unintelligible through the translator, something the translator could not translate.

"I love it when he talks that way," Helio smiled broadly.

The console lit with Old Face's lights. None of this was particularly new to Soarer.

The Modallians broke formation, peeling themselves off, each meaning to pass Soarer head on. Borter dodged, firing as he did. Soarer's wings retracted to a more swept position the flyer becoming more of a projectile. Helio spotted for him and Parnak plugged his recorder into ship's sensors. Old Face could enjoy the show later.

"What?" As Borter made his first hit, the lights flashed together, and bells and even a dinging rhythm announced it. Helio traced one of the enemy flyers as it spun toward the ground, engulfed in flames.

Soarer's new weapons responded to every command, no matter how slight. He fired again and again. Borter sat intently, meeting every challenge, until they landed, bells following them all the way, leaving a sky full of Modallian ashes.

"Safe," Borter sighed deeply, his shoulders drooping.

The attack had suddenly fallen off, the sky around them a darkening, fathomless gray. Beyond it, somewhere ahead, the forces of Modallas marshaled beneath. Shortly, they would break cover, this time on the underside. All three hoped they would not find the remaining Modallians waiting for them.

"What sort of obstacles are there between these ridges?" Borter looked over wearily at Helio.

"Unknown," the Dillisome responded efficiently. "We'll have to wait and see. After we break cloud cover, I'll be able to let you know."

"I'll be able to do it myself, then." Borter snarled. "Until then, we'll have to take out chances." It would do no good to push Helio. It never had. Borter was just spent reacting to the adrenaline in his system. He hoped there was more left. He would have to wait.

Parnak made his way into the conversation with the type of statement that Borter always liked to hear but never quite knew how to handle. The journalist was heard and thoroughly ignored. "Your flying is magnificent, the both of you."

"Uh… Do you mind? We're not done yet."

Helio nearly laughed out loud. Parnak was silenced.

Borter returned to his work.

Soarer swept along the belly of the clouds in a deep valley, close between its steep ridges. The valley floor was lush. The grasses leaned forward and back as the winds coursed them. Aside from the winds, there was no other disturbance in the grasses or on the ridges. It was to prove a deceptive calm.

The sensors painted perfect three-dimensional images of everything that they flew toward and passed above, ahead, and beneath the interior of the cabin. All three had the sensation of winged free flight. After flying through such an intense fighter screen, it would disappoint them to fly aimlessly into one of the nearby hills.

"New fighter contact," Helio announced quietly. "From behind - coming fast."

Borter muttered something better left unintelligible beneath his breath at the news.

Soarer began to wiggle and dodge as Borter put her through the gyrations necessary to evade the enemy fire bursting all around them.

"Apparently, you've made them angry," noted the Dillisome.

"Maybe it was something I said," Borter snapped back.

"No," Parnak interrupted, "It was I you made angry, Borter."

"Really," the pilot turned, giving the journalist a quick and disparaging look up and down, "If you can remember what I said…"

"In addition to the Modallian fighters." The words from Parnak translated into perfect Universal.

"…write it down, will you? Maybe I can use it again later," Borter replied.

Soarer dived toward the ground. Borter extended the wings almost to full and angled the shield aft. Helio seconded everything and read off the altitude as it declined.

Soarer's rear gun-quad began to fire at the coming fighters. As angry bursts from the Modallian guns snapped at them, neither man looked up from his business – keeping the small freighter and themselves airborne and on course.

The bells and whistles annoyed again, clattering as the Dillisome scored hits on the fighters with the rear guns.

The new sensor array directed him to the most likely targets. "That's annoying," the Magnean sulked. Parnak surveyed the action in the cockpit with his small recorder. Everything was transmitted to his news services and anyone else who could pick up the signal.

"They're going to keep coming," Borter said. "They probably know the terrain better than us, too." From above and ahead, more came. Both wings of fighters overflew them as they slowed and dipped low against the landscape. Soarer's broad wings were as before - magnificent.

As Borter prepared to do battle in front, Helio fired at the receding fighters behind. The Modallians wheeled front and back and coming about looking for this most elusive prey, coming on from the front, then from the rear, taking turns.

Borter allowed the forward sensor to find and lock on one of the coming Modallians. He fired. The Modallian obediently disappeared in a hail of flaming wreckage and black smoke trailing off toward the ground.

Old Face's arcade buzzers and whistles assailed their ears. The assault went on, Helio taking another fighter behind them.

Borter rolled, retracting the wings and quickly gaining speed to avoid another attack. Energy snapped around them all the time, but Soarer remained unscathed.

As they broke away from the treetop level, the fighters were gone. Parnak leaned forward, recording the competent Helio on his screens. No one relaxed in the slightest, continuing to look for whatever The Helmsman might have in store.

34

The Ground

S oarer wove a path between the highest ridges. Nothing was to be seen of any kind of fighter screen in the sky.

Barreling down the narrow canyon between the ridges, it would take only seconds to reach the assigned landing field.

"Didn't we already do this?" The Magnean demanded.

Tall blue grasses shuttered at their approach driven to all sides as the ground air escaped their path. Borter matched the terrain staying close to the ground. Helio watched the sensors carefully.

He piloted, and Helio read off any new piece of information that came across the screen. There were no tall trees or any growth tall enough to impede their flight. Ahead of them, something moved, still several seconds distant. It was in the grass. One could tell by the way the stiff blades bent in its path. Slow moving, it made little headway. As they came closer, it fanned out in a wide angle.

"Targans — on the ground." Borter pointed, though he did not have to. What they had been wondering about was a huge column of Targans moving down the right-side slope to the valley floor.

Soarer rocked brutally. "Ground fire," Helio announced flatly. "That's why the fighters didn't follow us in. Probably afraid of being shot down by their own people. The Helmsman must have gotten them worked up into quite a pretty state for this attack."

"Not The Helmsman," reported Parnak, "But their own leaders and their own biology."

"Biology?" Both flyers turned at once. Parnak was trying to think of some way to answer a question when fire from below rocked Soarer again.

"Small arms fire, medium blasters." Helio recorded another fact. Borter did not want to pull up into the clouds. The fighters might again be encountered there. He attempted to scatter the Targan by strafing ahead.

It did little good, the Targan stood their ground and their fire intensified. Soarer's shields below, had gone up automatically to protect them.

"We're getting by them," said Helio, "a small band left ahead, just beyond the others." He hadn't finished his sentence before Borter assaulted the last set of ridges to the landing strip.

On the way, they encountered more fire that did them no damage. Parnak stood silent, peering down into the sights of his recorder.

"They're heading the same place we are," Parnak said. "We had better alert Marcellus Control to advise the commanders in the field, or I'm afraid they're in for a very bad time. Very unusual for a Targan to range this far from the forest. I suppose it might be expected, though, since they are making an attack against Marcelleans, not each other."

Neither pilot took particular notice of the statement.

"So much for objectivity," He gave a clipped observation as Soarer careened faster above the most difficult terrain yet encountered. Smaller bands of Targan could still be seen along the way. All seemed to know in advance of their approach and fired at them.

Meanwhile, Hello contacted Marcellus Control, which patched him directly to Marcellean battle command in the field. The voice on the other end was terse and filled with authority. Helio gave locations from his screen. The voice demanded all the information. When there was no more, the voice signed itself off.

"Didn't even say *thanks*," Borter complained in a low voice. "I suppose he knew already and was ready." He shrugged. Helio laughed at the episode.

Parnak spoke. "He doesn't have to be polite - that was Lord Soal.

"Didn't sound much like him," Borter countered bluntly.

"He's probably in the field somewhere or other. I guess the bad connection that distorted his voice slightly was the patch-through. He would never tolerate a malfunctioning Shoulder Falcon."

Around them, the terrain grew more angular, a proper setting for battle, Borter thought. It looks like a passage from the smattering of heroic literature he'd managed to read. Sharp outcropping of rock passed close by the streaking flyer. Borter, once again, paid full attention to his work.

They shot by more troops, several lines. Borter supposed

that they did not have or had not time to bring any fire to bear on them. It was just as well, in his own estimation. He'd run other blockades, and now, he'd run into this one. Once it was done, he'd come this way no more.

He swooped and wiggled Soarer away from the nuisance of their small arms fire, dodging the ground and jagged precipices alike. It was certainly an elegant new machine Old Face had given them. The whole thing seemed easy. The valley deepened below them. It was a sudden sloping, very steep going, on foot.

He heard Helio's voice. "Massive obstruction ahead." His voice became a cry wrung with urgency. "Coming visual. Too late to dodge."

Faced by the sudden, sheer impossibility of the approaching obstacle, Borter realized there was no place to go. He looked to Helio, who looked back, awaiting a decision, and at Parnak, who watched from the bulkhead.

Borter shrugged, again, theatrically, raising his eyebrows, one cocked higher than the other as if measuring something that had struck his pilot's eye oddly as if from a different point of view, the same thing would aid in the judgment of it. "Hang on," he muttered to the journalist.

Abruptly, Soarer tilted over, standing on one wing as Borter tilted his head to right things for his own perception. Parnak scrambled for a foothold. Helio was very surprised to be alive at all. Borter, in his manic genius, had flown them into the narrow passage to one side of the great oncoming pillar of stone, wide enough for them if they flew one side up.

Cabin lights came on as they lost all light in the deep crevasse. Bright lights beneath the wings came on as well. Sensors read a long, deep corridor ahead, open only at the top and at the other end. Borter kept the angle steady, he felt suddenly as if he were making some insane dive to nowhere.

He got the idea that both Parnak and Helio, too, had stopped breathing, frozen, afraid their slightest movement would hurl them into one wall or the other.

Light showed just ahead at the end of the corridor, dimly, at first, hauntingly dim, tantalizing, recent memories of safer, brighter light. The rock walls rolled by on both sides, etching the echoed roar of Soarer's engines in the back of his mind. Borter imagined the Targan would have to come through here, too.

"How far to the end?" He croaked out the question to his co-pilot.

"Three seconds."

"Count me."

Helio began the count. The information flickered across his screen. At *no* seconds left, Borter released a space mine at the spreading mouth of the chasm. Righting itself, the powerful flyer sailed upward again into the sky.

A blast ripped the sides of the chasm. Ancient rock shook and tumbled downward to the place where a more ancient stream cut its way into the rock. The entrance was sealed against this Targan invasion for all time. Now, only one side remained.

Borter, seizing all his courage, went back to close it. Helio and Parnak were amazed but said nothing. The little ship dived like a bird of prey at the remaining opening. Borter fingered the release, and another mine launched itself at the target. Momentarily, it was closed against the Targan. Soarer turned steeply, getting back on her old course. The second exit from the deep ravine crumbled.

Beneath him, on the plane, Borter saw a force on Marcelleans staring up at them. The tall grasses around them were trampled and burnt away. They had, indeed, cleared the land all the way around the massive pillar, and they were ready to battle there to the death.

The crew of Soarer stared down, also, with curiosity. Around the Marcelleans lay a number of Targan dead, an advance party. They had placed themselves directly in the path of the invasion and fully intended to defend the Marcellean rear at the path and choke off the Targan column there. Parnak noted, still regaining himself from the narrow passage, in what passed with him as amazement, "Even on my world, they will not believe what I have just recorded."

On the ground below, the commander of that small, beleaguered contingent raised his worn ion blade in salute to the passing Soarer.

"Must be the off – world pilots we heard of, "said another, beaming joy at the prospect of continued life with another grizzled veteran.

"I thought they'd be bigger," another, who smiled as broadly, came back.

Not far, elsewhere on the field, Lord Soal marked the work of his new champions.

35

The Forest Campaign

They were clear of it. They would not have to worry much about Modallian fighters at their backs. Marcelleans on the ground meant Marcellean air control. Borter wondered at the Marcellean force already stationed at the gap. Parnak assured him that it would be a far – flung battlefield, enclosing many kilometers before all was done.

Parnak looked at Borter with new respect, Helio, too, but Borter especially. He was no longer the careless boy he'd known once. It had been many planets back they first met. He needed a ride, and Soarer was young, a new bird, and available. Something about the two pilots was now more serious, more somber.

Perhaps it was the change to maturity their classes of humanoid went through. This had been a difficult thing for him to accept about several other classes on intelligent beings, this long period of maturity and growth when his own race l was *brought to life complete*, as they said it. Through the time they spent together, he'd noticed no physical change in them. He had long ago shed the set of vestigial arms his race was born with but never used.

In a manner, Helio had always been the strong and silent one, treating Borter with great deference, even, at times, in a fatherly way. Had there been less difference in their relative appearances, one might have thought that this was actually the case, that Helio was his father. However, the difference in skin color would have been difficult to explain. Borter, then, had been a perfect picture of impetuous youth among humanoid races. On all sides, he spread mischief with the best of intent or no intent at all. He made trouble or had been in trouble on half a dozen planets before learning better. On most planets, this was something freighter pilots did not do, at least among those who were not their own.

He was an experienced heller and bar crawler. Now, he had been brought to this. He was a fine pilot or had become one those years ago and now was a better one. Magneans did that.

Parnak was deeply impressed with the way they had handled the emergencies of the day. Borter lowered Soarer from her harrowing flight far beyond the sight of any tribute.

A car met them as they came to a ragged halt on a makeshift landing strip. This new Borter, Parnak thought as they bumped to a stop, stealing a glance, has grown into a man of mysteries. I'm sure Helio was aware of this long before me, and I'm only just seeing it.

They traveled by car for the rest of their journey for a few minutes. Occasionally, one of the trio would turn to look behind them into the billowing cloud of red dust in the wake of the car.

The Techno Dwarf who drove them said nothing and apparently was not curious about them and spoke no more than the commonest of courtesies the entire journey. Borter, beside Helio, found himself dozing uncontrollably until, finally, they slowed to a dusty stop.

The car left them amid the leading ranks of another Marcellean force. The veldt grass was thick and luxuriant beneath their feet. By the look of the place, Borter thought it an obvious battlefield. The hillock, some distance in front of the first ranks, hid the edge of the Targan Forest from their view. No Marcelleans were on it.

Their quiet ranks drawn up to the little slope had the same appearance as those he'd passed over as they waited for the Targan to emerge from the crevasse. Those, however, were far fewer in number than these. For a long time, they had driven past them in the car, all standing the same, waiting.

Borter and Helio supposed they would be somewhere to the rear of things. They had no business in the action, in the front lines. Marcellus was still just a name as far as fighting was concerned. They were Parnak's flyers, nothing more. The hillock's distance presented a false safety to them. Parnak said nothing, and they followed the directions given to them by the Techno Dwarf who had driven them.

He promised them Lord Soal was not far away as they'd left the car. Parnak had been all business, turning away toward the front immediately. "These are the finest warriors in the galaxy," his words floated back on the dust as they passed by. The descriptions that followed this were terse, perhaps for the benefit of his recorder and its audience rather than his companions. Helio noted there were no Techno Dwarves in the ranks.

Having gotten used to seeing them among the Marcelleans on most of their important occasions, he mentioned it to Parnak. "The Techno Dwarf are not warriors, but are Marcelleans just the same." Parnak turned from the lead to tell him.

"They make everything you see and much more you do not. The relation between them and the Marcellean, those who are warriors, is ancient, primordial, in fact. Without each other, neither would exist as you see them today. The relation is mutual, dependent - symbiotic.

It is beneath the Marcellean, who are the most expert of fighters, to do anything else since the relationship is made necessary. From the other end, they protect the Techno Dwarf from a common enemy. Many warriors have fallen, keeping that bargain."

Parnak continued the description as he moved quickly forward. He had no time to dally and knew it. It was as necessary to view the preparations as it was to see the actual battle. The Targan could spring from the forest in the blinking of an eye. To miss that or ignore its descriptive opportunity would be to lose much of the bestial aspect of the Targan as a race.

Borter wondered where Lord Markham would be. He had developed a keen interest in his former captor. He drew a sharp contrast between the shrewd gallantry of Lord Soal and the calculated malevolence of Lord Markham. To see him react in a pitched battle would be most enlightening. He would like to see Lord Markham brought down. The Magnean did not know why.

Parnak suddenly pointed to a dark figure in the distance. On all sides stood aides. Lord Soal stood looking straight ahead, hands clasped behind his back, his feet spread widely apart, in a stiff military attitude. Behind him were his handpicked troops, the Reds, the elite of Marcellus. They were silent, icily watchful, detached. That day, the faith of The Heart rested in their hands. All that was to happen was the will of The Heart, and they would play their part as directed. Parnak was immediately admitted to the inner circle around Lord Soal. Borter and Helio stayed behind him. The small recorder flashed against the deep black of Parnak's hand as it recorded the events taking place.

The insectoid stirred no outward curiosity among the somber Marcelleans gathered at the army's lead. Lord Soal noted their presence but made no welcoming gesture. Once, he glanced at Borter from the corner of his eye, and though it was covered by the ever-present battle mask, Borter knew the look intuitively and nodded cordially, smiling from one corner of his mouth.

The shoulder falcon present as ever, as ever present as the battle mask and armor, blinked its eyes studiously. Its sensors probing everything around them and even into the forest, watching, waiting. Lord Soal was fed information from everywhere through it. The ion blade, too, was in place. Its anger would be felt by the Targan before that day was done.

Borter looked at the long ranks made from the Marcellean elite Rangers. Besides the array of blasters, all carried ion blades like that of their leader. Parnak panned his recorder up and down the line. Their rank comprised the center of the Marcellean front line. It stretched far out of sight on both the left and the right. There was not enough room between them to let a single man pass. In such a multitude of Marcelleans, shoulder falcons, that little box on every shoulder, were evident, more so among them.

"We'll be safe enough here for the present. Lord Soal will reserve his elite from the first part of the fighting. They will not be used until the time is right. Of course, that barring the fortunes of war." Parnak returned to his recording. Lord Soal waved one of his officers closer. He pointed to the three of them still standing together.

The Marcellean approached them, "Lord Soal has asked me to inspect your weapons – to be sure you command enough – firepower to look after yourselves."

Borter stared at the man for an instant but produced the Reggian blaster from his side readily, "We're not going to be right out here," he gestured to the forward part of the field, "in the fighting." The blaster came back to him. Helio handed him over next.

"Of course, it is merely a precaution." The officer smiled in a friendly way. Parnak had no weapon, nor did he want one, but the Marcellean insisted he take one. Parnak accepted a standard-issue Marcellean infantry blaster. He turned again to Borter, speaking with some admiration in his voice, "That is an interesting weapon you have."

"I got it in a bar - actually, I took it in a bar fight - from a Reggian pirate last year." Borter won the fight using his fists but saw no favor in leaving the weapon to the original owner. Later, when he had a chance to look at the blaster, he noted the power level, far in excess of legal ratings for the Inner Galaxy. It packed the wallop of a small field piece at its highest setting. The custom grip was, surprisingly, his size, too. He'd come out ahead in the deal twice.

He had some practice with it but had never the need, before Marcellus, to fire it at anyone. He hoped that day also would show him only as a spectator. Beside him, Helio added a standard issue blaster to his own, also provided by the same officer, and received, besides the weapon, instruction in its use.

36

The Forest Campaign More

When we are called upon to move into battle, you will have time to move back." The officer thought an instant longer before turning to rejoin those around Lord Soal. "Do not refuse a direct order or try to get through an advancing line," he said.

"You will be cut down." Then, recalling something else, "Lord Soal has asked me to extend thanks for the action you took against the Targan air cover and - the ground forces, of course — as you approached for your landing. He further congratulates you on your superb skill as flyers — and warriors." The man nodded to them. Parnak's recorder entered the whole scene into history.

The Marcellean turned without another word. Borter holstered the Reggian blaster he was so proud of. "In a way — it sounds as if he just said — *goodbye*"

"That's a comforting thought," He added without looking around," keep a path clear for me to Soarer, will you?"

"That might be a good idea," Helio smiled at last, one of his rare smiles. It was, as usual, the odd times that Dillisome selected to show their good disposition. A rare release for stress withheld, Borter thought, very unhealthy.

The order of battle was drawn up on either side of the Marcellean overlord. Borter could venture a guess, with some accuracy, the total width of the line since he'd flown over some of it coming in and supposing Lord Soal to be the center of all things. But. he did not care to place a number the depth of those lines or the number of the staunch Marcelleans standing behind the icily disposed Marcellean lord.

The forest swelled in the distance with Targans they could not see. In his more poetic moods, he would have described it as a snarling beast hidden within a deep vapor of green. Awaiting only the command from the spirit of savagery to leap, taking its prey. Borter found colorful descriptions uncharacteristic of himself and rarely chose to give them a voice.

The Marcellean army numbered in the hundreds of thousands that day. There was nothing weak in their military design. How many, that day, were the Targan? How many times the Marcellean number were they? Borter thought of the impossible numbers assigned to stars in the galaxy and wished to be elsewhere among them.

With a great howl, the forest lost its torrent. As if the sky above them burst, letting numberless drops of rain plummet down to smack the armor of the Marcellean and run in swift rivulets around their feet. The roiling mass of bodies rushed outward from the underbrush toward the line on the right.

There, the ranks of warriors knelt in their firing orders, weapons ready. They waited until, at last, the screaming savages were almost among them before slaughtering the first to have broken from the forest. Lord Soal turned quietly in that direction. He could see no Targan leader. Knowing Sorel would change his position, the center of the line, where Lord Soal made himself conspicuous.

Dead and dying Targan soon heaped the ground in several wide broad areas along the line, and they kept coming. The forest held no end to their numbers. Where one fell, another took his place.

Parnak watched calmly as his recorder claimed everything happening for his viewers. Borter and Helio watched minute after minute as the battle's fury increased. Those holding the center of the Marcellean line stood unmoving, waiting for the attack that must surely come.

Meanwhile, the battle that raged between Marcellus and the Targan Forest escalated quickly. Lord Soal watched his warriors meet the challenge that hurled itself against them. Ranks opened to admit Targan, then reformed to cut them off, trapping them from aid and retreat. Then, tramping forward like a bristling. Armored machine dividing the enemy, suddenly turning against its flank sealing the fates of all Targan caught between.

Still, that was not the end of it. The Forest Spirit sent his minions on in greater numbers. Lord Soal watched this endless tide dash itself against the Marcellean ranks. Only moments away, Sorel would receive his command from Markham to throw his men against the line's center. If the line broke, the slaughter among the Marcelleans would be great that day as the Targans turned their own tactics against them.

Above, in the sky, Marcellean air cover had been sufficient to keep the Targan from the Marcelleans on the he ground. Defeat of the Targan horde on the planet would mean certain retaliation from Modallas above. Lord Soal had prepared an expeditionary force to counter this eventuality one going to the cylinder world itself.

This, he promised himself, would be the final battle, the final victory or defeat. The shoulder falcon plotted time precisely, feeding information directly to Lord Soal. Borter and Helio stood watching nervously for some time. They were painfully conspicuous among the Marcelleans and their practiced air of confidence. Borter fingered the butt of the Reggian blaster hoping things would not be so desperate he would be forced to use it.

The main bulk of the Targan force welled in the forest directly before Lord Soal and the center of the Marcellean line. Though hidden by the forest, their strategy was predictable.

These Targan would see action soon.

A second great shout was raised in the forest. Targan made ready with their war cries. Sorel was at last allowed to bring his attack against the center of the line. At first, there was only shouting. A great racket went on for a time, drowning out even the sounds of the struggle already engaged nearby. Borter watched the dark edge of the forest, expecting some special movement there. For a time, nothing happened only the cries of war coming, growing in intensity with each second.

After late prayers to the Forest Spirit, he decided finally. Nervously checking his weapon, he noted that Helio did the same. Parnak did as he always did – he recorded. The pit of Borter's stomach swam.

"Your eyes are better," He motioned to the Dillisome, "what's going on?"

"They're trying to frighten us, I believe," came Helio's unbelievably calm reply. "It is an old trick."

37

Punishment of The Heart I

Sorel's Targan bled from the forest in quick streams. Streams that soon became torrents which, then covered the plain dividing the forest from the Marcellean line. The howling pack surged onward without resistance from the Marcelleans who waited, silent, without emotion. They seemed like ocean waves crossing the uneven grounds heads bobbing as they ran, faces contorted in all sorts of unnatural shapes in savage anticipation of battle.

Parnak turned to Borter and Helio, "I believe it is time for the non-combatants to leave." The pilots gave quick agreement and were already turning, on their way to the rear and Soarer. But, something startled them, stopped them short.

Lord Soal's shoulder falcon spoke to him. The tone of it was different, as if it had suddenly taken life and was no longer a device made of tiny circuits.

"Lord Markham has taken the field." It was a deadly note received by the whole of the Marcellean line at once. They moved forward as one, ready to give themselves, each, one by one, in the attempt to destroy Markham. Borter looked at Helio, not quite believing the moment. More resigned to the development, Helio wheeled himself about, blaster drawn, rejoining Parnak.

"Oh, well," the journalist tossed his shoulders, "so often, in the individual search for destiny, all we get is fate. Come along, Borter."

Parnak called to him cheerfully, "You'll see what you've been missing all these years."

In another instant, Borter was beside them. The three formed a miniature line of their own in the vast Marcellean ranks, but one not of choice. In the front ranks of the Marcellean line, ion blades left their scabbards in a flash of blue. Lord Soal was nearby.

The first Targan reached the line at a dead run. If there was any honor among them for being first, it must have been worthwhile to the dead, for that is all left.

Their drill was worked to perfection, a defense formed on both sides of their overlord. Borter, Helio and Parnak decided it was a good place for them, also. No one knew where Lord Markham was. Borter did, however, know where his Targan was, and, just now, they were coming faster toward him. Borter pointed his weapon forward at them. Neither he nor Helio had ever fought in a pitched battle on the ground. They watched Parnak and did what he did.

Borter picked off Targans, moving in his direction, as did Helio. They crumpled in the grass before him. In the air, elsewhere, the Marcelleans worked their ion blades in whispering arcs, cutting down the thick, struggling masses of forest men. Bodies from both sides began to heap, but still, the Targan came, and the Marcellean line stood.

Barely perceptible at first, the rush of Targan began to slow. Then, at length, they slowed and began to pack together, firing Modallian blasters blindly. They could not breach the line, nor could they fall back and regroup in their disorder as others pushed against them. Solemnly, Lord Soal signaled the advance faster. To hold any posture of defense would have been to invite disaster.

The Marcellean force moved quickly in the field but moved efficiently, deliberately, like a reaper in the field, leaving nothing standing at its passage. The Targan crushed one against the other and were easy prey for them. Their blasters became useless. The three off-worlders kept pace with the Soal.

Markham had not yet been seen. He was behind his army with Sorel, who had not run out to attack the Marcelleans. Sorel wanted a confrontation with Lord Soal but was held back by Markham. "Let him come to us," Markham counseled him. "There will be time later and a better chance to see an end to that one."

Sorel stepped out and signaled. Word was sent to others who led for him in other parts of the field. Reluctantly, they began to fall back. Markham instructed them when to fire their blasters, pinpointing various targets. Not far, in the distance the blue tinged ion blades of the Marcelleans could be seen individually. The time drew nearer.

The Marcelleans pushed harder, taking up slack developing between themselves and the retreating Targan. They wedged themselves into their enemies. With Helio and Parnak, Borter saw some opportunity to pull back. Parnak refused. Lord Soal was near enough, allowing them still to hover close by, enjoying the benefit of his heavy guard.

He remained aloof from the fighting, keeping his communications open to other units in the field. Coordination of all surface elements was in his hands. His shoulder falcon assured him of Markham's proximity. The drive to reach him continued. It cut tirelessly into the reeling wall of Targans.

Borter looked around quickly. Marcellean ranks stood all around them, but no living Targan. Moving forward, sometimes quickly, sometimes with difficulty, they went on. Units moved up and fell back, relieving those who had been in the front ranks longest. No relief came for the center of the line. It appeared their calling was something special, one not entirely shared by the others.

He was able to distinguish Marcelleans in their armor among those dead on the ground. There, they no longer appeared so proud and invincible. It, at least, was not a quality given to the enemy who could lay claim to only a certain brute savagery. Borter wondered how many more Targan were left in the forest. He was growing tired and wished it was done.

Lord Soal would continue this fight until the Targan was forced from the field or were entirely annihilated or until he was cut down himself. Helio watched his stride purposely forward to strike at his age — old enemy. It was the same warrior who had rescued them in

Toth. The same who amazed him with his skill in breaking the trap set there by the same Lord Markham.

Marcelleans cut a deep salient into the teeming horde before them. Targan everywhere fell dead in great numbers. Each Marcellean cost them hundreds. Parnak was glad these Marcelleans never had designs on the rest of the galaxy.

Ion blades whooshed through the air in precise arcs, leveling the resistance in their path. Masses of the forest savages melted away, so much ice before so much fire. They came, on and on, more from the forest. Their numbers seemed without end. The more killed, it seemed, the more came. The flashing ion blades of the Marcelleans made room for them.

Again, the Marcellean flanks turned, and once more they did, trapping more surprised Targans for whom the fatal edge of the planet suddenly appeared at their feet. For a time, they struggled with an uncontrollable urge not to be thrown into that abyss until the inevitable ion blade appeared before them, closing darkness over them. Ion blades became the engine of vengeance in all quarters. Their wielders sometimes struggle over heaps of fallen bodies to reach farther into the field. In the end, they joined forces with other Marcelleans engaged in the same task and would divide again to face this same enemy who pressed against them endlessly. Targan leadership appeared to have lost control of any strategy on the battlefield.

38

The Sky Above

Above, The Helmsman's Modallian flyers were engaged heavily by Marcellean fighters. Air battles contrasted with those fought in the red dirt below as the sleek and speedy fighters made their passes at each other, heavy blasters poured out power. Targans were better trained and took a heavier toll among them.

It seemed that the air of the planet was becoming full of the quarrelsome, quick and powerful gnats. At every level of the atmosphere there was an engagement of one sort or another. The fortunate or, perhaps, only the very skillful, blasting the less fortuned from the sky. Flames and smoke scored the air.

Over the city of Marcellus itself, defenders in the air swept the attacking Modallians away, challenging them before they could inflict damage on the magnificent buildings below. Air cover held the city safe, an umbrella in the storm.

Other Marcelleans reached out as far as Modallas itself. Modallas held greater sway, and Marcellus suffered. Its gleaming surface was untouched, far away from the planet itself, in orbit. All the same, following the Marcellean sun with the planet as if it were its own and not an alien orb hanging in some distant quarter of the galaxy.

Marcelleans swept in, as low over that surface as they dared. Before they could reach a target, the Modallian fighters appeared to drive them away. The spinning cylinder stayed behind them, invulnerable, unscathed for all their effort. Time and time again, they would have given their lives to reach it, just once, for their overlord and the planet below. There was no chance. Modallas was too strong at home. Only Soarer had got closer.

From its massive airlocks, all down the turning cylinder, fighters came. Squadrons of efficient Modallian fighters pressed and counterattacked, happy, at last, to strike at hated Marcellus. Targans became proud flyers in Modallian service. They learned quickly enough when removed from the forest.

The Targans swirled, unable to break the Marcellean formations. Units to the left and right again performed their flanking maneuvers, cutting off more Targans for quick slaughter. Everywhere, the ion blades came down one after another. Heavy blasters reinforced the leading ranks.

As the battle wore on, Lord Soal went forward to claim victims of his own, the blade in his hands moving with that ease of long practice. At one point, several Marcelleans went down in front of him. a number of Targan bearing blasters charged at him, firing as they came.

The Marcellean overlord met them as he'd met the others, swiftly, without hesitation. The powerful Modallian weapons did them little good as he stepped among them. Borter, Helio, and Parnak watched with new amazement at his skill. The Targan were stopped in their tracks, hardly knowing he had been there by the time they died.

They added to the growing number of dead heaped together in grotesque mounds across the field everywhere the Marcellean had advanced. Targan, however, still came from the forest, as quick and undiminished in their ferocity as those before them. There was growing order in their movement that was worrisome to the three off-worlders, but there seemed to be no central scheme to give more weight to their fears.

The Targan in front of them seemed to boil, running up from all directions and falling back, having attempted to breach the line. Sorel appeared in the throng. He directed movements against various points in the Marcellean lines and came forward to meet Lord Soal in battle.

He strode forward purposefully, a powerful blaster slung from shoulder to opposite waist aping the Marcellean manners he envied in Markham. A vanguard preceded him. Lord Soal noted the presence of Sorel in the battle and directed his troops to hold him out – for a while.

39

A Legend Takes The Field

Sorel increased the pressure against the middle of the line until he realized he was being kept away from the victim he desired. It was to be his day, his day to wear the ears of Lord Soal as battle trophies, in glory before the Forest Spirit. He would not be denied.

Lord Soal watched the Targan offensive build, when his line appeared unable to bear more, he ordered them to let through.

And through, they came. The Marcellean lines moved around him. If Sorel wanted to meet the overlord of Marcellus, then he would. The lines crushed inward like an armored vise.

Lord Soal stood alone in a clearing, ion blade in hand, at the end of a funnel of Marcelleans down, which poured screaming Targan at him.

At the other end, Sorel moved forward, a way made through his own fighters, his eyes firmly set on Lord Soal as be came on, appearing as though he could not have be less concerned with anything else around him. This was to be a personal duel, for his own glory.

Lord Soal, however, planned otherwise. He held no care at all for Sorel, hardly knowing of him, except as a leader among the Targan. Markham was the real quarry he wanted and The Helmsman. To end his charade quickly was his most pressing desire.

Down the trough, he propelled himself against them, ion blade flashing out everywhere, spoiling the point of the charge he had allowed to break his ranks.

The confrontation came quickly. Before Sorel realized it, his vanguard had melted away and he alone faced the rampaging Marcellean lord. Lord Soal allowed Sorel only an instant to raise his blaster before ending his existence.

The open ranks had swung almost completely, firmly, around once more, before the shoulder falcons, as one, let their voice be heard in the ears of the overlord and all Marcelleans in the field, Lord Markham has taken the field. The message repeated itself again and again, in their ears. Knowing the signal to mean not only that the renegade Markham was present, but could only be moving toward him, Lord Soal ordered his troops forward.

Ion blades cut their way across the plain, driving the Targan before them. They were soon a torrent stemmed, driven back to their forest source. Lord Soal seemed to be everywhere at once, urging his men on. Helio and Borter followed with Parnak, barely able to, at times, keep him in sight. An impressive number of Targan fell.

At last, perhaps after several minutes of fighting, no one could be sure, the Targan rose up in a great wave and once more thrust themselves forward. As they did, the Marcellean fighters could see Markham raised up on a platform, carried along by the surging Targan. He, like Sorel, seemed not the slightest concerned with the vast carnage surrounding him but bore on.

The sight caused a great rousing of effort in the Marcellean lines. Angered, Marcelleans merely increased their slaughter of the oncoming mass. Nor did Parnak miss the event with his recorder. Borter and Helio, meanwhile, played the disagreeable parts of his bodyguards against the Targan, for whom all were the enemy.

Under Soal's tutelage, a bloody path was cut toward Markham. It was much like that sprung to kill Sorel, but much more intense. Lord Soal, now, watched calmly as his soldiers went before him to greater slaughter against their old enemy.

Shoulder Falcons registered with greater intensity as they approached Markham. The little machines seemed to be much more than any ordinary calculator or sensing machine. The red dots that were its eyes lit continuously and brightly like a steady beacon and blinked, then, only slowly.

The time to come to terms with their errant Markham had come, and every Marcellean seemed to know he had come and where he was as Lord Soal strode forward into a path cleared for him at a walk. Lord Soal's elite Reds took a greater toll on the Targan, fighting with a madness equal to or surpassing those followers of The Forest Spirit.

It was time. Lord Soal walked behind his Reds, ion blade glowing a deep blue as did those of the soldiers who went before him.

Here and there the weight of the Targans broke the line, the ragged holes closed quickly, to the surprise of the Targan who found themselves trapped for their effort.

The three off-worlders followed after Lord Soal. It was no longer difficult to keep up as the fighting toughened. Borter, as did Helio and Parnak, kept a close watch for breaks in the line ahead, so far, the Marcelleans had held them safe from harm.

The blaster was held tightly in his grip. For some minutes he had been glad at not having to fire it.

Several times, the Marcelleans let its gangs of Targan break through the ranks but were quickly cut down. On one side of Parnak, Helio fired several shots far to one side, ending the battle for several of the invading forest men. Borter glanced over as Parnak recorded the event.

The roiling cortege bearing Markham came on. Markham, himself, was quite aware of Lord Soal's presence and whereabouts. With a shoulder falcon of his own, location was easy. Ordering the willing Targan ahead against Marcelleans was no problem.

In fact, word of their victories at the ranger camps had spread through the forest. It made good talk around cooking fires and drew others on to greater deeds in battle.

Ahead, Lord Soal's Reds seemed lost in the general mass of bodies. Some of them fell, others took their places to defend Marcellus and themselves to the last. Markham was not far off, obvious in the sunlight as his dark armor caught it. Still, he came on, carried on that large platform by his willing minions.

While Marcelleans systematically littered the grounds with dead, none attempted to take the life of Lord Markham. His life and the honor of taking it was long reserved to Lord Soal. They simply were to clear a path for Lord Soal to him. Markham regarded this as a certain immunity to death. Little else prevented a direct confrontation between the two brothers. The field between them had narrowed sufficiently.

Lord Soal and his Reds hacked a path farther toward him through his Targan vanguard. He watched the arcing blades of ion force ripple toward his position, then, the prospect of doing battle directly with Lord Soal brought a giddiness to his head and to his walk a swagger.

The platform lowered carefully and the renegade Marcellean stepped contemptuously the short distance to the ground.

Markham gestured swiftly to both sides. This time, better the charge of the Reds. Lord Soal was to be let through, then let the battle rage as it might.

Here, Markham stood his ground, content to wait and do no work meeting his brother.

His phalanx held their fire until they faced only the red-armored Marcelleans. their firing orders allowed only directed, well — aimed volleys designed to hold back any who would interfere with the battle royal. Markham waited patiently, smiling in anticipation beneath the opaque battle mask. The event was long awaited. Marcellus was soon to be his.

The Targan before these phalanxes thinned, until finally there were none. Lord Soal saw, now, that his soldiers faced quite a different problem. before the main organized unit of Targan opened fire on them with heavy blasters. Many fell. Lord Soal directed covering fire from the flanks, moving closer until the Reds exacted a toll of their own.

With them, Borter, Helio, and Parnak opened a three-way nucleus of fire. Feet rushed up from behind. They were not the heavily shod feet of Marcelleans. Borter found himself sprawled on his back, separated from his formidable blaster. The first living Targan he had seen close that day hovered dimly above him. The man was large, dank smelling, and well-disposed to send Borter to his death. The heavy stock of the Modallian blaster need only crash down on the semiconscious Borter a second and final time.

With the pirate blaster in his grasp again, if unsteadily, Borter lurched forward, aided on each side by Helio and Parnak. Lord Soal in the lead, they went forward. There was no other choice. Borter rubbed his head, groggy, and looked back at the Targan Helio had killed. Now, he had to control himself, find his legs, and continue to defend himself. Soal dealt with the last Targan to momentarily confront him. Then, he turned to deal with the problems of pilot Borter. It would not suit his plans to lose the man now.

As he reached out to kill the Targan, a beam of photon energy struck before his iron blade. Lord Soal looked around for the source of the blast. The Targan fell back into a large smoking hole where much of his chest had been. Helio gave off another of his strangely more frequent smiles before helping Parnak get Borter to his feet.

Borter still weak from his injury, his footing difficult, tried to raise himself. Helio with the aid of Parnak steadied him between them as he fired.

For a moment, there was a bright light, as if something powerful had burst close by. Borter was alive, he was sure. He was not as sure of the others. His vision was returning but blurred. At least, he expected a deep crater from the blast and his friends dead, around him.

Helio a very surprised look on his face stood only a few feet away and Parnak beside him, camera as usual, recording everything. Borter got to his feet next to a huge, roiling form.

5D raised a bloody maw, defying the savage throngs around him, managing an ear-splitting roar at the same time. Resistance melted before them or at least kept its distance. A legend walked the field of battle.

40

Punishment of The Heart II

It was Lord Soal who was drawn into the trap. However, he was a victim who went with his eyes open willingly. Markham took some offense at the impertinence, at the ease his brother offered himself to death. It was no mere sheep coming to slaughter. He expected some apprehension to be shown when he turned the tables on any opponent. Instead, it was he who warranted fear.

The Red Warriors attacked the flanks hard with disturbing effect. Lord Soal came nearer with each stride. Each step exuded confidence. Markham did not move. His own ion blade remained sheathed, his hands far from it, though when the time came, he, too, was capable of the same blinding speed of all Marcellean warriors.

In the blink of an eye, 5D appeared beside Lord Soal, maw dripping fresh crimson, as red as the Red Warrior's armor. It was only a short distance to Markham when Lord Soal stopped the great beast and made him remain behind. Had 5D his own way, he would next materialize his jaws already at Markham's throat.

Markham was no match for the animal. 5D was larger, more powerful, and could avoid any cut or blast instantly, with his natural ability. Lord Soal came the last few meters forward, his blade ready.

Markham drew his blade – held ready. There was nothing left between them to be said. Only the death of one or the other would satisfactorily conclude the encounter. For a moment, they circled, carefully stepping, watching each other as they felt for the proper footing and the proper advantage. It could be over in a single stroke.

Blades met with a loud snap. Lord Soal parried a cut at his legs as Markham spun and returned a well-aimed overhand at his thigh which was stopped, also, short of target. For another long interval, they circled, each again looking for that single, deadly opening that would spell doom for one or the other.

When young, as children, they had played out this game many times. Then, it had been only learning and practice.

When they were grown, the lessons learned at such play were meant for Targan, not each other. The fighting continued around them.

The Marcellean line pushed against the Targan. Stray fire blurted close by, through the air, but did not touch the two brothers in their mortal combat.

Punishment would be heavy. The Heart sought retribution for the lives of many of its own. The day had yet to exact its tolls, however great, on either side. In what seemed to be an empty space, a weary trio sank to the ground. Parnak was interested in recording the battle between the last Marcellean titans only. Borter and Helio had no choice except to agree as they posted themselves on either side of the preoccupied journalist and fired at whatever came close to them that was not Marcellean.

The recorder's eye took the battle between Lords Soal and Markham as even. Blades flashed only a short distance away. It seemed to Parnak that the sound of this encounter alone rang over the entire field, that it was for this personal struggle alone the Marcelleans had come and given so many of their lives.

No words were recorded between them as they circled in the grass, then thrust at each other in earnest. Both were grim and remained so, intent on the job at hand.

They seemed to attract no special attention at all from those who battled around them. No strain of battle showed through their armor. Borter, again on his feet, and Helio were forced to defend themselves and the busy Parnak. At another time, later, they would be unable to remember a more fierce battle. Parnak, too, would be at a loss to remember any greater and none of such magnitude or, for that matter, one fought for such obscure goals.

Neither Lord Soal nor Markham gave ground. It was a hard battle, skillfully so, a battle of proportions. Both knew their business and were quick at it. The formal Marcellean manner was most evident as the duel resembled more a ballet than a deadly battle for one another's life. Each movement seemed expected and planned to the smallest degree, one man knowing the other's thoughts, nothing out of place.

On their tiny patch of ground Markham and Lord Soal teetered back and forth between victory and defeat. On such tiny patches of ground the fate of worlds were fought over and decided. The fire of the heavy blasters hurtled closely overhead, lighting the sky eerily, reflecting beneath the thick cover of dark clouds, looking as if this battle, a fierce second battle of duplicates, raged there as well.

Parnak moved cautiously around the scene, recording everything with Helio and Borter in close attendance. Above, in the cold sky above the battle and beyond the dark clouds, Modallas rose in the sky, invisible in the heavens.

All was well aboard the giant arc. As the turning cylinder traveled its path flawlessly, each system hummed with its own perfection. The Helmsman sat in Control, in his armor, poised, ready, following the duel below.

There had been no errors in many, many years. Modallas had traveled her course straight and true. It had been his accomplishment alone. Orbit was no special trick, a minor adjustment now and then, all completely expected and prepared, long in advance. It had been entering this galaxy, choosing it. That had been the real trick. No other could have done it – no Modallian and no Marcellean.

Events below on the planet arranged themselves well. His own sensors picked up the battle in detail between the Marcellean brothers. As usual, Markham disgusted him. Lord Soal, if he was to give any merit to those on the planet, was far in the lead as a recipient of that honor. Markham was tolerable so long as he could be used — and useful he was. Their association had been long.

Markham's intrusion upon his own efficiency was marked. Eccentricity was tolerable only so long. This string of pitched battles was not much to his liking. Results had been spotty, goals questionable, the action to please Markham's whims, his wildness. Like every action, his actions would have reactions. The Helmsman wondered just what form this reaction, this mad vengeance on his own kind, would take. From the Marcelleans, it was only a question of time before retaliation.

He pondered the likely results. If, by chance, Lord Soal could be eliminated - that would be different, even reasonable, though he could not fathom the particular logic that made it necessary in Markham's mind. Recall, should it prove needed, was almost instantly possible; there would be no great loss of materials or trained Targan, and Markham could be teleported to Modallas before any real harm could come to him. If, in fact, he'd left instructions for just such an event.

Slowly, his mind passed over the controls. Something afoot, something he did not understand, something that played foil to his best calculations, roiled his thoughts. Feeling that he saw only what the Marcelleans wished him to see, he hesitated, passing over the impulse to recall Markham instantly.

His gaze floated across the vast space housing Control. The bitter dispute between Soal and Markham was of no consequence. Only the Marcellean Heart mattered, more than a weapon, it was the instrument of galactic dominance. Only The Heart mattered, and this tiny battle was not getting it for him. The destruction of one man, no matter what his stature, the man, on a single obscure planet meant nothing.

Of course, if Markham managed some way to destroy his brother, he would be the remaining wearer. Once the hiding place of The Heart was known, both Marcelleans could eliminated. The science of Modallas had, at some length, been unable to develop its own wearer for The Heart.

It was a technological wonder that pleased him when he thought of it. It would allow him access to the power that created a galaxy, the power to make the galaxy his own. Once The Heart was his, planets and whole star systems would fall to him. There was not enough power in the galaxy, all combined, to oppose him.

Such a concentration of power was this Marcellean device, whether or not it did contain the life force of all those called Old Marcelleans. It did not matter, nor did that concern him at all. The object was power, not planetary mythology. Those prattling planetary systems and star federations of the Inner Galaxy merely toyed with it. He would show them real power.

To the Marcelleans, he owed a minuscule but grudging debt. Theirs was the hardest resistance he could meet in establishing the galaxy as the new Modallian home. It had been long, long and, now – not much longer.

41

The Punishment of The Heart III

The old home was gone. It had been a galaxy much different from this. Civilization there was Modallas, everything was Modallas. In all that galaxy, among all those stars, there was nothing else. In a billion stars, there was room left for nothing else. When the end came, it had come swiftly, so swift there was time only to build one arc, one Modallas, one final refuge, and bring aboard those chosen and leave the dying galaxy. He alone had been the one to guide them.

His hand steady at the controls, they'd crossed the void between galaxies. The long, empty years of searching for a suitable home, one to subdue, one worthy of bringing to heel.

He had piloted Modallas to that destination, this galaxy. The others who were Modallians slept below as they had for all of what seemed an eternity.

Of the three broad land strips extending the length of interior Modallas, they occupied just one. There, none were allowed save The Helmsman himself. Markham and the others, his Targan, as The Helmsman liked to call them, were excluded from all contact with that land mass. Most would not go there. Markham certainly knew what was there. When he'd asked, he'd been told, but he'd never set foot on the Third Plain.

It was shortly afterward The Helmsman offered him an alliance with Modallas. Asked what would be his price, Markham replied simply, Marcellus. That was his price, nothing else. The Helmsman agreed. Marcellus was his necessary point to begin the quest, the necessary point of beginning. Markham ruled Targans who were repulsive to him and repelled by him, who destroyed the very Marcelleans he wished to follow him.

Lord Soal delivered a fierce downstroke, cleaving only air where Markham's head had been an instant before. The Helmsman's hand released the control. All of Markham's personal guard surged forward as he teleported away. They were slain as quickly as they came forward. An angry Markham materialized inside Modallas' teleportation chamber. The Helmsman would not see him.

Lord Soal turned, unfazed by the slaughter around him. The trio of off-worlders behind him were stunned. Teleportation was new to them; its mechanics were highly abstract. A sort of thinking preferred more by Helio than by Borter or Parnak. Their wits finally returned to them, and they realized once again they were surrounded by protecting Marcelleans.

So taken by the contest between the Marcellean lords that the exertion of the larger struggle never overtook them, a fatigue they had not seen coming. Lord Soal turned to them as if nothing had happened and ordered his Marcelleans forward. Once more, the three had no choice except to pick up and move with them.

Soal was very near driving the Targan back into the forest, but it required a final determined effort. The drives from the left and from the right had come a long way, but the battle between himself and Markham had eaten away at the advance from the center. As he returned to the fighting, he was a different Lord Soal, somehow deflated, somehow reduced.

The endless struggle became the mundane, painfully mortal. The expectation of the conflict had gone. It seemed that all things left were of no more importance than routine matters, things to be performed at a regular basis by menials.

The center of the line advanced at pace with the left and right flanks equaling them, then leading. In their lead was the Marcellean overlord himself, his own Reds still close.

The troubles of the previous fighting seemed nil. The arc cut as ion blades zipped through the air. More and more strokes fell from them into the raging Targan before them. One after another fell beneath the arcing blades. The force of the renewed Marcellean attack stunted for good the wild, headlong Targan charged from the forest.

The contest was one of frustrations. Lord Soal, unable to win his prime victory, now settled for something less. Targan he had fought before, they were always defeatable. Their new Modallian weapons made little difference, they were crushed beneath the heels of the finest warriors ever known in the galaxy. They would stop at nothing less than driving their primeval enemy back into the forest.

Lord Soal, beneath the confinements of his battle armor, was tense, anxious to carry the effort of this battle to this logical end. That end, today, was Modallas itself. With the Targan threat quelled for even a single day, his already prepared forces could themselves pounce on the real enemy. Only a matter of time existed between himself and this one goal. Once the Targan was within the bounds of their forest, their ancient and rightful place, he would give the order all awaited.

The Helmsman played the game of cat and mouse by proxy, using first his mad brother, the Targan and, in its turn, Marcellean honor itself. It had never been misread by the Marcelleans once it began. Now, were they ready, in their own time, to strike back properly at the cunning and powerful Helmsman?

The pace moved easily forward, as if there was no resistance as if there was nothing in front of them. The photon energy from the blasters still raced frighteningly back and forth overhead. Borter glanced around himself occasionally, trying to decide where they were, from where they were aimed.

Unable to decide, perhaps those points were beyond the range of his natural senses, perhaps the beams dissipated far out in space having gone the paltry distance represented by planetary atmosphere.

He could not keep the thought. In the deepening shadows of the day, he was forced to the defense of his friends nearby as well as himself. The advance continued unabated. The horde of forest men bent back like tall grass in a great wind.

The streaks of hot energy swept impatiently overhead as if they were weary of the fighting, too. Their trials left an afterglow in the eye only as they streaked away. They seemed to go toward the forest only. Rarely, at last, was there a reply from that direction.

To the Marcelleans, it was merely work; a second or third or even one-hundredth Targan standing before any of them was merely a repetition of the one before. A few Marcelleans fell on the field. To the Targan, the Marcelleans they faced were far more individual, for the one they faced, almost always was the one sending him into the afterlife, to the dwelling of the Forest Spirit.

Within the hour, it ended, and the Targan faded away before them into the distant forest. The space between opposing forces grew until contact no longer existed. The Marcellean warriors slowed until they stood still in the field wearily and alone. The forest stood before them not far away. No sounds came from within, all silent as it had been before.

Lord Soal gave new orders. The glowing eyes of the shoulder falcon everywhere showed in the dingy aftermath of battle, blinking off and on as he stood there. As Borter and Helio sank exhausted to the ground, Parnak continued recording.

"Rest while you can," he said to the pair, "we'll move again soon. This is not the end of it, you know?" The last words were said with a certain gravity that was unusual, even for Parnak.

Neither flyer made a comment, happy to let the statement go unquestioned.

42

Soarer on Modallas

It seemed as if Marcellus had come to a stop around them. More casual to the eye, the attitude seemed regular and peaceful.

Turmoil, the horror of warfare was over, it seemed, suddenly. Looking back, the day seemed unreal. Later, a private showing from the memory of Parnak's recorder. It would be as if they were seeing those things for the first time. They would remember nothing of the things they saw themselves do.

Minutes passed, and the force of the attack died away, leaving them feeling at one moment both elated and depressed the next as if they depressurized quickly. Normalcy felt odd.

Borter struggled to his feet, nudging Helio as he rose. A large transport rumbled up, offering them a ride back to the ship.

Helio caught the idea quickly enough and was on his feet, ready to go. Other transports arrived on either side of the first. His Reds began boarding all three. For the moment, Soal was content to stand outside congratulating his warriors.

Parnak dutifully stood by, recording. At last, Borter remembered he had the Reggian blaster clutched in his hand and, with some difficulty, opened that hand and holstered it. They boarded and found places to sit among Lord Soal's Reds. The battle helmets came loose in the large hold of the transport, and the faces of Marcelleans could be seen. There was not much conversation. Borter looked from face to face, several near him. One after another, they returned the glance without emotion, perhaps without even knowing they did so.

Borter regarded them a little differently as he looked at them this time. The Marcelleans before the battle were a curiosity, more like children than warriors of the caliber he had just seen. Now, they seemed older, more solemn. There was none of the light chatter among them. Save the roar of the transport engine, there was little else to be heard. He thought they were like children, shone something horrible for the first time in their lives, like children who had lost something intangible but real and missing, all the same. In the end, he supposed them all to be very tired. Minutes later, the transport rumbled to a stop, halting with a rough jerk.

The pilots let the Reds get out first, then wandered down the ramp themselves. They moved toward Soarer's newly blackened hull. Oddly, the cargo ramp had been lowered already. Borter strained, looking up into the tube before going in, trying to make out who had gotten there ahead of them. The tube of Soarer was tightly packed as a number of Red Warriors crowded in. Lord Soal came in after them just as Borter was about to tell them this was a private taxi. Looking around, he nodded to them without speaking. Helio faced around in the cockpit hatchway to Borter, who was seated at the controls in the cockpit. Parnak rushed in, brandishing his faithful recorder.

The cargo ramp raised and sealed itself. Quick arrangements were made through Parnak for the use of Soarer, though Borter knew it was useless to resist. He wondered, remembering Tyrus, if the Marcellean would allow them to take off and fly Soarer themselves this time. It was not business that caught Borter's fantasy or Helio's. They'd seen enough action for one day. Parnak was the only one who craved more excitement. The bruise on the pilot's head was still painful.

He wanted to rest. The prospect of invading the enemy's stronghold, even in strength, was not inviting when announced moments later. However, the agreement with Parnak was made to stick.

Seconds later, the sky swallowed them up. Sensors found the orbiting Modallas. Helio turned to Lord Soal in the tube. "There seems to be a fighter battle going on around Modallas." A reply was quick in coming from the Marcellean, who, like the others in the cargo tube, had removed their helmets and sat a short way behind the cockpit stiffly.

"Our forces there shield activity on the planet and the expeditionary forces coming to invade Modallas itself." The elder warrior appeared more grim, speaking the words.

Behind him, the others remained silent, now equally grim. Soal gave directions to Borter for landing on Modallas.

Rather, the computer had them and, at his signal, gave them to the pilots. Then, neither pilot would have dared refuse his orders, though they seemed more suicidal than any other they'd accepted that day.

They had been invited to invade Modallas at its most prominent and obvious breech, the mammoth air lock stationed at the leading pole of the cylinder. The rest of the expeditionary force would follow them in and drive toward Control at the other end of Modallas. The forces there would soften all outside resistance.

Soarer sped toward Modallas. Monitoring the heaviest concentrations of fighters, Borter kept them well away from the fighting. Modallas was still far in the distance but appeared more than a shining object waiting for them in space.

"It's moving away," Borter informed Helio. "What's her speed?" He demanded.

Helio read it out. He added, too, that there had been no readable acceleration. Modallas had the capacity to drive its massive bulk to maximum speed in an instant. Borter found himself agog, amazed at this. He began to realize how alien Modallas and The Helmsman were to the galaxy.

Even at that pace, thought the Dillisome, it would require several lifetimes, as they understood life, to enter only the outer fringes of the galaxy from their next, nearest neighbor.

Just what sort of creature was this Helmsman? The chase continued. Soarer moved ahead faster.

Borter and Helio found it necessary to avoid swarms of the still slower Modallian fighters sent to block their path. From around and behind Soarer, the challenge was met by the other vessels serving the Marcellean invasion as transport or escort.

They had begun to string along without notice taken aboard Soarer.

Borter glanced at his co-pilot with the same realization that they were, truly, the flagship of the Marcellean invasion. Both were beginning to feel a trifle used. Modallas stayed far out ahead and pulling away, until Borter shoved the speed to maximum.

Helio occupied himself, returning fire to the blurring fighters outside. They were becoming more and more of a nuisance as they neared Modallas. One end of the great cylinder was completely visible as the rest of Modallas angled away from them. The port they wanted was the farthest away.

Soarer matched Modallas' movement perfectly. Each turn was copied, bringing them closer. They evaded fighter after fighter, Marcellean on either wing were less fortunate. Several big explosions rocked Soarer despite her set shields.

Parnak commented, nodding backward to the tube from his place at the cockpit hatchway; they would give themselves a thousand times over to allow Lord Soal to get within killing distance of the Modallian master. The pilots and Parnak had little time to discuss sentiments on the destruction of living beings, for they had, at last, maneuvered in front of the speeding cylinder.

Brought about in a wrenchingly tight circle, Soarer was aimed at the wide portal serving Modallas as a spaceport. It stood helpless before them. Modallas and The Helmsman were open to them. A horde of Marcellean ships followed them in.

Heavy guns greeted them from the area surrounding the port. Lethal photons reached up for the new black hull.

Before the shields could bear no more, Soarer burst into the vast expanse of the enclosed cylinder, her wings already spreading for flight in the atmosphere. Five hundred kilometers lay ahead to Modallian Control, The Helmsman, and those who called themselves Modallian.

Ahead, there was no sign of resistance, no deadly, oncoming bolts of light, no fighters. The inside surface of Modallas' hull alternated three land areas of equal distances of clear enclosure blinded only by the forever opening and closing system of shutters, allowing natural light to enter. Below, on the land strips, vast enclosures of buildings covered much of each area.

Shapes flooded by above and below the invaders. There would be time, later, to examine them at a more leisurely pace - if there was a later for them, from Parnak's recorder. Coming quickly near the end of the cylinder's length, Borter saw it, a clear tract of land, one large enough to land them.

Heading down, they dropped from the system of clouds in the zero gee center of Modallas. The landing gear snapped down at roof top level. Helio checked for any malfunction before landing. Everything was right – in place. His computer console provided the data. Borter let them down gently to the flat ground.

The horizon widened quickly. Indeed, it appeared to be no different than landing anywhere else. With a faint thump, they were down and sitting far forward as Soarer braked quickly to a halt. Around them, several other ships touched down, coming to the same shortened halt. More landed, not far from them, on the other land masses of Modallas.

Lord Soal was the first to debark, after Parnak, who set himself up quickly to record the historic event, the footfall of the second Marcellean to reach Modallas, and the first to reach the cylinder world on a mission of vengeance.

43

Borter on Modallas

They were about their business quickly, once on the ground. Not far away, the massive control center rose vertically along the trailing end of the cylinder. Here, it was thought, most likely, The Helmsman could be found. Lord Soal led his Reds forward to mete out the vengeance of an entire race, decimated, resisting the evil hidden there.

Marcellean flyers returned to the air above, hovering like anxious mothers, protective of their young. They followed the advance slowly, ready to warn the ground of any attack or to defend them from it with all the weapons at their command.

The Red Warriors and their covering entourage of flyers were not long at vanishing into the distance and Parnak with them. The two flyers remained on the ground, as ordered, safe, looking all around themselves, taking in the sights. Borter left the cargo ramp down. It was time for a walk.

"Remind me to talk to Old Face about those bells and whistles he's got installed – they're beginning to make me crazy." Helio nodded.

Sharp eyes peered out as Borter walked down the lowered ramp. They had seen all except this one strange ship move away as the troops they brought moved out. This remaining curiosity intrigued them. The Targan crept forward until they were beneath Soarer's dark hull.

Borter came down the ramp. As he did, the two were behind it. Beneath, they craned their necks upward against the restraining Modallian body armor. The powerful Reggian blaster swung on his hip. Since a force such as the Red Warriors left the spot without trouble, there was probably nothing to worry about.

Perhaps The Helmsman had no defenses inside Modallas, that of all the places he could have chosen to be in the galaxy at that moment, he might now be in the safest. A quick mop up of the guns that fired on them as they entered and that should be all, except for The Helmsman himself.

Modallas was weaker than he imagined, a paper tiger. Things seemed peaceful. Borter laughed bleakly. He'd seen too much death that day to think seriously that Modallas would be lightly guarded. He would enjoy the peace while it lasted. The landing gear had to be checked, fire on the way in had damaged one of the pods. The gear had lowered sluggishly, but it had worked.

He moved down the hull, checking for more damage. Old Face's friction-free coating seemed to work well. He kept his full attention on the black hull as he walked toward the pod. The Techno Dwarf had done a good job, he had to admit. Helio had already known that, of course, having made an inspection while Borter had involved himself in emotional outbursts.

Within the small flyer, Helio dutifully checked his instrumentation. All was as it should be and his mind was at ease. Occasionally, with curiosity, genuine for a Dillisome away from home, he looked out at the artificial world surrounding him. what he could not make out with his eyes, ship's sensor picked up. In some ways he envied the technology of such a place, he wondered at the simplicity of it all.

The Targan crept toward Borter. Bred on Modallas, still they had lost little of their forest stealth. Borter found himself struggling, his arms clamped to his sides. The pilot found himself lifted from the ground by the pair of Targan. Others emerged from the nearby edges of the field.

The spin generated gravity for the place. Helio was about to say to himself that all here was made to duplicate the conditions of the alien world that built the actual structure of the place. At the last moment, he realized it did not have to be so. The Modallain environment was completely flexible. It was anything its creators desired.

A certain rudimentary dedication to the work of piloting saved the Dillisome from danger more than once. The unseen, heavily shod but near silent feet running up the cargo ramp turned him around with a start. The chances that Borter had already been killed were great. The invaders would not have reached the hatch had he been able to use the Reggian blaster.

But the gangway swept away from Targan feet spilling them roughly on the ground. It was similar to what Borter had once done to Jibba on Menad.

Borter would have been proud. On the edge of the makeshift airstrip, the pilot was being held down by three very large Targan. They grappled for his blaster.

Soarer's engines came to life somewhere in the distance. The Targan lifted him up a second time. Borter struggled in their grip. Startled by Soarer's engines, they lost him. The pilot crashed to the ground. Somewhere nearby, Targans opened fire on the freighter. Helio responded with a potent blast of his own.

Opposition melted away. Borter raced away, his would-be captors in pursuit. More than a match for these armored Targans, Borter widened his lead on the trio — a good dose of fear did not hurt.

Soarer leapt into the air after a short run on the air strip. Helio took the battle to the air where the advantage was his. The long wings that sustained her in flight at lower speeds, extended, the Dillisome turned back searching for those who chased his partner. It had not taken long for them to get away.

Borter reached the first row of buildings before the three Targan, outdistancing them on account of their armor and his own fear. Helio swept the flat plain, looking for him. He'd sent the three sprawling for cover.

The buildings were the first thing in the near distance that broke the flatness of the plain. Once there, they presented him with sheer faces of a masonry he'd never seen before.

Helio made one more pass before he reached the comparative safety of the buildings. There was no time for another before the pursuers reached them, too. Roaring engines sped him away toward the stationary, floating clouds at the core of Modallas.

Borter held the blaster easily in his grip, searching for a target. The sound of Soarer drifted away. He could tell the direction Helio had taken her among the flat walls.

No windows or doorways were apparent. He ran, looking over one shoulder, zig-zagging in the narrow alleys between buildings. At times, he thought he could hear the Targan running up behind him.

His first thought was to get back to the field where they had landed. There, he was sure Helio would spot him. Had he any wits about him, he would have worn a communicator with his translator. Helio was somewhere, perhaps far away by now, looking for his own way back to that spot.

There seemed no way out of a deepening maze for Borter. The deeper he went, the more things became the same.

Overhead, Modallas' sky appeared deep and uniform to his eyes, an optical illusion included by Modallas' designers to relieve the appearance of a cramped vehicle, even one so large, against the vastness of space. Helio watched for any signal from Borter.

The chase continued, Targans relying on their forest-bred stealth against Borter's swift cunning. Borter chose to slow down and await the eventual confrontation before expending his total strength in a useless flight. The Targan relied on themselves, individually, splitting their small force to attack singly. There were few beings who could avoid their senses.

As Borter searched for a hiding place, they closed the gap given to him by Helio. Between the buildings, they knew there would be no chance for a second rescue from above. The pilot's knowledge of the Targan was limited, but he entertained the illusion they might pass by him. He would have to wait for them to come.

For a long time, he waited, straining for any sound. The building tops offered no clue. Though it would be preferable to defend from above, there was no way for him to climb even to the lowest of heights. He hoped Targans found the sheer walls equally difficult.

Of course, that was too much to hope for. He had seen the Targan's ability to scale things as easily as another could walk. His memory held forth the time in Toth lost there on Marcellus; he'd been so stunned to see them rush downward on him from all sides. Lord Markham was, also, part of that memory.

Time for supposition dwindled, and Borter thought his pursuers were close behind. To rush ahead would have been the obvious course.p However, the continuous maze through which he would have to pass was no longer inviting. Wondering at the thickness of the walls, he raised the Reggian blaster and fired once, then twice.

Concussion knocked him back amid a shower of debris. A new, jagged opening in the wall appeared, before him. As Borter stepped through the opening, three sets of savage eyes followed with much apprehension. Glancing, first at one another, the three cautiously surrounded the opening. None entered. Instead, one pushed a stud on his armor opening a communications link with his commander.

44

The Bargain Unkept

Borter ran down long, windowless corridors blindly. Lighted dimly, they led into a far distance. It was as if one building connected with all others, providing a long, long covered causeway. But, Modallas was sealed, why the need for such complete privacy?

His footfalls echoed down and back in the vast halls. Fright overpowered his curiosity for the moment. There was no wish to face the three Targan in him. On Marcellus, they had been such wild fighters, he was not sure how to tackle them at close quarters. The wound he'd received to his head throbbed as he ran. Borter wondered where the might be the slightest cover, a single corner where he could make a stand.

Sweat soaked his clothing and stuck it to his skin. At last, he came to a stop, his breath coming in gasps and pants. The corridor behind was still empty as far as he could see. In front, there was, also, nothing. Silence, it struck him as odd. He wished for Helio.

The Dillisome was good in a scrape. He had never been sorry for bringing him aboard. In fact, he remembered, with a smile, Helio, too, was quite proud of announcing they were partners - at times.

Many thought of them, as Helio's people, as somewhat slow or passive. Nothing was further from the truth. He was glad that Soarer, as powerful a weapon as it had become, was in Helio's hands if not his own.

He turned, first one way then the other. There was no going back. Behind him, the Targan surely waited, if they did not follow. He moved on. Walking this time, looking back over one shoulder briefly, the corridor led on.

The walls around him, white and stainless, glistened around him. The Targan, all of them, would be looking for him soon if they were not too busy with Lord Soal and his formidable Reds. He thought for a while about blasting through another wall and letting himself out. If he blew it out, he didn't have to go through it, just make the search more difficult for those who followed him. Then, it was done. The wall buckled inward with a sharp crash, and Borter walked through. He was becoming good at the – making.

Within was far different than without. The Lights were dimmer. At last, there was the corner where he could wait for an ambush for those who came after him. He wondered exactly where he was. Without better lighting, the new chamber seemed more mysterious and uninviting. There was a more profound silence than in the corridor, demanding more than the unsure footsteps of a lone Magnean to disturb it.

Used to the frigid darkness of space all around, Borter felt something different in this darkness, as if something lurked nearby, waiting to swallow him whole without warning. For the first time during the chase, Borter felt the sweat on his body. Looking out into the darkness, he stood ready for whatever came, though it might be able to walk up to him before he could see it.

The perspiration on his face cooled quickly in the new room. The air was different here, cooler and dry. He had no time to consider anything else. The Targan would pick him up again soon enough. Borter decided to press on, to work his way back to the landing field.

Helio, if he was able, would keep an eye on that spot for him. The bared halo of dim light where he'd blasted his doorway offered nothing except a certain return to his three Targan without acceptable odds for success. A lighted opening, Borter wavered for another second, then turned away.

Markham burst into the Control center and face The Helmsman, his manner, full of the usual bluster. The Helmsman's manner was cool – cold, and well calculated. He addressed Markham matter-of-factly, infuriating him more.

"Yes, Markham, what is it?"

Battle mask still drawn, he came as close to The Helmsman as he dared and let his anger out. "I demand to know the reason my sacred battle-to-the-death with Soal was interrupted?" By what right was that battle curtailed? A battle, for that matter, that would have won us the planet, is now very likely lost because of this interference."

"You demand nothing here, Markham. It is I who demand - not you." The tone was imperious, larger than life, and calculated. "You tread dangerous ground bearing small matters. You have failed to keep pace as usual," the dark figure loomed closer.

Markham brushed past the insult easily and its implications as well. "I hardly think winning the planet by the death of a single man is possible." He added, "And I have kept my part of our bargain."

The Helmsman mocked him. "You fail me once more – subtly, this time. Things have changed, Markham." He paused menacingly, letting his words sink in. "You see, Marcellus is no longer of any use. The Heart of Marcellus is no longer there. It has, at last, come here – by itself, little thanks to you. Neither you nor your brother are necessary any longer."

Markham stood stunned for a moment, unable to move. "You no longer require a Wearer?"

"Ah – at last, a light glows in the darkness," The Helmsman mused darkly.

"I assure you that you are mistaken." Markham rushed to his own defense.

"Not I, "The Helmsman reassured him quietly with an easy coolness unusual even for him. "It is you who are mistaken, Markham," a sharply pointed finger emphasized, reassuring the mad lord. "Modallas has duplicated – the unique qualities of a Wearer."

"No," Markham cried.

"I'm afraid so – yes." The cruel mask bobbed up and down before Markham, convincing him of The Helmsman's complete confidence. "However, it will not alter our original agreement."

The Helmsman stood. "As promised, the planet will be yours, though you might find its character somewhat altered.

And, I have only one more small task for you, one you will, I think – enjoy."

Markham asked warily, "What do you mean?"

"Since your services will no longer be required for the conquest of the galaxy, I have work for you suitable to your talents – the task requires the abilities of a meat cutter – a butcher. Yours, if you want the planet."

Markham, insulted, degraded, but with no alternative, his prize nearly in hand, but tarnished, barely nodded assent.

"Good." The Helmsman went on. "Only a little service,

something to prove yourself once again." The featureless mask seemed to smirk at him, though it remained as opaque and rigid as ever. "We have had some unusual opportunities presented to us in the last few moments. I'm sure you'll agree.

Just now, I was reviewing the Marcellean withdrawal from your little adventure on the planet. There seems to be no point in their continuing once you were gone, you see. Most odd for Marcelleans to withdraw from a critical battle, don't you think? In effect, they've abandoned the city and the planet to me. It seems, as well, that they have mounted a considerable force to invade Modallas itself. In leaving – I believe they have come for us."

"You seem strangely delighted at this turn of events," Markham countered, still angry.

"We engage them now on all but the Third Plain. They have landed a relatively small force there, of the warriors designated – Red.

"That means Lord Soal leads them," Markham gasped, forgetting his anger.

"Of course, he will be my gift to you a second time."

The Helmsman nodded graciously, "However, there is that small problem I want you to take care of – first," he said raising a finger holding Markham back from his prize, "a small thing really – a flea. One of them has become separated and managed to enter the White

City. You will deal with that one yourself, then you may re – engage Lord Soal."

Markham brightened at the prospect. First, he would deal with this minor opponent in the forbidden White City. Then, he would deal with his brother. Targans would barely enter the Third Plain, let alone the White City. This was the Modallian citadel, they were nowhere else on Modallas.

Markham had never had occasion to enter there but held no fear of the place or its inhabitants, those The Helmsman had guided across the eternity of intergalactic space.

"You know this one," The Helmsman went on. "He's one of the off-world pilots who has escaped you twice before." He paused dramatically, "See that I do not have to resolve this small annoyance myself, Markham. It would make you quite useless in my sight - more than now - do you understand?" Markham turned and left the presence of The Helmsman without speaking.

Reentering the teleporter, he was instantly at his assignment. Teleportation held little discomfort; one was simply unassembled in one place and reassembled in another.

Marcelleans gave little thought to technical workings. That was something that fell to others, Marcelleans considered themselves above such work. A flash of light and Markham arrived at his destination, the hole blasted by Borter in the citadel wall moments before. He entered the building after him.

45

The Battle

Not far on, they entered lush gardens, a surprise. Soal noticed the garden, looking around himself. It was an odd mix, part Marcellean, part alien, most unseen before, never imagined, side by side. No doubt, at the behest of The Helmsman's manic but efficient technology.

The place was a wonder. No Marcellean, before, not even the disgraced Lord Markham, had entered. None who had ever emerged to tell a tale. Many kilometers away, far from them, nearly out of sight, the containing wall vaulted up, forming the curve of the giant cylinder.

Above them, perpetual clouds, caught in the zero gravity of the tube's center, kept hidden anything of the remaining two land masses that could be left to the naked eye.

No word came from the other branches of the Marcellean force to these two plains in the sky. Would the sound of battle carry that distance intercepted only by free-floating clouds, more of The Helmsman's creation or, perhaps, the creation of the other, more illusive Modallians? Perhaps, happenstance? He assumed they had made contact with their enemy and would soon join him.

Though Modallians had ever been seen and were not to be seen that day, there were no Targan, no matter how well trained, able to stand before them. He counted on their presence.

The garden became less dense, then slacked altogether. A broad causeway spread before them. Lord Soal made his decision quickly. He could not wait out the enemy on his home ground. It was either attack and take his losses or retreat through the maze to the landing strip and begin again. He had not come all that way, all those torturous years to turn back. He moved his Reds forward.

At his command, The Red Warriors broke from their thin files ready to take the causeway. The Targan would rush them, trying to push them too close together to fight effectively, where they could be killed easily. A fight would be difficult, there was no cover.

Lord Soal looked at the perimeter, fanning out on either side of him two by two by two, ready to fight in a broad front in the direction they'd been moving, but no longer in the long files following the Marcellean overlord. Now, they flanked him on either side. He looked at them, stepping forward to lead. They had already made their place in the Heart. Not even he could guarantee their lives in such a place. However, that was not their main concern. Dealing with The Helmsman was that concern and at any cost.

They had not seen what had happened to Borter. Targan did not allow themselves to be seen. The sharp sensors of their collective shoulder falcons showed them to be all around, their calm voices whispered into ears all down the line. They passed into the city of closed, windowless, doorless, white buildings, finding their way with Lord Soal in the lead, as always, quite naturally, without incident and no hesitation.

They were not attacked on the causeway. On, through a complex ground way intersecting smooth, tiered walls of the pyramids, they finally stood at the center of the White City.

A new prize, it held itself out, singing its siren song to them, tantalizing them with all the sweet lure of Marcellean vengeance. They had run the maze and were ready to take their reward. Before them lay the ultimate goal, all for which they had lived and died.

Their overlord signaled a halt. Thus far, they had met no resistance and seen no Modallians. There, too, had seen no Targan, though they were all around according to their ubiquitous shoulder falcons. It was all too easy. None of them knew the use of the buildings around them.

Silent feet came closer. Their sensors gave more intense warnings. Lord Soal could guess the essence of the orders from The Helmsman that day to his officers. Lord Soal motioned Parnak forward and ordered his men to form ranks around them both. For a brief moment, they stared, perhaps trying to recognize some familiar internal counseling emotion in themselves.

The overlord spoke. Parnak was ever ready with his recorder to catch every movement, every word, for those who would see them next.

"The time has come," he said. "The enemies of the galaxy are here. The fulfillment of our very existence is near. Whether any live beyond today is nothing. Paramount is delivering the vengeance of The Heart. Today, there is nothing else."

The old warrior turned, then issued more of his usual, calm orders to the Red Warriors, who went swiftly to obey them.

Parnak gazed into his recorder and muttered a few carefully chosen words of his own. It was more extraordinary than usual that he should do so. The thought patterns of his own race were so distinctly similar that no explanations were necessary to accompany what the recorder brought them.

Suddenly, they came. It was as if the city itself lunged out at them. The ground, too, seemed to have at them, revealing fast-moving Targan. The attack was from all sides this time. The Marcelleans found themselves with no safe place to rest their backs except against one another. That would have to be good enough.

The Helmsman's own Targan, the elite he'd trained for use aboard Modallas, were a better lot than those left behind on the planet. They fought well with a plan. They were better armed and uniformly armored. Against them, the Red Warriors fought together as a single unit around Lord Soal, closing in when one of their numbers went down. Parnak, in the middle of it all, kept one hand on his recorder and the other on his Marcellean issue blaster to protect it.

The Marcellean overlord marched them all forward toward the place of The Helmsman. At last, the disease that had all but killed an entire planet was to be confronted. Lord Soal would press ahead and see him done to the end, though it would be a poor vengeance for Marcellus.

In front, by some distance, they were cut off by another force of Targan. For a moment, they eyed one another with unusual restraint. Each seemed to regard the other with curiosity and caution before anger. Lord Soal moved forward with more speed. The Targan stood firm. They clashed suddenly.

Elsewhere, Borter crawled along the dark corridor, looking for a way out. A way out from what to what? He couldn't say?

Dead planets held more light. He cursed, wishing he was on one. The blaster slipped away for an instant, clattering across the floor. On his hands and knees, Borter crept after it with one hand leading, following the path of the sound.

As he reached it, he realized the search had been too easy. Lights were beginning to come on. Dimly at first, then more and more brightly, Things, strange things, took shape around him. The blaster firmly grasped in one hand, Borter hung close to the floor waiting. Nothing. Automatic lights perhaps? He still did not raise himself from the floor. Why had they not come on when he first entered?

As far as he could see were vast straight rows of nearly white tables. How many, a thousand, a million? He did not know. Yet, there was no exit in sight. There was no other sound than his breathing. The source of light was still a mystery.

Above him, far up, the white tables rose away into the air, confined only by the limits of the building. Catwalks joined and crisscrossed them all high into the building. The tables seemed to be all the building housed.

He wondered if they were all that the other buildings held. There were many, and his legs felt as if he'd run by them all before breaking into this one. Borter kept his head well down as he moved among the tables, crossing, never staying in the same row.

Light came to the chamber more quickly. Borter decided caution outweighed foolishness as a case for valor. He stopped beside a table. Something chilled him; some unknown dread crept up on him as he looked upon its blank surface.

It was the fabled sixth Magnean sense that stood the short hair on the back of his neck straight up. Few lived long who did not trust it.

Whirling, he let the blaster lead him. There was nothing to be seen. Still, the back of his neck stood. It would not let him alone. Eyes wide, he followed the blaster, looking for the cause.

46

The Chase

Nothing came, or anyone. Raising his eyes above the level of the table nearest him. Borter registered the new limits of the chamber. Lights were coming on everywhere. The air was still and smelled oddly of long disuse. Borter inspected the gleaming blaster held in his hand. Finally, sure he was safe enough, he let himself get to his feet slowly.

Where was there a way out? The barrel of the blaster, now, led his eyes. Modallas was a place of wonders and certainly great danger. The vast chamber, still lighting itself, presented a serious puzzle with its winding tiers and catwalks set atop one another. Sooner or later, he would trip some sort of sensor if he already had not. He did not relish the thought of the three Targans again picking up his trail. Would he ever get out? Aboard Soarer, things were quite different.

There, Helio experienced an odd peace, something new, even for him, a Dillisome. On one hand, battles raged everywhere, on the other, Borter's uncertain fate. He had to search for him. It was the way of their partnership. But, hope for Borter's rescue faded with each passing minute.

Helio had taken Soarer directly to the center of Modallas, its weightless core. There, ship and pilot drifted effortlessly, shut down, silent, hidden amid carnage on all sides. The Dillisome waited for — he did not know what, perhaps something to touch his shoulder and move him into action. For long moments, sensors probed the clouds in the zero-gee core, trying to locate the lost pilot, his friend, and his partner, Borter, in turmoil.

With no trouble, Lord Soal's Reds were located some distance away on the Third Plain. Borter was not among them, he showed nowhere on the surface. Lord Soal and his followers were heavily engaged by The Helmsman's forces. The pilot had to be inside one of the buildings. Nothing moved, except the battlers toiling against one another.

Borter climbed higher into the pyramid. The vast building ascended to a point far above him. Markham followed closely, dogging him quietly but staying far enough behind to avoid confrontation, waiting for his moment. Markham was playing him, waiting, baiting his trap. To Borter, the Marcellean's plan was unknown. He could not yet see the top of the pyramid closing in on him.

The chase went on. No matter how Borter changed his direction and varied his pace, Markham was always somewhere close behind him. In Modallas' Control, The Helmsman watched as Markham teleported from place to place, harassing his quarry. "Markham," he ordered, "end this farce. You are needed elsewhere." Markham passed again and again through the machinery of the teleporter.

"He is mad," The Helmsman growled. "Bring this to an end," he repeated his command more loudly.

Then, suddenly, the fleeing Borter raised his blaster and fired without aiming.

A white table beside Markham shattered. The ever-present ion blade left its scabbard with a blue flash. Now, Borter faced his death. Panicking, he fired a second time and ran.

Materials from another, disintegrating white tables clattered against Markham's armor unnoticed. The disgraced Marcellean moved forward for the kill, blade in hand.

"Soal's pet," Markham snapped behind his battle mask. Markham shut off the ion blade, favoring stealth. Teeth gritted, eyes bulging, he drove toward the interfering off-worlder who ran before him. Borter turned and fired at the charging renegade or just ran. The path of the flight became littered with materials from the destroyed tables.

Markham vowed to cut Borter, once caught, in half, from top to bottom or side to side.

The mad dash moved upward, Borter choosing a different route of escape from the Marcellean as often as possible, hoping to come out at a place Markham could not follow. Out of breath, the pilot arrived at a new level, each level smaller than the last, the mad lord nearer or farther than the one before; he looked around, the blaster always ready to counter an expected lightning attack from any quarter. Markham did not want to appear on the same level as Borter. Instead, one or maybe two away.

Once, he caught Markham looking the wrong way, already ahead. Instead of firing, Borter was content to lower himself back down to the previous level, doubling back to avoid danger altogether.

However, a confrontation was inevitable. Markham turned up, sooner or later, ever on his trail. By chance, they emerged, one landing from each other, one in full view of the other.

Borter cursed his poor luck and ran away at a heavy sprint. Markham cursed Borter and his lightness of foot. Peering around opposite corners, they missed each other again. Misreading his self-contained sensors, Markham went up as Borter, quite by accident, turned his path of escape once more downward. The pilot, realizing his good fortune, quickly ranged far.

Looking over one shoulder, he ran, leading himself to the chamber's edge, a journey requiring some investment of time. He reminded himself of the pyramid shape of the place, an attribute more apparent from the outside.

Disappointed, he swung his course upward, if there was a way close by, it would be at the top or near it. Borter resolved that, if he had to, he would blast a way out as he'd blasted his way in, and climb down the white gradually slanted exterior to safety, wherever that might be.

Markham whirled around a corner provided by a convenient pillar, staunchly planting himself two levels above Borter, having been sure he was hiding nearby, perhaps stalking even the Marcellean lord himself. He cursed again. There was nothing in sight, nothing except the ever-present orderly rows of white cases. This fleeing off

– worlder had damaged many in his flight. Markham termed it regrettable, but there was nothing to be done. Modallians could certainly repair their own toys, he thought.

For the moment, he had to think to clear his mind. Centuries had drifted by, with only The Helmsman and his barely acceptable, trained Targan, who, no matter what or how strict their discipline, at the Helmsman's hands, had to be treated chemically to subdue their natural impulse against him.

Restricted areas, control principally, kept others trained for warfare on the planet, away from him, the teleporter always trained on him, ready to sweep him away to safety at the untoward blinking of an eye. There, too, on the planet, they were wild and unschooled, awed by the simple technical displays arrayed for such purposes by The Helmsman. There, he was regarded as a god, a messenger of the Sky God.

Markham moved silently despite the enclosing battle armor. Borter crept quietly, his breath hissing between his teeth. Going up one level, he noted the pyramid reduced its area; nothing there except, again, the tables. Their greetings were silent, peaceful. That's welcome, he thought, it's coming.

Markham was transported just beyond the edge of faded darkness near Borter. His Modallian scanners swept the aisles with lightning swiftness. Within his armor, he could hear his prey's fearful scurrying, the sound of feet just beyond an adjacent row of tables, not far away. His own ion blade remained sheathed, so satisfied was he of his superiority and certainty of the kill. His quick trap set for this minor event in his day, Markham waited in silence, watching sensors behind the battle mask; Borter came nearer.

Borter climbed, unaware of the short distance between them. Markham was silent, his prey coming closer. It would be easy. He would no more than reach out, press the button, and it would be over. Lord Soal would be next. And Marcellus would be his, after all, that glittering jewel hung in space. Marcellus would rise like the light of a star beside the glory of Modallas.

He realized, suddenly, that the coming footsteps had stopped. Somehow, the pilot had found him out, and his daydreaming had made him the fool; the hunted, instead of the hunter, tables turned. His nerves exploded with unaccustomed stress. Indeed, what kind of being did he face?

He activated the blade and sprung his trap. He guessed Borter had opted for the most obvious means of escape and crept upward toward the pinnacle of the pyramid. Now, the plan was given away by the flash of his blade, the stealth, caution for nothing, and this back world upstart, leaving him looking the fool. It was intolerable. Borter was not there, at least there where he was supposed to be.

Markham rounded the pillar to face the not – quite – surprised Borter; for the briefest instant, blaster and ion blade leveled at each other as the opponents appraised the other closely. The blade cut the air, too far away, a feint, testing the nerve of his opponent. Borter found himself stepping backward. His knuckles tight as he gripped the blaster. Markham, feeling control again, laughed behind the faceless battle mask.

Taking a large, bold step toward Borter, he struck again, this time closer. Borter, off balance, managed to get off a wild shot in the Marcellean's general direction. Markham charged, pressing his regained advantage.

47

Modallians

Entering that last level, things were not as Borter would have had them. His shot destroyed another white table, and still, Markham did not pause. Markham had not been easy. Getting away alive was again something else. Borter fled with Markham cursing at his heels, belittling him for not having the courage to, at least, stand and die as the Targan did.

Fortunately, Borter was the quicker and more frightened in the foot race. Far enough ahead among the white tables, he turned, losing a volley that forced the rogue Marcellean to dive for cover. Though, in an instant, the race was on again, in earnest.

Half falling over himself with fatigue, Borter flagged, hurling blast after blast at the dodging Markham. If only he could rest for a moment, he thought, or find some safe place to hide, but his strength was suddenly gone that day, going to other places. The battle on the planet, the long run from the Modallian landing strip, and the strain of pursuit in this running battle with Markham all had their effect.

He turned and went suddenly to one knee and let go another fusillade of shots at Markham. Markham, close, not having discounted Borter's hope of any hit, even a lucky one, crashed to safety. Pieces of white casing fell around him and, with it, something else. Borter stopped, lifting his barrage.

Markham was unhurt, he knew. In the instant of Markham's confusion, Borter surveyed the roof. It was only a meter or two above him. This was as far as he could go. He raised the pirate blaster and fired. Flames erupted briefly and a rain of debris showered down as the blaster opened a door for him to the outside. The face of a Red Warrior looked through at him as the air cleared. "Get me out of here," he bellowed.

What had stopped Markham, he didn't know, nor did he care. Safety beckoned. He did not care to face Markham as an opponent on any terms. A slim line reached down to him. He wrapped it around himself once and tied it loosely in front, sitting down in the loop as it tightened against him. They were pulling him up. Red Warriors gathered around the hole in the roof. "It's the pilot," they said among themselves, amazed to find him there. And, Markham.

Markham sat dazed and motionless in the rubble of several freshly destroyed tables, nodded back and forth, muttering some childish sing-song. Borter glanced back as the rope twisted under the steady pull from those above.

"Dead – all dead," he muttered on the floor to himself, "All dead. All this time." He collapsed, totally, no longer himself. The ion blade rested thoughtlessly, dangerously untended, beside him. Around him, in the debris of the shattered cases, were disjointed skeletal remains, the remains of the Modallians he'd never seen. In a broken table not far away lay the nearly intact form of a Modallian. Of it, Borter could make neither head nor tail. It was grotesquely curious, unlike anything he had ever seen, a being utterly strange – alien.

Borter was finally hauled up. He stood by himself, a little more shaken and tired but not the worse for wear among the Red Warriors. "Thanks," he gasped. Together, they gazed down at the scene.

"Shall we take Lord Markham, too?" One asked. No commander was in the group. Borter spoke up quickly, saying they should leave that decision to Lord Soal. One of the Reds went to find the Marcellean lord.

Turning away from the hole, Borter asked where he was. A Red Warrior told him, pointing the way. Lord Soal had chosen to make his stand before the broad terraces of the pyramid. They were the first to reach the top. Below, a vast army of Targan gathered. "How does it go with the other parts of the invasion force?" The pilot wanted to know.

"Hard," was the quick answer. "But that does not matter." All around him, Marcelleans stood. Then came the Marcellean overlord. His own battle flag fluttered close behind.

48

Red Flag

Marcellus' millions packed, along with themselves, their future into the sky. Certain necessities left the evacuation fleet quite defenseless against Modallian reprisal. Therefore, an invasion of Modallas was planned and executed. Waves of Marcellean fighters pounded the cylindrical terror in the far sky, keeping it and its Targan fighters occupied.

A new planet awaited them; those Marcelleans left behind were long dead. Now, wild Targan owned all the prime real estate and belonged alone to the planet. How they would fare was a matter of unimportant speculation. Of importance was the prospect of Marcellean survival.

As the fleet moved in, they took back the planet for the last time and at the great turbulence of their former lives. Of all the millions of refugees, none cared to speculate on the future of their race. Instead, thoughts turned to the invasion forces and how they were doing against the evil force of Modallas.

There, reporting was Parnak, as always, the voice of the Inner Galaxy. There were those who would have committed themselves to the action, even then, had they been able – but, that was not the plan. Their parts were elsewhere to be played.

Their faith in the Marcellean overlord was undiminished. If he was able, The Helmsman himself would fall beneath his iron blade. Those surviving would follow along as a rear guard.

The destination, it sounds so odd to say, was finally to be an end to their suffering. What lay before them was perhaps the final tranquility promised by The Heart. Although forbidden to reveal its location, scouting teams had landed and had sent back information. Sent by The Heart to the planet, It was said that The Heart itself would lead the greater fleet back. On the great voyage, the last great formations gathered and, at last, rocketed toward a place said to be near the galaxy's edge.

Looking one last time behind themselves, they went. Some left their lives behind them; others brought it along, and all the escape would permit. Life sought a new place in the galaxy and would meet whatever was there on its own terms. Time for them, on Marcellus, had ended.

Julia placed her hand on Old Face's shoulder, a singular honor from one of her stations to one of his in Marcellus' society.

They looked into each other's faces for a moment, realizing the future. Then, turning their gaze to the planet fading behind them, fading into the void becoming their past. The mood was somber, each going to their own thoughts.

"Keep the pilot safe," the overlord commanded.

A warrior moved Borter away from the center of the Marcellean line brusquely, Borter felt dragged away. He did not argue. Ranks of Marcellean Red Warriors formed in front of him, spoiling the view. Checking the Reggian blaster, having nothing better to do, for damage and reserve power.

Glancing toward the hole in the pyramid, he wondered about Markham. Marcellean ranks formed there, too, though it held little interest for them. The renegade Markham seemed forgotten. And, They were far too busy with the Targan.

As Borter looked backward from his new position, Parnak raced to the edge of the opening and pointed his recorder into it.

He looked to neither side, concentrating solely on his work. What happened there was not known until much later. For now, the presence of a red flag and what it meant took his attention.

He had not come to die, he promised himself. Lord Soal gave orders to all sides. His captains moved their ranks efficiently in quick drill squad order. Many silently consigned themselves to The Heart reaching no reservation in commitment for the coming battle. Masses of The Helmsman's Targan approached the pyramid. The style of the battle would not be much above the most savage hand – to – hand combat.

Markham spent his final moments kneeling in the twisted rubble that had been the destroyed white cases. His battle mask and helmet lay aside. His face looked much like that of his Brother. The mad spirit within him was crushed totally.

Remains of long dead Modallians lay where they had fallen from their shattered cases, all nearly dust despite the eons long protection by the white cases, themselves long past any function, their resources shut off by The Helmsman.

Behind Markham, the form of Modallas' master appeared, materializing from the teleporter. Without speaking he moved toward the insensible Marcellean. As he came closer, he could hear Markham mumbling in barely audible tones.

"Yes, you weak – minded fool, they're dead." The Helmsman spoke the word dead contemptuously.

Markham did not notice. "Dead," he muttered in a voice he no longer recognized as his own. "I've labored all these years for the dead?"

The Helmsman closed the distance between them in a single stride, knowing the business he was about. "Weakling," The Helmsman jeered, "killer of fools and old men." Above his head, he raised the ion blade of the Snow Beggar, glowing, activated, deadly. "Your stupidity has served me well – until now."

The doomed Marcellean did not turn to meet his slayer. On The Helmsman's part there, there was no moment of regret, no hesitation. The stroke was clean and swift. Markham and his armor fell to the floor, the dead among the dead, those he'd served so long.

Sounds of battle reached from above. The smashed roof revealed the hated forms of Marcellean Reds. All ignored him, intent on the battle below. The Helmsman stood for a moment longer, watching them. Pressing one of the many studs on his armor, he found himself far from the building. A dusty heap of corpses was left alone.

He arrived instantly at Control. There, he reviewed the beginnings of the battle at the pyramid. He regarded the Marcellean position with interest and considered ways to smash it into nothingness.

Parnak hurried to Borter's side. "Where's Helio?" The insectoid asked in the din. "Where is Soarer?"

"Where we landed," Borter, angered by Parnak's attitude, answered coolly, "I think," he added with perfect nonchalance. If Parnak's face could have reddened, it would have. Instead, Borter thought he heard a kind of rattling sound through his translator.

"You didn't get him killed and ourselves stranded, did you?"

"Targans attacked us where we put down," Borter answered, having fun with Parnak's nerves. "We got split up. He had to take off. He'll be back."

"He'll be back? Parnak barked the question. "You do have a contingency plan, don't you?" Borter no longer seemed to listen.

"Borter, you do have a contingency plan, don't you?" Parnak demanded this time more loudly. Borter seemed only vaguely aware of his questions. "Don't you?"

Borter was still preparing the Reggian blaster for battle but finally looked up to answer Parnak. "Sure," he said, nodding. "Sure. We got a plan."

Looking confused for a moment, then angry, Parnak went on, "Inexcusable." Borter merely shrugged and finished checking his weapon. He lifted it, feeling the heft and its balance as if it were a new weapon to him, and took leisurely aim past the journalist at a big Targan who had just broken through the Marcellean ranks some distance ahead. He carefully squeezed off a shot, killing the Targan, who jerked backward, going down with a crash.

"Yeah," the Magnean smiled to himself, not knowing if Parnak listened any longer, "a plan!"

"Couldn't," Parnak grimaced, "you say something more enduring?" Parnak motioned toward his recorder. "I have the whole Inner Galaxy on link up." Borter smiled and gave the recorder a halfhearted wave to the multitudes watching. Another great mass of Targan rolled against the Marcellean line.

Lord Soal pointed to another rank of Marcelleans, then to a spot in his line. He moved forward as a man to that spot and met the enemy. Looking once more around himself, measuring his reserves, the overlord of Marcellus motioned the red flag forward, signaling a general charge.

49

The Voice of The Heart – Ending

Lights dimmed, within Soarer, Helio sat. The sights of Modallas delighted. Nothing else was like it in the galaxy, perhaps the universe. The vastness of it stretched beyond his sight, far away. More and more, he realized it was not a thing that could simply be destroyed but a thing to be escaped and avoided, like a wild beast. Modallas smelled of something he had never liked, never gotten used to, it smelled of death.

Below, somewhere, were Parnak and Borter. If nothing else in this folly, he was loyal to those two and, through them, to the Marcelleans and Lord Soal, who brought them to the place.

The onboard computer scanned everything below and all around them. Finding the pyramids of the White City and the landing strip or what they had used for a landing strip was easy. The actual heat given off by the weapons of battle was too easily found by sensors.

Borter had not yet been located, though Parnak's whereabouts were long known. Fighting was everywhere in the cylinder world; if it could be called a world, Helio mused at the question. All around, on all three of the vast land masses, the invasion force bore on in numbers larger than he'd realized.

Helio knew something of Marcelleans and was aware of the destruction of which they were capable. Of Modallas' real power, he'd seen only the Targan arm. What more did Modallas hold in store for them? He worried.

He imagined the great number of Targan, trained by Modallas, ready killers, to ravage a planet for The Helmsman and those he served. The Helmsman? Of him, the Dillisome knew little, nothing really. He had never seen the Modallian master. What would be the final power of such a being? The clouds of Modallas stretched out before him as Soarer hung within them, her new shields defying detection.

Movement would certainly bring the enemy down on him. The moment must be right, he thought, to reappear – very right.

Borter still had not emerged to show himself to the wandering sensors of his own ship. The Dillisome mulled just what kind of blip The Helmsman would make himself on the screen were he to appear. Still nothing. The cloud tube became singularly monotonous. In the curious physics of the place, Helio began to feel an indescribable strangeness; his attention began to drift. Other thoughts rambled through his mind.

It was as if something else altogether held him. It felt totally unlike Soarer or any other vessel he'd ever been aboard.

Strange voices spoke to him, strange voices in odd, unknown languages. Others rang familiarly to the hours of recordings he'd viewed in Marcellus' library.

Something held him; nothing held him. He was everywhere, and he was nowhere – all at once. The infinite, he had learned to call his home, and to revel in, approached without hurry as it had always. Sounds, other than voices, reached out to him; he reached back feebly to all. There was contact.

He was there. The first strongmen, Marcelleans, they were, yes - he recognized them, knowing them by their ion blades. It was a far different time, a time to which he did not belong. They turned suddenly toward him, at last, aware of his presence. Helio went on. The clouds before him turned without explanation.

New scenes approached with greater and greater rapidity. Helio went headlong, tumbling, feeling as if he were breaking down the most difficult force fields with ease – just passing through. Then, there was only open space, the open void of stars clustered around and – the one voice speaking to him and only him.

Helio felt the presence talking near his shoulder in soft tones. He trusted the voice immediately. The soothing tones, not words any longer, like a melody to his ears. It sang to him. Soarer's cockpit, Modallas, and the battles raging nearby all slid farther away. The voice, if it was a voice, had spoken, and Helio understood. It was his name he heard in the music; something, someone knew his name and beckoned him.

"Come," it called.

Soarer turned, slowly yawing, nosing down from the clouds - zero gee suspension faded. Unused engines in zero gravity kept silent, and her pilot was oblivious to the changes around him. In the cockpit, instruments melded. No longer were there problems demanding his attention.

The voice of The Heart sang to him its own song, sang the galaxy - the universe, its own way. In a different place, far below, the great struggle in its name went on.

Lord Soal, with Borter and the ever-faithful Parnak close by, strode before the Modallian pyramid. Irresistible in battle, surrounded by his elite corps, nothing kept him long. The air filled with the deadly craft worked by ion blades.

Everywhere, death enveloped the oncoming Targan. Blades avenged eons of Targan atrocities. They could have picked no better place for a final stand.

Soal worked the combat; the Marcellean number diminished, given even their ferocity. Across the line of battle they refused any other weapon than the ion blade, weapon of the ancients, their own. They closed with the enemy. For a while it went on.

On other, remote parts of Modallas, it began. Marcellean commanders received orders to break off contact with the enemy. Reluctantly, they did so and moved away toward their transports. The job was done, they had been told – it was time to go.

Orders were given and obeyed with a deft proficiency, though, later, commanders wondered in their own minds just whose orders they'd followed. They crowded invasion craft, oddly assured every objective had been accomplished. A rear guard dealt with pursuit.

Red flags, often tattered, trailed along their promise of glorious death in battle against an implacable enemy unfulfilled.

Whose voice was it that commanded, the supreme overlord, for whom all were pledged to give themselves a thousand times, if necessary — faithful, unswerving to the end? That end had been called off by a greater power. Marcellean ships began to fill the air inside Modallas.

Lord Soal himself ordered his Reds away to the landing field. With reluctance, they went his Reds, sure he was coming behind them.

He was not. The Targan massed before them waiting, licking their wounds, ferocious, willing to pay more greatly for another attempt at the Marcellean overlord. Borter and Parnak were still protected within the retreating ranks. It was then Soarer broke from the clouds.

The initial burst from her new guns cleared the Targan from before the Marcellean. A second cleared the way for the exit to the landing field. Soarer emerged in the Modallian sky, an angry lover of those she carried.

Borter was quick to turn toward the landing field. Parnak followed, having carefully left behind a remote lens from his recorder. Soarer hurtled by low overhead, her engines drowning out the clamor below. The two hurried toward the landing field where transports were hovering. Lord Soal stood, his back to the pyramid. The gigantic backdrop issued awe.

Around him, the mixed dead of Modallas and Marcellus lay. A few meters away, the Targan waited.

Informed of his brother's death by shoulder falcon, Lord Soal spoke quietly, "May The Heart reclaim you — and ease your madness. It is over for you, brother — and soon for me and all the others of us, too." His was a sort of prayer that reached up for whatever gods might be listening and The Heart. At last, Targan gathered themselves for a last rush. Roaring at the horde before him, defiant 5D appeared.

Beside Soal, a shifting quick vortex of black and white triangles serving as a body for the creature came roiling into view. Triangles stretched, pulling toward the beast's mouth, his central point, dark, unseen, deep within his dimensional form, one side up, one down, at the opposite axis, left to right.

Another, then, right to left, again and again. Soal reached up to pet 5D's bloody maw, "Get the smell of this place in you, old friend," he said. "So, you will be able the find it in the coming days – when that last day comes for its helmsman." 5D snorted heavily as if taking up the meaning, snarling at the Targan.

Chilled, each to the bone, the Targan reached something in their deepest being. 5D set forth another roar. It was a sound they would hear again. Things did not look as easy as before. There were only two against their great numbers.

What could go wrong?

Borter finally reached Soarer. He ran aboard, quickly greeting Helio with a playful nudge as he went into the cockpit.

"My plan worked nicely," he said, going by.

Following him, Parnak stopped, frustrated, unwilling to enter a verbal blind with the Magnean. The Dillisome sensed the traditional discord between the two. He glanced at him, an eyebrow raised, from the co-pilot's seat. He offered. "What plan?"

With a great shout, the Targan charged. With an even greater roar, the beast of five dimensions and its master reached them, both awesome, both deadly.

"I got no plan," the pilot jerked an impatient thumb over his shoulder in Parnak's direction as he took a seat in Soarer's cargo bay.

Helio twisted in his seat instantly, "Oh – " he nodded, smiling, reassuring without enthusiasm, "No plan. Right."

"No passengers!" A second later, a glib Borter closed the cargo ramp, "What's happening there?" Borter turned, remembering Parnak's remote. "Can we get them on my screen?"

"They go a different way from us," the journalist stated.

Borter looked at him curiously as if never having seen him before. "We may never see them again - ever. Take my word for it," Parnak grumbled, "I have it from a very good source."

Lord Soal and 5D, among their enemies, left death all around. That more ragged invasion fleet rocketed from Modallas than had come to it that day.

In the galaxy's most distant parts, all could be seen from Parnak's remote. Targan moved away. Those alive dropped their weapons and ran.

"Nothing? But – Modallas still exists." Borter spoke suddenly, saddened as they rejoined the fleet. "Marcellus did not destroy it!"

"True enough," the journalist spoke. "That is now the problem of the galaxy at large - not of Marcellus. They have done their part."

"Can the galaxy handle that?"

Parnak turned to him, much weary of explaining things to the pilot, "Can we handle that?"

"What?" Borter mumbled through a fading smile. "Does that mean we're not done?" Parnak did not answer.

A moment later, The Heart itself drifted away, the Marcellean lord and his pet its only passengers. They were gone, away from the battlefield and the white pyramids of the Modallas' Third Plain.

"And, this plan of *got – no – plan*, explain, please." Without enthusiasm, Helio turned a hazy glance into the bay, carefully avoiding Borter's look of pain and the look of Parnak's disappointment.

"It means – The Heart has sung its song," Parnak complained," here, in full voice, and you have missed it – both of you, the only two in the galaxy, who did." He walked toward the cockpit, his recorder in hand. He showed them what they had missed.

THE END